FIRST YOU TRY
EVERYTHING

ALSO BY JANE McCAFFERTY

Thank You for the Music

One Heart

Director of the World and Other Stories

FIRST YOU TRY EVERYTHING

A NOVEL

JANE
McCAFFERTY

HARPER

An Imprint of HarperCollins*Publishers*
www.harpercollins.com

This book is a work of fiction. References to real people, events, establish-
ments, organizations, or locales are intended only to provide a sense of au-
thenticity, and are used fictitiously. All other characters, and all incidents
and dialogue, are drawn from the author's imagination and are not to be
construed as real.

HarperCollins books may be purchased for educational, business, or
sales promotional use. For information, please write: Special Markets
Department, HarperCollins Publishers, 10 East 53rd Street, New York,
NY 10022.

FIRST EDITION

Designed by Fritz Metsch

Library of Congress Cataloging-in-Publication Data

McCafferty, Jane.
First you try everything : a novel / by Jane McCafferty.—1st
ed.
    p. cm.
    ISBN 978-0-06-621062-9 (hardback)
    1. Middle-aged women—Fiction. 2. Married people—Fiction.
3. Identity (Philosophical concept)—Fiction. 4. Pittsburgh (Pa.)—Fiction.
I. Title.
    PS3563.C33377F57 2012
    813'.54—dc22

2011028528

12 13 14 15 16   OV/RRD   10 9 8 7 6 5 4 3 2 1

For Patrick, Rosey, Anna, Josh, and Jordan
With special thanks to Charlotte

FIRST YOU TRY
EVERYTHING

EVVIE

THE DAY WAS shot through with silver winter light, an almost eerily beautiful light that was unusual for Pittsburgh. It was a light that sent people rushing outside with cameras to capture an old, naked tree, or their bundled, red-cheeked child, or a bike leaning alone against a wall. The small brick houses on Chislett Street in Morningside were flooded with this light, and inside one of these houses, on the corner of Chislett and Gael Way, across from a view that looked down upon the Allegheny River, Evvie Muldoone was listening to music, her dark hair hanging down in a single braid, her brown eyes happier, calmer than she felt, because she liked the song she listened to quite a bit. She was the sort of person who derived consolation from playing the same song over and over again, walking around the dining room table in a trancelike state her husband had once found charming.

The song was "5 Days in May" and featured an old couple driving toward the sea. She had the sound turned up, too loud for most people's taste, at least people who were past the age of twenty. Lately she needed an auditory shelter from the storm of her own thoughts.

You didn't hear too many songs about old people like this.

Old people were sort of embarrassing and becoming even more so these days, and Evvie noticed that even people in their late seventies dressed up like young people on their way to the gym. It was likely a positive sign that people had stopped capitulating to the tyranny of numbers. But more often than not it seemed that geriatric youthfulness was dependent on considerable money, so that only the poor were looking old. Last year, when Evvie Muldoone was in a book club, all the women but one had said they'd get plastic surgery when the time came.

"In a heartbeat," a few had said, emphatically, and Evvie, feeling herself step onto a soapbox she couldn't resist, captivated the room with a little speech about the beauty of old faces, how depressing it was that they were all planning "to erase themselves," how she didn't care if she was the last person on earth who looked old, she'd wear her age proudly, like a medal, and wasn't it really sick, when you thought about it, that people poured all this money into letting some doctor butcher their face—the denial of death was at the heart of almost everything, *don't you think*, and wouldn't it be shaming when only the poor looked worn down, as nature intended? The atmosphere in the room had shifted, not because her protest was original—at least a few of them had this argument with themselves on a regular basis—but because the passion behind it unsettled everyone. Evvie had never been good at self-modulation. "Give that girl a Valium," good-natured Teresa Moncada finally said, and everyone laughed. *Lighten up, sweetie*, said the hostess.

THOUGH EVVIE WAS only forty-one, and looked mostly the same as always—same long dark hair, same dark eyes, slight overbite, too-pale face with circles under her eyes that she tried to hide with makeup these days—the number jarred her lately when she recalled her mother at forty-one, a functioning alcoholic in a housedress and blue Keds, driving to the grocery store with Evvie and her sister and brother. Evvie could see herself and her sister Louise flashing peace signs in red plastic sunglasses, rosary beads and scapulars around their necks, the two of them still close in those days, making too much noise in the back of the car, her mother turning up the radio on the way to hunt down the Salisbury steak and iceberg lettuce and electric orange French dressing.

Her mother's life had been full of part-time jobs and friends who were also raising kids, and they were in and out of one another's houses all the time. Somehow she'd taken care of Evvie, Louise, and Cedric, who were her second batch of kids—the older three were already launched by then.

Something heroic about the way her mother had shuttled her kids ten miles to the pool at night for all those swim meets out in the suburbs, her back so bad she could find no relief, not even when lying down, not even when she wore a brace. Evvie went to call her, even as she knew the mother she missed did not exist.

"Ma?"

"Evvie!"

"How's everything?"

"Well, let's see. I won third place last night at karaoke."

"What'd you sing?"

"Something you'd hate."

"Come on, what'd you sing?"

"'Country Roads.' Bob Denver."

"John Denver. Bob Denver was Gilligan."

"Right."

"So I was just thinking how you came to our swim meets in the summer. How you'd stand by the fence and watch us, even though your back was killing you."

"I don't remember that."

"Yes, you do. The suburban pool. Near Uncle Gus and Aunt Irene's?"

"I don't remember standing by a fence at a suburban pool. I remember you kids at the pool across from our house. How's Ben?"

"Fine."

"OK, that's good. And you're fine too?"

"Yep."

What Evvie wanted to say—and would have had she known how to bridge the gulf—was that it was odd to be forty-one and have no real idea who you were. It had been all right when her husband, Ben, was beside her, not knowing who he was. But now Ben wore a suit. It no longer looked like a costume. He had been told he'd soon be promoted into something called *knowledge management* at the medical equipment firm. He would rise. He was forgetting their years when they'd worked a push-cart in fresh air, selling Middle Eastern food so they could get home by three and do what they really wanted to do—make art, play music. Not get trapped, as they used to say.

BEN APPEARED IN the dining room doorway, dressed in sweatpants and a T-shirt, his arms recently gym-sculpted. His dark hair was overgrown the way she liked it. He had deep-set eyes that were both green and brown, and often when he looked at her, or at anyone, he'd squint, as if everyone was just a little too much for him. He hadn't shaved today, and she liked that too.

"I need to use the table to do the bills," he said.

One vigilant region of her mind heard a quiet contempt in the tone of his request; the other willfully deaf part leaped to battle, squashing any perception that interfered with what had always been the truth. He loved her, adored her, really, and she adored him too, so all was basically fine. Despite his exasperated sigh, she left the room without a word and began to pace back and forth in the so-called family room, which was really a small storehouse for her animal rights literature and a disarray of icons: owls, Buddhas, pigs, small marble elephants, a framed picture of Virgil Butler, the Arkansas chicken rights factory worker turned activist. She'd meant to hang Virgil Butler up months ago as a reminder that transformation was possible. "Yeah, Ev, you mean to do a lot of things," Ben would've said.

(Actually, Ben would say no such thing. This was Evvie's projection.)

Ben had a point, she told herself, regarding this thing he'd never say that she imagined he would say.

It was true that she was still not a follow-through person, but rather one of those often befuddled souls who seem paralyzed by the exorbitant weight of their own good intentions.

Also in the "family room" were hundreds of cans she had collected in an old red wagon for the homeless. She'd gone door to door with Freddy, the cute "Hi, I'm Fweddy!" neighbor child, his presence assuring people she was not crazy—for what grown woman would walk around pulling a red wagon? She did this because Ben had suggested she cared more about animals than humans.

She'd gone to the suburbs and gathered up a bunch of fur coats to send to Afghanistan after the bombing too, through Animal Amigos. Amazing how many people had handed over their fur coats out in Fox Chapel.

Ben persisted, unappeased.

"It's interesting," he'd said a few months ago. "Animals light up your face these days and people usually leave it in the dark. Like you don't *expect* anything from people anymore."

"That's a horrible thing to say," she said. "I love people!" But reddened, feeling accused.

She did love people but didn't see too much of them these days; her good friends lived far away now, and she'd lost touch with two of them (out of three), not just because time and distance made everything a bit strange but also because she often felt it was challenging enough just to handle the life in front of her.

Besides, to keep in touch was to resurrect old selves that had their own demands, that collided with new selves who were trying to live out days that were almost impossible to translate.

That was it! She didn't have stories she could *translate* to people outside of Pittsburgh. The city was its own universe, somehow. It wrapped around a person's mind, especially in winter, and Evvie couldn't explain that particular, persistent gray to a person who didn't live there, who didn't walk the long streets day after day, or ride the buses, or circle the Highland Park Reservoir on evenings when snow settled lightly on the dark face of the water. She'd settled into something routine and perfect with Ben, and while she sometimes missed whoever she'd been without this delicious structure, this life composed of work at the Frame Shop and volunteering at the shelter and wildlife center and watching movies and reading books and sometimes getting together with the Klines, she felt—though she was hardly aware of this—that most any other life was both unreachable and somewhat threatening. Her old friend Lorna, a six-footer who taught ESL and was an avid bird-watcher, was always trying to get Evvie and Ben to go white-water rafting. She was a white-water rafting freak, had rafted every river in the East and Midwest. She would handle all the details, she would even come all the way from Michigan, pick them up, and take them down to West Virginia in her old black Mazda blaring the Decemberists. They could sing themselves down to the rapids. And Evvie wanted to go. Badly. But she loved Lorna too much, and thought with even minimal contact Ben would love her too, and then Ben and Lorna would get in the raft together and head downstream, leaving Evvie on the bank saying, "Hey! What about me?" She'd pictured this in exquisite detail several times and knew it to be a crime against her own imagination, not to mention a crime against her marriage and against Lorna. She believed her fear of abandonment was only partly rooted in childhood experience. It was also, as she'd told Ben, "probably just the way I came in to the world."

"Yeah," he'd said, back then. "Me too."

And so Lorna and Evvie's friendship had been reduced to a few phone calls a year and a few e-mails. Mattea, from Wisconsin, e-mailed Evvie about her kids and her job, and Evvie always wrote back, but to be married with kids—that was its own universe, with its own language and incessant demands, and Mattea said as much. A third friend, Declan Moore, was an artist in South Carolina, living in a tiny town he'd transformed with murals. He and Evvie had traveled across the country together when they were eighteen. They'd made friends with everyone on the Greyhound, they'd slept in fields under stars, they'd read *Soul on Ice* and *Slaughterhouse Five* out loud to each other, under the North Dakota moon, with flashlights. Now Declan had three kids and a wife whose real name was Elvine Dishes. She was a singer and a glassblower. Evvie visited Declan once, but he could hardly talk with all those kids around, and Elvine Dishes in the bedroom behind a closed door practicing opera in a robe and the slippers the oldest child had crafted out of felt and duct tape.

In a smaller country, she imagined, life would be more ingrained, textured, rooted. She could hop on a train every other weekend to dine with kindergarten friends into their nineties. "Remember that day eighty-five years ago when we ate paste?" Such seamless continuity would certainly have been her preference.

Still, sometimes the past could rise up so vividly in Evvie, the present would disappear. She was affected enough by the sweep of memory that she'd been prone to things like car accidents (three in one year) and wearing two different shoes (only once, but very disturbing) or talking to herself in public (regularly, which was OK, since everyone just imagined she was talking on one of those headset phones). But still. *She* knew she wasn't. She knew she was alone in T.J.Maxx with words streaming out of her mouth without her consent. She'd catch sight of her talking self in a mirror, soul utterly detached from body, like a strange face peering over her shoulder.

"Do you talk to yourself in public?" she'd asked Ben.

"Sure. You know me. I always talk to myself."

Just like that. He didn't second-guess himself at all these

days. He was fine with being a guy who talked to himself in public. Big deal.

THE DOG, RUTH, watched from various corners while Evvie tried to straighten up, singing "5 Days in May," picturing the song's white-haired couple pulling the car up to the edge of the beach and watching the wild waves. The man slings his weary arm around his wife of forty-odd years, she leans into his wiry frame, and they're thinking about their grown kids, how they all hardly visited more than once a year. You raised them and they took off.

Evvie, who'd not been able to conceive a child despite years of trying (after one drastic late-term miscarriage) and had finally agreed with Ben to stop trying for adoption, attempted without much success to protect herself with visions of how dismally the child-rearing story often turned out these days. And congratulated herself that at least she'd be doing her part to keep the population down, not to mention saving a brand-new soul from having to endure the pain of having to be somebody.

Not that she didn't absolutely appreciate having to be somebody. She'd had moments of shocking gratitude for her life—not lately, but they'd branded her, and even catapulted her into serious trouble. In the wake of one of those grateful moments just two years ago she'd flown straight out of a high red tree into a lake she'd imagined was deep. A wild and celebratory leap in the blinding sun, a leap of gratitude for the sometimes unbearable mystery of life itself, but she'd broken her leg in two places.

"Can you turn that song *off*?" Ben called. "I'm trying to get things in order."

She froze. "Order is good!" she called back. "Order is very good."

He said nothing more. She went to the dining room doorway to look at him. He was pinching the bridge of his nose. His shoulders—beautiful, unpretentious shoulders—were tense.

"Today I feel like I've had a heart transplant and the new organ isn't taking," she told him.

Silence.

"You say *nothing* to that?"

"What do you want me to say, Evvie?"

"Why do you hate this song?"

"Could it have something to do with you having played it a hundred times?"

"Oh. But don't you see? That's you and me in that song, Ben! The old couple is *us*. We'll swim naked. With our dog. We'll stay strong and be best friends and camp out on the beach with a fire."

For a moment she was embarrassed, her words had fallen so flat. She had not been embarrassed in front of him this way for years. Early on, it had happened frequently, when all she'd wanted to do was impress him, and now it seemed she'd been returned to that state of extreme vulnerability. "Ben, I'm—" He didn't look up. Something was dreadfully wrong here, said the odd, vaguely British documentarian's voice that often resounded from the deep marrow of her breastbone. The voice had been recurring for days. She punched herself there, hoping to silence it.

"Are you *angry* at me? You've been so—"

"I thought you said you were going to do something today. You said you were living for Saturdays. What about the—"

"So that's why you're acting this way? All distant? Because I haven't worked on my stuff?" Her "stuff" was a sketchbook where she was mapping out an idea for a documentary about a guy who worked in a convenience store on Highland Avenue. She'd made one documentary before, eight years ago, and two short ones about city garbage for a cable station, so this wasn't entirely unimaginable. "It's not like I've been sitting around doing nothing!" she cried. "I was up at five o'clock cleaning cat cages, for one thing! Not that you'd care about a bunch of caged cats."

That wasn't fair at all. Ben was tenderhearted about cats. If it weren't for his allergies, they'd have adopted several.

She went to the banister to retrieve her coat; she was bundling up. She had to get out of there. Something in the air was like a thin, gray, long-fingered spirit choking her. Her face was blazing hot. He was leaving her! For a moment she could feel that.

"Something's wrong with this place! And you are so . . . so *different* now!" and then she was out the front door, leaning into the wind as she walked, sudden tears in her eyes. She was inexplicably happy to discover a red Rome apple in the flannel-lined pocket of her coat. She stood on the corner of Chislett and Leon and ate the apple and watched snowflakes hit down on the deep red roundness. Would he follow? The husband she *knew* would. He would burst out the front door without a coat and rush to pull her back inside, generous even when angry. He would yell at her, offended love flashing in his eyes. *Why do you just walk away? That's so fucking immature and you know I hate it, so why do you do it?* But this new husband, this person with this barely controlled *attitude of exasperation*, desperation, who was he trying to be?

She listened to the apple crunch inside her mouth, eyes open but mind attending to a childhood memory that visited in the way of recurring dreams.

The old milky gray cafeteria from Immaculate Conception grade school. The mother-daughter luncheon. And Rosemary Bates, three years older than Evvie, showed up with her father. He was bald and older than most fathers, he moved awkwardly in a loose brown suit without a smile. Rosemary's mother, said someone across from Evvie, had died. Isn't that a shame, someone else said. Evvie's own mother was out of her seat, talking to Sister John Helen, who was praising Evvie's sister Louise, as all teachers did. Evvie minded that, but not as much as she would have had she not been fixated on Rosemary Bates, a sick twisted knot forming in her stomach each time she looked across the room and saw the pale, frizzy-haired, gangly Rosemary with the serious bald father.

Evvie kept walking. The apple was so crisp, so deep dark red, the sky above so gray, shaking free its long mane of snow. She breathed in the cold silence. Strange. The strangeness of life! This was the feeling that had permeated all of childhood. At the dinner table, looking at her brother and sister, or walking through the small backyards of the neighborhood, or just standing by a window at night, the strangeness of life had often pierced her, pinned her in place, set her heart pounding.

She would like to see Rosemary Bates right now. She'd never known her, really, beyond "the motherless girl at the luncheon," and yet the girl had taken root inside of her so long ago she had the intimate weight of an old friend or lover who'd altered her life in mysterious ways. The memory of that luncheon came to her two or three times a year or more, rolled in like an unpredicted storm that was itself a harbinger of something.

BEN'S EARLIEST MEMORY—Evvie sometimes remembered it as if she'd been there—was sitting in the sand by Lake Erie on a blanket, playing a bright-colored toy xylophone, in love with the sounds, which he imagined the water could hear. He'd been a gentle child, his mother had said, "the kind who liked to sit alone with a pile of rocks all day long, and just be a happy little guy." This statement had astonished Ben, who had no access to childhood memories that weren't burdened by a sense of isolation.

"EXCUSE ME—WOULD you like to protest the war?"

She'd gone all the way down Hampton to Highland Avenue. It was the nice enough but disturbing guy from the coffee shop whose dislike of George W. Bush had become a little obsessive. Something sad about him, as if he'd imagined that gathering all his energies into detesting a figure that so many others detested at this moment would somehow win him respect, or friends, or at least company. Meanwhile most people ran when they saw him coming: Evvie had quietly witnessed this at the café, where he spoke too loudly and eagerly.

Evvie couldn't bear the sight of someone trying so hard to be loved. She resisted her instinctive recoiling from him, made herself look him in the eye.

"You mean the protest down at the church, right?"

He nodded; his face had broken into a mildly astonished, wavering smile, he was so used to rejection.

Evvie thought of Louise Jacques, the French mystic: *These are two different things: when you are kind to a soul whom in the bottom of your heart you do not esteem, or when you use your kindness to seek and find the beauty in a soul you are not inclined to esteem.*

"My education message will resignate amongst all parents," he said, in George Bush's voice. He was actually a good mimic. Maybe too good. He'd even somehow made his face look like the sorry president. But his peculiar brand of loneliness drowned out the humor. Besides, Bush wasn't funny anymore. Those days were gone.

"I know how hard it is to put food on your family."

"He said that?" she said.

The guy continued. "I mean, there needs to be a wholesale effort against racial profiling, which is illiterate children."

He smiled at her as they walked through the falling snow; she smiled back.

But her heart was splintering.

She wished she was alone now, that she could veer off down the street to the gas station to further investigate the nature of a man who happened to work as a cashier in the convenience store there. She had overheard a man from the Tazza D'oro café, weeks ago, saying that this clerk had *sustained* him last winter when he'd go there late at night for a candy bar.

"I didn't even want the candy bar. I just wanted to see this Indian dude," the man in the coffee shop had said, leaning forward toward his confidant, and his face had stilled Evvie, who'd been at the next table. "I mean, I'm not even *gay* but I felt like I was falling in *love* with the guy. And all he'd say is stuff like, 'Thank you, come again.'" Evvie, struck by the man's intensity, had gone to the convenience store herself later that day and found herself mesmerized by the clerk's face, the bright, black eyes calm and intensely alive. She felt the man emanated a warm silence. She felt the man knew things he couldn't put into words. She felt instinctively the man could be, should be, the subject of a documentary. Guy behind a counter making minimum wage, and all the difference in the world.

THE AIR WAS so cold it hurt her lungs and gave a focal point to her psychic pain. On the corner of Jackson and Highland she saw a tall man who happened also to be eating an apple in the snow. Evvie recognized him from somewhere. The man had his eyes closed and his face looked oddly ecstatic. She asked him if he would like to protest the war, and his eyes opened. She held up her own half-eaten apple, expecting him to recognize what? The kinship of outdoor apple eaters? The ecstasy, had it existed, was gone. His gray eyes filled with distance as if the sky had invaded them.

"No," he finally answered, and walked off in his large black shoes.

"It's just me against the world. Good thing half the world's on my side," said George Bush, still beside her.

She laughed. "That's like a weird Zen koan. I gotta tell my husband that one. By the way, did you know Bush's speechwriter is an animal rights activist?" she said.

The guy shook his head.

"You might want to read *Dominion* by Matthew Scully."

"I just might do that."

"Because every day, all day, underneath all of this plentitude, all of this absurd *abundance*, tortured animals are screaming to be heard."

"Yeah. I bet that's true. But aren't tortured people screaming to be heard too?"

"Yes, but maybe not so consistently."

Evvie didn't care enough at that moment to explain about the interconnectedness of all things.

THE PROTEST WAS small. The church flew rainbow flags and had a shelter in the basement. They joined the thirty or so people, many of whom held signs, but it was a protest devoid of chant and song, it was thirty-odd people pushing diligently against the futility that rose around their shivering legs like dark, polluted American waters. Evvie, who always wanted to believe in the worthiness of protests but could not today, stood silent. She thought of her husband's new glasses (worn only on weekdays at his new job), and for a moment they seemed responsible for her fear. He looked *suave* in those glasses, one of those executive square jaws in a magazine who might be photographed in black and white reading Proust and sipping cognac in an armchair.

An older woman, silver haired and beautiful in sturdy shoes, the type who Evvie imagined could count the nihilistic moments of her life on one hand, began to sing, "*This little light of mine.*"

Evvie deeply admired the woman but also disliked something she saw in her face, a pride, a willful ignorance inflaming her solitary, anachronistic voice as it tried so admirably to attach itself to this spectacularly elusive and brutal historical moment.

I'm gonna let it shine.

Not to mention a kind of wretched vulnerability to death and the specter of meaninglessness that she seemed not to recognize.

Why am I seeing things this way? It's a corrupt way of seeing.
I'd rather be dead than see things this way.

Evvie closed her eyes and begged God, who she still tried, with no success these days, to believe in:

Make me silent as the tundra.

Make me quiet and present as a leopard, or a dog.

Get rid of me, God.

This last prayer was imbued with an emotional violence that was cause for alarm. She took the cold gray air into her lungs. She closed her eyes and lifted her face to the snow.

A flag-flying car screeched to a halt, and a woman jumped out of a gold van and screamed, "You assholes! You asinine assholes!" Then she got back into the flag-plastered golden SUV and sped away. A stunned silence circled them.

Evvie reached into her inside pocket for pamphlets. Mercy For Animals had recently targeted rodeos in Ohio. Another pamphlet was older, but relevant as ever with regard to factory farms. *Even if you like meat, you can help end this cruelty*, the front of the pamphlet said. She handed them out now, asking people just to take a look. One man put his hand up. "Been there, done that," he said, winking. Others grabbed and began reading immediately, nodding and thanking her.

Evvie wanted to go home. She missed her husband as if he were on a large ship in the Baltic. She would remember this whole day as filled with surrealistic omens, a million miniature crows with human faces filling the air. This was the sky inside her too. Probably she was just getting the flu.

"Can I borrow your cell?" she said to a kindly-looking thin man whose jaw was wrapped in a red scarf.

She walked a few steps toward the church wall and called her husband. "I'm protesting," she said. "Down at the church. Wanna join me?"

"I'm still doing bills."

"Really? Oh. Wow. Well, I have a question."

"Yes?"

"Do you still love me?"

"Of course I love you."

"Is something wrong? You're so distant."

"No. Just come home."

"I miss the old days," she said, and clenched her eyes shut, turning away from the crowd. "I miss our pushcart and the house on Rosewood and even being broke. I miss our old customers and how we used to be." The words brought with them a gut-roiling torrent of longing.

"Yeah," he said, and let go a sigh.

"Do you too?"

"I don't miss being broke. But yeah, maybe sometimes I miss the pushcart."

"And all those crazy customers we loved! They were a part of our life for all those years, and just like that they all vanish. We don't even mention them anymore!"

"Evvie, come home."

"My heart's going a mile a minute. I think it's about to explode. Something's wrong. It isn't normal."

"Don't be scared. Just come home. You're just—everything will be all right."

"It will?"

"Yes, I promise, just come home, Ev."

She explained to the Bush impersonator that she had to go. He nodded, and she saw some hopeful light flicker in his face that told her all was not lost, he would maybe each day find someone in the world who would befriend him for a little while, and his loneliness would be alleviated occasionally, in small spurts, and his strangeness—whatever it was at his core that made him one of life's impenetrable outcasts—that too would be pacified little by little, she hoped.

On the way back she walked to the convenience store, but the saintly clerk (she'd started thinking of him that way) was not working today. The hefty clerk with a crew cut and a Russian accent and small blue eyes told her he usually worked nights, and that his name was Ranjeev. "But we never call him that." And then the Russian man shook his head, unsmiling. Evvie wasn't sure what he was attempting to communicate. That Ranjeev was a problem of some kind? A joke? Her face must have looked puzzled, because the Russian man stopped shaking his head, crossed his big arms, and signaled with his eyes that their interaction was over.

"What do you call him?" she tried.

The Russian man peered at her. "We call him Apu."

"Apu? Like the guy on *The Simpsons*?" Evvie smiled.

The Russian man nodded, arms still crossed. "Apu like *The Simpsons*."

Evvie smiled. She wanted the man to smile back. She was fascinated by his tremendous ability to refrain from smiling, and by her own perverse need to stand there smiling at him in spite of this. "Good night," she finally sang. "Tell Apu I said hello!"

BEN

BITTERLY COLD MORNINGS in Pittsburgh sometimes resemble evenings. People get themselves into cars and go to work, or stand on corners and wait for buses, and just below the surface of their complaints about the brutal cold, they learn to covet their weather, and feel superior to people in sunnier, sillier climates.

Ben was tired of all that. Not Evvie. She loved Pittsburgh the way the natives did. This after years of wanting out. If Ben complained about the weather, Evvie liked to remind him that an architecture critic from the *New Yorker* named Pittsburgh, Saint Petersburg, and Paris the three most beautiful cities in the world.

But he'd grown up in Erie, and these days felt tired of Western Pennsylvania, architecture and all.

This morning Ben was grateful for Cedric's sleepy silence in the car. His brother-in-law was almost always quiet in a car, as long as there was sports talk on the radio. The talk show host rattled on about the coming Steelers game. The low sky looked like a bruise, and Ben drove fast against the feeling that nothing was right.

"I'm not looking forward to this game," Cedric mumbled when a commercial came on.

"Baltimore's overrated," Ben answered.

"I don't know about that." Cedric cared so much about his team he had to take nothing for granted and assume they'd be beaten, so as not to be crushed by the possible disappointment.

Ben pulled the car into the lot of the Aspinwall Giant Eagle.

"Thanks, man," Cedric said, before getting out. He looked at Ben with his usual mix of innocence and apprehension. "You all right? You seem a little tense."

"It's my job, I guess."

"Being tense is your job?"

"Seems that way." He gripped the steering wheel, leaned forward, blew out a stream of air.

"No real pressure here at the old Giant Eagle. You would make an acceptable cashier. Or you could choose to be a low-rung loser and unload trucks in the back with me."

"I just might, someday."

Cedric nodded his encouragement, smiled, and got out of the car. Ben watched his brother-in-law head across the parking lot. Cedric had dropped out of college, where he'd been studying electrical engineering, had chosen to work at the Giant Vulture (Evvie's nickname for the supermarket megastore) because it was low pressure, involved little interaction with a boss or customers, and because, according to Evvie, he had depended on such stores since his childhood in Philadelphia. (Evvie had told Ben so many vivid stories about Cedric as a child that sometimes it seemed he'd been there as witness, an invisible sibling who'd seen Cedric walking on his toes toward Pantry Pride, where apparently every day for years he'd bought red licorice and bottles of iced tea.) Those shopping ventures had been distractions from home life (where nothing was predictable) and school life (where peers considered him the freak to torment). A popular girl had once stuck a dead rodent in his Batman lunch box, for instance. When he was ten, a teacher kept him after class and told him he would never amount to anything if he didn't find a way to stop *being so weird*. Did he think it was "cool" to be *weird*? the teacher had said. Was he looking for attention? Did he practice being weird at home? No doubt Cedric had stared at her, unblinking, able to see her ineptitude but too stunned to name it or know it was cruel. (Ben and Evvie both wished they could walk back into the past and deck the woman.) And then, when Cedric was thirteen, he'd been given a concussion by a boy in gym class, the same boy who, the year before, had started a rumor that Cedric regularly gave the janitor, a portly guy who smoked cigars, blow jobs.

And yet, according to Evvie, the Pantry Pride checkers in those days had greeted Cedric as if he were a celebrity. *Ceddy! Where you been?* And his presence—something so golden and pure about Cedric, and he was beautiful too—had unified them. According to Evvie, his presence had rendered the checkers in an impersonal grocery store as momentarily intimate as the mom-and-pop shop people two blocks down.

Evvie's loyalty to her brother was something he'd fallen in love with. He'd absorbed all her stories about Cedric, the ones she'd told when the two of them were holed up in that first tiny third-floor apartment where the fire escape led to the back entrance of a bar where Evvie's old band had played when she was twenty. Maybe he would drive by that old place later today, look up at the old white door, or even climb those steps and peer in at the kitchen. Maybe whatever devastating love had been born there could be felt like a reviving tonic. He needed some kind of tonic badly.

Ben watched Cedric walk through the glass doors and disappear for another day. Sometimes Cedric was his favorite person in the world. He did not get involved with others but regarded them from a natural distance made of his sincere inability to comprehend what all the fuss was about. Though he was highly intelligent, he possessed the gift of simplicity that seemed rooted in a radical innocence.

Sometimes Ben wished this innocence was something he could contract himself. To walk through the world that way seemed a worthy, if unachievable, goal. Other days Ben thought of Cedric as a compulsive and self-absorbed filthy squatter, teetering on the edge of eviction, oblivious to the needs of others. He'd said he needed a place to stay, and they'd said sure, but that was five years ago. He'd slowly trashed their attic. "What does it matter?" Evvie said. "Like we ever go up there." But Ben felt the chaos over his head like something that itched. "If someone else had made that mess, you'd hate it," he told Evvie. "Maybe," she'd admitted. On certain days, the relationship between Evvie and Cedric struck Ben as pathological. She loved his dependence. He loved the routines he'd developed, the crappy little nest he'd made in the attic, the way she made him buttered muffins and gave him money she didn't have, and called him *Cedrico*. Lately every time she called him *Cedrico*, Ben wanted to say, *His name is Cedric*.

The attic was probably infested. Evvie said it was a good sign if spiders and mice wanted to hunker down with you. It meant you weren't too toxic yet. She actually whispered, when she found webs in their cabinets, "Spiders, you're good. You're very good." She refused to kill the moths that overtook their kitchen twice a year. She didn't mind kitchen moths. "They're so harmless." She'd try to cup the moths in her hands and set them free, but after a few egg-hatchings, the kitchen would fill up with great swarming clouds of the white, winged crea-tures (a neighbor had come in one night, unexpectedly, and seen Evvie eating a plate of noodles as if in blissful ignorance of what the neighbor told Ben "had to be a good hundred of the little bastards"). Finally Ben won the battle of the moths, setting up little cardboard tents that lured them in with sticky black stripes of pheromones that promised sex to the males and instead trapped them in place, their wings protesting un-til they died. "Imagine that," Evvie said. One of Ben's darkest thoughts regarding Evvie was that she was a pheromone trap. That he'd entered the trap fifteen years ago and some part of him had slowly died because of it.

THIS MORNING, OUT of nowhere, Evvie had given him one of her old hugs, lifting him off his feet though he was fifty pounds heavier than she was, and four inches taller. She'd done that a lot when they were first married, proud of her strength, which seemed to issue forth from a sporadic mania. Now she was do-ing it again. After years of not doing it. Couldn't she sense that he wasn't in the mood?

He'd broken free.

He'd turned away, walked to the sink. She'd followed him, putting her arms around his waist, then leaped back, as if he'd burned her.

"I'm really in a hurry," he'd explained, and he ran out.

———

TRAFFIC WAS HEAVY. The sky still dark, clouds packed with snow sailing in from the West, moving slowly across the sky. He put in Keith Jarrett's *Koln Concert*, something he'd loved in college, and turned it up, driving down the gray highway for work; he worked testing and selling medical equipment now, a job he'd had for almost two years. A friend had recruited him, and it was a decent salaried job, and he found himself enjoying the way it felt to glide down the street in a coat and tie. He looked surprisingly good and sometimes didn't recognize his reflection when he passed by glass storefronts. A man in his prime with dark wavy hair, his long stride more confident than he felt. He passed others on the street dressed like him, headed to offices, and felt affiliated in a way he'd never imagined possible when he and Evvie had set themselves apart from all this, working the pushcart four hours a day, proud to be out of the mainstream. They'd been like travelers, even though they'd never gone anywhere.

Now, when he walked down the street in his coat and tie, he was a person among people, fortunate people going to work, accepting the limitations of their jobs, accepting the world and its demands and limits, and none of them, Ben imagined, cultivating the idea that they were somehow special and deserved something other than this. None of them pretending to rage against the machine that fed them.

For years he and Evvie had lived without much money, thought they didn't care about money, and suddenly, there it was—nothing compared to his friends in law or computers, but enough that now he could entertain thoughts of vacations to places other than New Jersey. He'd paid off their credit card debts, and the last of their college loans. He'd bought a decent guitar. He wanted to go to Greece.

"You think you'll do this job forever?" Evvie asked last year.

"Don't be judgmental," he'd snapped. They were walking the dog, but now they stopped. "This money allows you to defend your pigs and ducks."

She'd blinked, silenced, reddening.

"I'm sorry," he said. "I'm really sorry."

"I wasn't even being judgmental," she said, then called the dog. "Really. I was just being curious." Her voice was soft, stunned. She pet Ruth and looked down.

He'd been frightened of himself then, unable to understand why she'd called forth such anger. It was something harder to pinpoint that filled him with restlessness he'd never known before; he just couldn't admit to himself that his infatuation with a woman who worked in an office across the street from him had anything to do with it.

They headed down a long street, letting Ruth sniff the world, and Evvie had started telling him a story about an old friend of hers, and he made all the right sounds. Everything in the landscape—ordinary road signs, a white metal chair on someone's front porch, pigeons on a wire lined up against the blue—seemed to be charged with a strange light, beckoning him. All of it interesting in contrast to the woman who walked beside him, his wife, his best friend.

To battle this, he'd stopped her in the middle of the street, folded her into his arms, and kissed her hard on the mouth. Then stepped back and told her, "Someday we'll travel around the world together." Her dark eyes flashed up at him, beautiful, and for one second, strange again—he could remember in that moment the first time he'd seen her, and his body flooded with love born of all their history.

NOW HE CALLED Lauren.

"Ben!" she said, unfurling the name, stretching it out like a warm blanket. The voice was a little hoarse, always, and he loved it.

"Look at the sky," he told her. "It looks like day is done."

"I kind of like that day-is-done look."

He laughed and she started singing. "Day is done, gone the sun, from the lakes, from the hills, from the sky, all is well, safely rest, God is nigh."

He'd never heard her sing. She was a little off-key. "You have a good voice."

"Learned that one in Girl Scout camp. Also learned to hate Girl Scout camp."

"So what are you doing now?"

"Soaking in the bath." He tried not to imagine this. She was the type to get up extra early in order to start the day with a hot bath. She'd have her coffee in the tub while the sun rose and her daughter slept in the next room. She highly recommended hot morning baths, the tub filled to the brim.

Evvie would have a problem with that. All that wasted water a crime.

"I might try it," he said.

"I'm getting out now."

"OK, you do that."

He knew she had a soft white robe with *LAUREN* on the

pocket. He imagined her flushed body, stepping into the robe after the bath, and slammed on the brakes, just avoiding a collision. If he didn't watch it, he'd start to become the kind of driver he'd always hated.

"You all right?" Lauren said.

"Yeah."

"So last night I dreamed we were hiking in a foreign country and found a cave in the side of a mountain, Ben. It was so beautiful."

"Stalactites, stalagmites?" Ben said.

"No. It was really strange. It was like van Gogh's bedroom in there!"

Ben pulled over to the side of the road. Van Gogh's bedroom had been Evvie's dream of the perfect space. Once she'd said, "If you ever left me, I'd go rent a room and turn it into van Gogh's bedroom. I'd be a hermit with a dog."

"You still there?"

"Yeah."

"You sound a little funny."

"No, just wishing I'd had more sleep. Better go. I have a meeting way up in Cranberry today."

"*Cranberry?*" she'd said. "OK, have fun up there and don't take any wooden nickels, kid. And call me later."

"OK."

"Or sooner."

"OK."

HE DROVE ON. Keith Jarrett was too sad. As was silence. Turned on a talk show. Too manic. News. Worst of all. Went back to silence. It was starting to snow again. He leaned forward and squinted up into low, dark-bottomed clouds so thick they looked permanent.

January was a problem. It wasn't just the lack of sunlight, the oppressive skies, the scraping ice from windshields in the bitter morning darkness before work, the landlord refusing to turn up their heat, though all of this was certainly the perfect backdrop of gloom for memories that seemed to return to him every year at this time. This year they were more pressing, and a part of him remained compelled and hopeful that through such memories, a key was being handed over, and all he had to do was take it and open the door and then he might understand his life. How he'd arrived here.

There were January days when the essence of childhood returned like thick vapor and he'd feel himself transported, back to a family room with a picture window, the twins, Russell and June, his cousins Murphy and Al, who was deaf, and a few neighbor kids, all of them playing army, climbing on couches, while he stood behind the curtain, peeking out at his mother. That day she'd stood in her brown tweed coat and slippers, arms crossed, snow falling down around her, an expression of intense unhappiness on her face, and he'd slapped the window then, drawing her eye, making a funny face so she'd laugh, though this was out of character for him and only drew a look of puzzlement.

MEMORIES OF ERIE. *Eerie Erie*, his sister, June, used to say. Years ago, she and Ben had discovered that both felt that something bad had happened to them early on that they'd never be able to identify exactly. They knew that they'd been well taken care of, had gone fishing in the summer on a beautiful boat owned by their father's boss, had wonderful dogs, and had run on the beach together holding hands—Ben kept a photo of that to prove it. Under memory's *assault*, even innocent things— the time their mother helped them make a kite, the visits to a pumpkin farm, riding bikes in a yellow-leaf windstorm— seemed undergirded by darkness.

Ben's father, as it turned out, had enjoyed quite the string of affairs. Once he'd had the nerve to bring one of his "friends" home for dinner, a college girl (coed, he'd said) named James— James!—who'd broken down in tears before she left, embracing Ben's mother at the door and saying she was so sorry. "For what, James?" Ben's mother asked, taking a step back but still patting the poor thing's back. "For having sex with your father!" the girl had practically shrieked, and all of them heard it: June and Russell and Ben, all of whom had been trying to watch *The Partridge Family*, and heard too their mother saying to James, "You had sex with my *father*? He's *dead*!"

"You know what I mean!" the girl cried, as if their mother was being purposefully dense. And maybe she was. They couldn't have told the difference.

"Pack your bags," their mother said to their father, understanding everything. "Get out!"

James ducked out the door and ran.

Ben had watched all this from a doorway, the Partridges in the background singing, his father's lips compressed, as if hiding a smile, as if his mother's show of drawing this line was merely amusing.

"I'll give you three hours," she said. She was in green pants and a gray shirt printed with pink flowers. Her face was utterly calm.

He stepped forward. "I'll give you more than three hours," he said, and smiled, as if his charm would save the day again. "I'll give you the rest of my life."

"Mom?" Russell cried out. Ben turned. Russell looked small and paralyzed with fear, like an omen of all that was to come.

HIS FATHER HAD stayed in the house. His mother had gone away for two months—an eternity—to Oregon, where she had a cousin, a woman who nobody had ever met but who regularly called the house and said, to whoever answered, "Hiya, kiddo, this is Fat-Cousin-Sue." His father had confessed the long string of his affairs (describing, his mother later told Ben, each woman's physicality until it was like listening to a porn show) and after explaining how he had a healthy sex drive that "society" (a big word in 1972) couldn't and shouldn't dampen, he invited her into an open marriage. When she refused, he explained to the kids (the twins were only six) that "all was not well with their uptight mom." While he may have had some academic company in this attitude—he was a great reader of books—he alone, out of all the known fathers in Erie, had taken this public swan dive out of his marriage. Nobody in Ben's class had divorced parents.

His mother sent Ben postcards from Oregon that said she loved him and hoped he was holding down the fort. He'd walked around for months feeling like food was spoiling inside of him, though nobody but the closest observer would have known. His aim was to please. He pleased his teachers, his peers, and even the crossing guard, who'd called him "the gentleman."

It was hard work, pleasing, but he was no more capable of

stopping it than he was of flying away. Inside he was trying to make room for the deep shock of what had become his life—*His* father? *His* mother? He'd loved and feared his father—whose muscled form was so impressive two kids could hang on his arm at the same time—who'd been a great baseball player in high school and had trophies and photographs of himself winding up for the pitch, who'd also been salutatorian and seemed to know everything about everything. The kind of guy who quizzed you at the table to see how many presidents you could name. You'd work hard to memorize them at night, dying to impress him, and he would be impressed. Who cared if sometimes he was frightening, his eyes turning to ice if you disagreed, his bizarre habit of pinching June on the ass even when she begged him not to?

He could call his mother. She could assure him that falling out of love with Evvie—if that's what this was—did *not* make him a philandering ass, arrogant, deluded, or hard-hearted, like his father had been, all those years ago.

BEN WAS ALMOST in Cranberry. He was trying a new route to the office complex. Some guy from work had told him he could make new circuits in his brain that way. "We inscribe these maps in our minds when we drive! We need to burn them up and start over! We need to create new dendrites!" The guy was like a preacher about the brain. "Use it or lose it, buddy," he'd say, twenty-five years old and already passionate about not getting senile. He distributed little puzzle books. "Come on now, do us all a favor and stay sharp!" The guy was nuts.

He pulled over to the side of the road. It was snowing harder now. He called Lauren one more time.

"I miss you," she said, instead of hello. This surprised him. They didn't talk like that.

"I know. Me too." He wanted to be with her, tumbling in a warm field somewhere.

"When can you come?"

"Tonight. That's why I'm calling. Will you be home around seven?"

"I'll be there. I'll hold dinner for you." Lauren was a great cook—unlike Evvie, she didn't have a perverse need to refuse all measuring, and she still believed in the custom of sitting down for dinner. He'd watched Lauren prepare exquisite meals with a pure concentration he found humbling. He'd been compelled, then swept away, by the purity of that focus, which seemed a natural offspring of her compact physical form. She was the only person he knew who didn't seem to be in the grips of some kind of attention deficit syndrome.

And she loved meat. She'd thrown a fat steak on the grill the second time he'd visited, and still he salivated when remembering how together in her tiny backyard they'd eaten piece by piece of that pink filet, three paper lanterns on the table.

It's not that he didn't agree with Evvie's stance against factory farming, which any fool could see was a nightmare beyond imagining. But he understood that there would always be enough injustice and human suffering to make wrongs done to animals necessarily secondary. Such realism overwhelmed him, and he was sorry for that—sorry for how it seemed a product of despair that shot through his heart like a silent, twisted vine. Or was it despair? Maybe it was just weariness, or disappointment that he wasn't, and never would be, an empathetic chicken lover. A great wave of futility got in the way and dulled his heart.

(He'd told Evvie this, in just those words, the hundredth time she stood there asking him to feel outrage that fifteen thousand chickens were beheaded with every tick of the clock after living lives made brutal and short by what she called concentration camps.) He had to stop himself from saying, "So?"

Later, away from her self-righteousness, he'd argue with himself. What was happening was massive, unsustainable, and wrong. But people everywhere wanted cheap meat. Meat was history. Meat was *the bloody heart of culture itself.* He himself wanted cheap meat and wanted it more than he knew was good for him. He craved it, and this put him in the majority, and why did Evvie go around thinking humans were so different from other animals in their need for meat? What about that arrogance? He knew what she'd say to that. Humans didn't *need* meat. Like so much of what they took, they didn't *need* it at all. OK, Evvie, fine. So humans are terrible and shot full of greed. That's been established for quite some time.

HE AND LAUREN never took their clothes off or even kissed; it wasn't *an affair.*

The most they did was talk and extend a few quick hugs. Ben knew what Evvie would say to that.

And she was right. It was their talk that had created this impossible, intoxicating bond that had the power to lift him right out of his life as he knew it. Not the kind of talk he'd had with Evvie—not that soul baring, though there was some of that on his part after a few beers—but a smaller kind of talk, unusual for its ease. He'd never been good at small talk. Now, to find he could do it, was like finding a whole other self. They talked food, football (she loved it), people from work (she had favorite

eccentric customers the way he and Evvie used to have), co-
medians (like Evvie, she loved Chris Rock), the women from
Lauren's rowing club (they'd go out in kayaks at four in the
morning every Saturday), and Lauren's daughter (a character
with a dark mop of hair, a sharp chin, and her mother's laugh).
Sometimes they talked about work. Lauren was a teller in a
bank. She'd described the manager as *a barrel-chested dude
named Rob Rooter.* Rob Rooter made them all convene in the
morning for a pep talk about customer relations (*like they do
in Walmart!*) but usually ended up turning this pep talk into
a story about his wife, who was turning into a real be-atch, he
said, and did any of you girls have any advice about shopahol-
ics? He was the kind of guy who'd strut into the bank in his
pinstripes, with the air of a celebrity whom everyone should
recognize, and ask a crowd of strangers who waited in line,
"What do you think, people? Should I learn to ice-skate?"

Ben loved these stories. Loved how Lauren, a deep amuse-
ment in her face, punctuated so much of what she said with
"You believe that?" She had an appreciation for almost everything that came up. She had *People*, *Vogue*, and *Vanity
Fair* magazines neatly piled on a table. Sometimes he flipped
through these. Evvie hated magazines. Such a waste of paper,
such a cult of celebrity, such a distraction from what mattered,
such a celebration of all this excess. Yeah, yeah. Well, guess
what—Ben was really happy looking at the crazy clothes the
Vogue chicks wore, and why did Evvie hate *Vanity Fair* anyway, which had excellent journalism, including stories about
Iraq, one of which Ben read on Lauren's couch one night with
concentration that he hadn't known in a while. As if Lauren's

concentration was contagious. That night her house with its turquoise walls and bold red curtains, her vases filled with fresh flowers, the silence of order, had cast upon him a domestic peace he'd never known.

Sometimes they watched *Lost*. They stayed clear of politics, saying nothing while they checked the news on CNN. "I don't know." She'd sigh. "I guess they're all trying their best." And change the channel.

Tonight he would break it off with her. That was the way to progress. He knew it. The right thing was usually the hard thing.

Lauren answered the door with her hair up in a towel like a goddess. High cheekbones, crooked smile, wide, blue, startled eyes meeting his, filled with affection and humor.

"I can't stay," he said.

She hugged him, stepped back, and told him, "Come in for a bit." He could tell by her voice that her nine-year-old daughter was at home. Indeed the girl was sprawled on the couch.

"Hi, Ramona."

"Hi, Mister." Somehow she'd gotten stuck on calling him *Mister*. He didn't really mind.

She was a gangly tomboy, in red cowboy boots and a too-small nightgown. She lived nearly half the time with Carter, her father. Ben had no idea what that meant, since the only thing Lauren had ever said about Carter was "Carter's a bit of a dolt."

"What show is this?" He'd taken a seat on the flowered armchair.

"*Full House*, I told you ten times."

"I haven't even *seen* you ten times." He kept his voice jovial.

"Ramona's exhausted," Lauren said.

"I am not."

"Children never know when they're exhausted."

"She looks fine to me," Ben said.

"Well, I'm not fine," said the girl, wanting no alignment with him.

He couldn't resist. "OK, I get it. You're not fine. There's nothing fine about you."

Finally the girl smiled. The smile was brilliant and soft, and a little shy, and made him glad he'd brought her a Clark bar, which he now presented.

"Thank you, Mister!"

"THIS IS A work of art," he told Lauren. Rosemary chicken, sweet potatoes, salad, everything arranged on a simple yellow cloth, candles, flowers; this was just the way she liked to live. She created a *sanctuary*.

"It's like you're a landscape architect of the kitchen table," he said.

"I freak out like every night's the last supper." She looked amused with herself, but a little uncertain.

"That's the way to live," he said.

Ramona said, "Maybe this is the last supper. Nobody knows when they're going to die."

Lauren smiled. "That's right, babe."

"A boy in my class drowned," Ramona said, and her eyes were wide and accusatory.

"That's terrible," Ben said. "Was he your friend?"

"I sat at his table at lunch."

"He had a twin brother," Lauren said. "The family up and moved to North Dakota to live on a farm with grandparents. I guess they believe in the landscape cure, but I kept thinking how if you move, you lose everything. Every familiar face, and room, and banister, and light switch, and window view. I don't even like to think of that boy out there in North Dakota."

"And that's why I think God is mean," said Ramona.

Lauren shrugged and let out a sigh.

SHE'D MASHED THE sweet potatoes, then stuck them back in their skins. They were so good he ate slowly, noticing everything. Lauren's attention to detail helped him understand what he'd been missing so long with Evvie, who often ate a banana for dinner, dunking it in a jar of peanut butter, or some dark chocolate and a bowl of noodles next to a stack of books or newspapers. Evvie who felt so overwhelmed by material objects that she had sometimes taken the broom to cluttered surfaces and swept everything into the trash with a vengeance. "Evil elves are hauling this shit in when we're asleep! Nobody can tell me they aren't!"

When she got depressed she'd hold the sides of her head and clench her eyes shut. "I can't take it." She'd sit with a cup of coffee at the kitchen table, saying she should've been a monk because monks had no *things*. He wondered lately if maybe that's *exactly* what she should've been. But what monastery would take her? She'd flown out of a thirty-foot tree into a lake and broken her leg just because she was feeling good one day. That had terrified him, and the weeks he'd spent having to wait on her had been exhausting; she needed not only food delivered, but assurance. "No, Evvie, you're not crazy. You were just a little ecstatic. It can happen to anyone."

And it could. Not to him, maybe, but he'd known other people prone to proverbial ecstatic leaps. "You're just impulsive sometimes," he'd told her. "That's no crime." In fact, for years he'd envied her spontaneity. She'd always wanted to jump in the car and head somewhere. She was at her best in a car, soothed by motion and music, her eyes open to the world and shining, as if she saw an unraveling, ineffable secret.

But that Evvie was gone. Two years had passed since she'd broken her leg. Had that somehow marked the beginning of his detachment? Or had it happened even earlier, in the middle of all that effort that went into trying to conceive a baby he hadn't been sure he'd even wanted? Those had been an exhausting couple of years, watching Evvie inflate with hope and shatter with disappointment again and again. A great relief when they'd finally given up. They'd gone out to celebrate the freedom they would have lost had they conceived, in a restaurant they couldn't afford, got hammered, then walked through the empty streets of downtown Pittsburgh and down to the fountain where the three rivers met. Under dim stars they talked about beginning again. All the traveling they could do. That was what they'd wanted all along! They were free now. Still time to see the entire world if they got lucky.

He'd soon after quit the pushcart and gotten a so-called real job, both for the money and because he'd started to think too much togetherness was bad for them. Maybe, on some level, he'd been angry at her. Or maybe nothing had been quite the

same for him since she'd flown out of a tree he'd begged her not
to climb. If she did that, what else would she do?

And yet, wasn't it better to watch her fly from a tree than to
see her as anxious as she was these days, as if stepping out the
front door was a significant challenge? She was somehow turning into someone whose greatest desire was to shrink the world
or at the very least keep it from expanding.

AFTER RAMONA WAS in bed (Lauren had read to her, sung to
her, joked with her, told her a story), he sat at the round kitchen
table and drank some tea with Lauren, who was telling a story
about one of her customers at the bank. "He looks like Brawny,
the paper towel guy. But also like a robot. Like I seriously think
he might be a *robot*." As she spoke he felt he was looking at her
through the wrong end of a telescope; she faded, she became
tiny in the great distance, her beauty miniaturized and less disturbing.

"So, Lauren, for now, for now I think I have to take a break
from our friendship."

"You a robot too?" she said. She smiled. He thought he saw
a quick flash of anger on her face. But then that vanished and
she looked almost relieved.

"You're a married man, Ben. I'm not stupid!" She looked
down.

"Yeah, but you know the story. Look at me."

She looked up at him for a brief moment; her cheeks flushed.

"Doesn't change the fact that you're married," she said,
looking down, and for an instant he saw her as a child, a girl
who'd had to be brave. Is that why he loved her? She'd shown

him a picture of herself with her towering foster mother. He wanted that picture. She'd been six years old, with no front teeth, a fake smile, and a plaid dress with a lizard pin on the wide white collar.

"Look. You've been a good friend to me, and I'm grateful for that, but I could feel this coming. I'm not a dolt."

"This is hard."

"It's OK. It's not that huge a thing. It's life."

She knew how to skate on this thin ice with grace even if she'd had the wind knocked out of her. She stood up and said she'd see him to the door, that she'd been waiting for this moment, and it was a relief, in a strange way, to have it finally arrive. But her face was red, as if she was humiliated, and he couldn't bear it.

"But I love you," he said. "I'm in *love* with you. Really."

This stopped her. And a powerful sense of regret surged through his body, even as he'd spoken the truth.

She looked at him. She was not a romantic, but she didn't have expectations of her own love life ending in complex pools of secret grief and infidelities, despite a broken first marriage. She'd told him once she believed in love as a state where everyone deserved to live. It was a practical thing with her. If you fell out of love, if you found you were with the wrong person, that was a big problem.

"You're *in love* with me?"

"Come on." He wasn't sure what he meant by this.

"I guess I maybe did know on some level." Still, she looked shocked, transported. And delicate. She held her blue eyes wide, blinking

"I'm sorry. I'm confused," he said, looking off to the side. "I had no idea how confused until now."

Lauren smiled boldly and took a deep breath. "Ben. If you love me like *that*, you better deep-six your plan to ditch me for six months"—she had sudden tears in her eyes and was smiling—"because it's not *realistic*, Ben. And you need to ask yourself, is it fair to stay married to your wife if that love's gone?"

Gone? The word was hard. He wasn't ready for it. Not at all. But of course it wasn't fair! Evvie *deserved* someone who could really love her in return. They'd turned out to be a mismatch was all; this past year they'd sat across from each other in restaurants like old couples who've run out of things to say. *The Dining Dead*, as Evvie herself used to call them.

He kissed Lauren for the first time.

"I don't know where I am." He hated himself for a moment.

"You're right here."

"I can't sleep!" Ramona stood behind them, barefoot in SpongeBob pajamas, thumb in mouth like a much younger child, eyes wide and accusatory.

Lauren turned to her. "Well, you can go try your best. Go on."

She didn't budge. "I'm afraid I'll have another nightmare," she said. Ramona's eyes were filling up with tears.

"I'll talk to you soon," Ben said, and slipped out the door.

HE SAT IN the dark car now, on the edge of a tree-lined street in the park, and called his best friend, Paul. Paul lived in Chicago. He was an actor and musician barely getting by. He was also an unlapsed Catholic (having been lapsed for years), a recovering alcoholic, and a guy who had started a choir in a maximum security prison. Ben had known him since college.

"If Evvie wants to spend her life trying to save animals, being constantly freaked out about the world, she should *do* that, but

I can't," he told Paul. "She's great, but I don't think I can stay. I need something else. I don't even know if I love her anymore."

"Don't take this the wrong way, but have you prayed about it?"

Ben bristled. It was an absurd question, and passive-aggressive too. These newly sober people could drive you crazy, even if they were Paul.

"I've been the most prayerful atheist in town."

"What is it you want, Ben?"

"It's not what I want. It's what I need. I need to live with a grown-up."

"Evvie's not a grown-up?"

"I don't know."

"I mean, isn't she? As grown up as anyone else? Just because she procrastinates doesn't mean—"

"I don't know, Paul. I think she's turning into an agoraphobic. She barely goes anywhere, and she's always staying up late writing letters to senators she somehow imagines she can convince to stop the factory farms, or to huge companies like Merck or Johnson and Johnson. I mean, if I read you one of her letters, you might understand. It's like she has no idea who she's writing to. No idea what planet she landed on."

"I always liked Evvie," Paul said, simply. "Maybe she's trying to hold on to integrity or something. She knows the letters are futile, but why give in to futility? I just always liked Evvie."

"I like her too!" he protested. "Jesus, Paul. It's not about not *liking* her!"

"Maybe she needs therapy."

"She won't go. She had a bad therapist once and now she distrusts them all."

"Well, that's understandable, I guess."

Ben's temper flared. "Hey, bud, whose friend are you here? I need a little support!"

Paul was quiet for a moment. "You have my support. I'm just a little sad. You guys have been together for so long. And you're just following this trend I see where nobody believes in loyalty anymore. I'm just feeling a little bad for Evvie."

"Feel bad for me!" Ben shouted. "I'm in hell, Paul! Feel bad for me."

"OK," Paul said. "I feel bad for you!"

HE DROVE HOME filled with a simmering rage. Evvie had so skillfully manipulated him with her magnificent vulnerability that he felt like one of her beloved hogs or chickens who could hardly move in their cage. She had made him feel so indispensable, so responsible for her happiness! *I can tell you anything. I don't trust anyone in the world but you.*

Early on, when they'd been young enough to believe their alienation was unique—when Evvie had been recovering from childhood and a year in a punk band whose drummer had been killed in a car accident, when he'd only wanted to hole up with her and make his own music and outsize metal sculptures— he'd loved those declarations. Now, as his therapist explained, "If someone told me I was the only person in the world they could *trust*, I'd take that as my first warning sign that I was with a fairly troubled person."

(He told the therapist that he too was fairly troubled, that he and Evvie had always recognized and respected that trouble in one another, but the therapist had only said, "Hmmm.")

"The only therapist I'm interested in, Ben, is God, and unfortunately I don't believe in God."

"And that makes no sense!"

"Exactly."

"Just because one therapist screwed up with you nine hundred years ago doesn't mean they're all bad, Evvie."

"I agree. It's not *them* that can't be good at therapy, it's me. I blame myself. I'm afraid of assigning words to feelings. I'm afraid I'll just make up my memories. I do it all the time, even without a therapist. I've told you this a hundred times."

But it was like she was proud of being bad at therapy. That was it. She was full of pride, and it had her cornered.

He was home now. The bricks, the blue door, the statue of Francis of Assisi that Evvie, the proclaimed nonbeliever, insisted on having in the tiny garden, shining in the moonlight. Years ago, when they'd lived in Boston for a year so he could study piano, she'd wanted a whole flock of saints. She used to believe the spirits of the saints literally inhabited the statues, that the saints were powerless to resist the need people had for their presence. "Otherwise they couldn't be saints. It's what separates them from us regular humans—they can't resist love, and we can." Her Irish grandmother had told her that. In the old days, the remnants of Evvie's childhood faith had enchanted him, had almost been contagious. But when he'd looked around at the world without the lens of that initial blissful love, whatever faith he'd known vanished.

IT WAS HOME but it no longer looked like home. It looked like a memory of a place he had already left behind. The strangeness of this was exhilarating even as it stabbed him hard in the chest. He was headed for what some Buddhist writer called *the great longed-for catastrophe*. When he'd read that phrase he'd understood immediately how the sheer tedium of having to walk around in your own skin could fill you with the desire to burn it all down and start again. He'd tried to share that understanding with Evvie one night, and she'd bristled. "I'd prefer to dodge catastrophe for the rest of my life. Nothing in me longs for a catastrophe. The fact that everyone I know will die is catastrophe enough."

End of conversation.

The bright moon, almost full, shone on the bedroom window of this rented house where he'd slept for years. If Evvie was awake, she'd be under the covers with a flashlight, reading a book or writing her letters, Ruth beside her with her head between her paws.

Evvie wrote to politicians as if they actually gave a shit about the burden of animals. One letter he happened to see began like this: "Dear Senator, How are you? I'm OK, though it's been raining for eight days here." Like a kid at summer camp writing home to Mom and Dad. The letters always a barrage of agonized description about the lives of various brutalized farm animals. Or most recently, she wrote long letters to local politicians about cracking down on dogfights. He found a letter that Evvie had signed:

Blessings,
Evangeline Muldoone

Who the hell was she to give blessings? It would have been so much more honest if she'd sign off,

I'm fucking nuts,
Evangeline Muldoone

He walked upstairs and into their room. She was sleeping, with Ruth beside her, the dog's head on the pillow Evvie had made. Ruth was the most amazing dog on earth, half pit bull, half retriever, with pink spots on her neck and a sleek brown and gray coat, and a big, square, intelligent head, and eyes that revealed wisdom. Evvie had rescued Ruth from the shelter. He'd once told her that even if that was the only thing she'd ever done in her life, her life would've been worth it. If he were to leave, he'd need joint custody. He couldn't leave. Ruth would hate it. He wouldn't leave. He'd get through this. People got through times like this. He looked down at Evvie and softened. She was childlike when she slept. Her long black hair pulled back in a single braid that hung down her back, her mouth slightly open, her profile beautiful and so deeply familiar his chest tightened.

He steeled himself against the sorrow rising in his chest.

It was easy to freeze whatever feeling might have shattered him. Hardening his heart had become a habit. He took off his clothes and got into bed beside her, crossed his arms on his chest, and stared into the darkness. He let himself fill with sympathy for himself, for all the lonely nights he'd known in this house.

The bed split in half, a dark river ran between the two sides. He floated downstream.

Lauren.

He felt a yearning for her rise out of his chest and hover in the air above him, the great bold spirit of his future. Lauren wore an ankle bracelet; it sparkled in his mind, and he imagined running his finger down her long, smooth leg, then tugging on the bracelet.

He floated on down the river in his bed, his hands clenched together, his eyes wide open in the dark, sleepless.

"Is that you?" Evvie mumbled on the far bank, sitting up.

He looked over at her. "Hey."

"I just had the most beautiful dream."

"That's nice." Please let her drop back to sleep.

"I dreamed the Dalai Lama was sitting at our kitchen table in the middle of the night, quietly drinking a glass of water in the dark."

"That's a nice dream."

"In the dream I didn't even have to get out of bed to see him. It was enough that he was down there in our kitchen. I could feel he was filling up the whole house with love. Isn't that strange?"

She got out of bed and walked to the window. "Not ordinary love, Ben, but real love. It was the best dream I've ever had in my life." She was deeply moved, holding back tears. He wanted to put a pillow over his head. Not the Dalai Lama!

She turned away from the moon and looked at him. "Everything is going to be beautiful with us," she said. She walked over and petted the sleeping dog, her eyes downcast, waiting, perhaps for him to say something. But he could think of nothing he wanted to say. She went into the bathroom for some water. "We have to get back in touch with the everyday miracles," she said, back in their room, holding up a glass of water next to the window. "It's like we have to stop taking stuff for granted. Like water. Water's an everyday miracle, right?"

"I don't take anything for granted," he said.

"So maybe I'm talking to myself." Her voice trembled. "Maybe I'm just talking to myself. But that's all right. Sometimes in marriage, a person ends up talking to their self for a little while. While the other person maybe talks to his self. And then, some time passes, and they're talking to each other again."

She left the room. She was going downstairs. "I have to hear this song," she called. Of course she did.

If she goes downstairs and puts on any song other than "Fake Plastic Trees" (last week's insistent redundancy), or the song about the old couple driving to the beach, or *Purple Rain*, which she'd blared nine hundred times on Wednesday, I will cling to some final straw of hope, Ben told himself. He waited in the dark.

The music blared. Guitar. His heart surged.

The Replacements.

He hadn't heard them for years.

"Unsatisfied."

The song they'd loved together when they were first together. He remembered a summer evening. They'd gone swimming in the city pool, then drove down the highway toward the land's last drive-in theater, their dreams intact, the two of them so relieved to have found one another, their joy was nearly unbearable. Certainly it seemed more than enough to fuel their whole lives. He saw Evvie as she'd been that night, barefoot in some oversize Goodwill dress from the 1950s covered with birds. The memory was a splintering ache in his chest. He closed his eyes and listened. Evvie once said the song's expression of despair was so pure it almost became hope. A crying out so unmediated and necessary, it suggested the presence of a God who was listening.

He didn't want this last straw of hope. It didn't even feel like hope, it felt like pain, but there it was, shining in the darkness.

This song had played on a mix-tape years ago at a birthday party she'd thrown for him, in rooms she'd filled with hundreds of fresh flowers. She'd cooked excellent chili for two days and invited neighbors, friends, customers, and his family. His mother had come with her dogs, and his brother, Russell, from Chicago with a girl, Gina, who'd tried to kill herself a week before and had the scars to show for it. Gina was small and angular with haunted eyes whose expressions had traveled like dark streams underneath the surface of the party. When this song played, she'd stood by the window, looking into the dark backyard, and soon Evvie had gone to stand next to her, protective, compassionate, and unafraid. She didn't have to say a word; the girl had ended up laying her head against Evvie's shoulder. It seemed like a long time ago, even as the image came to him with surprising clarity and resonance.

He sat on the bed now, his head in his hands, listening.

The voice was a raw cry of the heart that became his own. "Come down!" Evvie cried now. "This song is as good as we thought it was! It's killing me!"

EVVIE

IT WAS CEDRIC'S day off, and Evvie decided to call in sick at
the Frame Shop so she could hang out with him in the attic and
watch movies (sci-fi flicks with robots she didn't care for) while
eating banana muffins and chips and thinking about how she
might change her life. For something was seriously wrong. In
moments it seemed that someone's cold hands were suddenly
clutching her throat.

Maybe the house was haunted. She didn't normally believe
in haunted houses, but the atmosphere of every room seemed
to be holding its breath.

And yesterday evening, rearranging sweaters in her closet,
listening to a horrific radio show about women in the Congo,
she'd felt a presence behind her. But it was nothing. Nothing
visible. Still, Evvie had gotten under the covers and hid after
that. What am I doing? she'd wondered, eyes shut.

And then, ten minutes later, Ben and Ruth were back. When
she heard them come in she sprang up and walked back to the
closet and began folding sweaters again, humming loudly.
"Have a nice walk?" she called down. He didn't answer; she
shouted again. "Nice walk?" and then he clomped up the steps,

Ruth following behind him on nails they really needed to cut. Click, click, click went Ruth and thump went Ben, his step unusually heavy, she thought, and then he stood in the doorway, saying he'd seen their friend Kline out there, and Kline had told him he'd been diagnosed with lymphoma. In the doorway Ben's pale face seemed to float. He looked down.

"Oh no!" Evvie said. "That's so awful. Was he with Nora?" Evvie's heart slammed against her chest.

"Nora was home with the kids. Kline was alone. Just walking alone in the dark."

"Prognosis?"

"He's got a good shot at recovery, or so they told him. Chemo, radiation. I just want to go to bed," Ben said, his eyes still lowered. "If that's OK."

"To bed?" For a moment she imagined—though nothing told her so—that this was an invitation.

"To sleep. If that's OK."

"Of course. Ben, are you—"

"Tired and sad. About Kline. Obviously. OK?"

"Did Kline look—"

"He's already lost weight he didn't have to lose."

"He must have looked like—oh man. This is terrible."

Ben was in bed, on his side, and had turned away from her. He still had his shoes on, under the covers, and she had to bite her tongue to stop herself from asking him to take them off. Not because she cared the sheets would get dirty. She just didn't like the idea of it. He'd never done anything like this before.

"Kline will get some good treatment," Evvie said. "It's not like we're in the Belgian Congo."

"What?"

"I mean, it's not like—"

"It's not even called the *Belgian* Congo anymore, Evvie," he said.

"Oh. Excuse me."

"Sorry. I'm just—"

"It's OK."

Kline and Ben had gone to high school together. Kline's wife was an architect and the mother of two small children. She also volunteered for Amnesty International, and earlier in the year Evvie had stopped wanting to go over there (she did not dare confess this) because Ben seemed to like Kline's wife a little too much, guffawing over her jokes, which were poorly delivered and which he'd heard before, and once even asking if he could hold the baby while she checked on the dinner, and always complimenting her on whatever she was wearing— some aggressively ordinary shirt—so that the compliment took Kline's wife by surprise and lit up her face before she dug them into a talk about Indonesian child labor abuses. Evvie worried Kline would die and Ben would move into the house with his auburn-haired beautiful widow and two adorable children, both of whom wore overalls, had big, startled eyes, and could sing Spanish folk songs learned at their nursery school immersion program. Evvie felt sick imagining Ben driving those toddlers and their high self-esteem to school, allowing them animal crackers in Kline's blue van, which had a TV suspended from the ceiling so the kids wouldn't have to be bored for one second.

She saw Kline's wife naked, spread out on a red bedspread, grief giving a poignant and irrefutable depth to her beauty.

———

EVVIE TRIED DISLODGING all of this, but the images only brightened in the sickening carnival of her mind.

The alcove window framed another snowfall. She was on her brother's bed, a quilt gathered around her shoulders, and Cedric was seated on the floor in worn green sweatpants, his curly gold hair a wild frame for his sleepy face. He was engaged in his routine, but not wholly oblivious to his sister's emotional state. He didn't understand much about why people seemed so devoted to making life so unnecessarily complex, but his heart was the most reliably tender a person could hope to encounter. Not that this compassion could budge him out of his routine.

"Yeah, I'm all right, but I need you to come with me to the foie gras protest this afternoon. If you're with me it'll be easier to leave the house."

"What the heck's the big deal in leaving the house, yo?"

"I don't know. I'm on this superstitious kick. Like if I leave, when I come back it will be completely empty. Or burned down."

"Evvie, I hate to tell you this, but that's something a schizoid would say."

"I know. But I feel like there's a phantom in here."

"What time this protest start and where it be at, yo?" Cedric worked with some black guys; sometimes he drifted into black dialect.

"Uh, down on Bryant Street, yo. At five in the evening, so we can catch rush hour traffic along with early-bird diners."

"I watch *my show* at five, son."

"So skip it one day, son."

"I think not."

"Skip it one day for me, please? I need you to skip *one stupid* television show for me today and I won't ask you for anything else for the next ten years!"

Cedric looked at her. Her fear had registered.

"So you'll come with me?"

"Yeah?"

"And what about the Latvian shoe repair guy? The cobbler? Did you call him back?"

"Yeah. He changed his mind. He wants to work alone."

"I'm sorry about that, Ced." She wasn't at all. Only Cedric would think that a career in shoe repair in 2004 was the way to go.

"Don't be sorry! Be sorry for people who starve or get their legs blown off in Iraq, or get shut up in asylums! Don't be sorry for me!"

This was his usual response to anyone's pity, including any trace of self-pity he noticed in himself. Sometimes when he showered he lectured himself at the top of his lungs. This had been hard to explain to Ben early on. "I guess it's a Catholic guilt thing or something," she'd tried.

Evvie smiled. Cedric was right. They were both so lucky, brother and sister, warm in an attic while it snowed, neither of them suffering terminal illness, hunger, unemployment, or even the ordinary abuses that every other person you met seemed to be enduring. She had to learn to breathe deep and calm down, and stop her brain from running amok.

"Let's go."

SNOW DANCED IN the pitch-black of five o'clock, and the usual duck liberators were already gathered on the corner

before La Foret, peacefully picketing. The air of these protests was always charged with a distinct sense of purpose, a
practical solemnity, and the confidence that came with knowing they'd already convinced two other restaurants to stop
serving foie gras. Evvie and Cedric walked up to the little
crowd of five and were warmly greeted. It was a real act of
love for Cedric to accompany her; he didn't like crowds, even
small crowds; he didn't like the cold, and he didn't get many
days off where he could stay in the attic with the TV. Plus,
he hated thinking about the ducks and geese with the metal
pipes jammed down their throats, the two pounds of grain
gunned into their guts, their livers so enlarged they couldn't
even walk, much less care for their plumage and their families. Evvie could feel Cedric trying to block all of this out as
she spoke with a tall woman in a blue coat about boycotting
the restaurant. "You can go home now, Ced. I'm all right."
Cedric didn't hesitate to run down the street. He could be a
graceful runner, but tonight he ran like Forrest Gump, and
Evvie stared after him in wonder.

THE WOMAN IN the blue coat said, "Isn't the so-called *delicacy
of despair* really big in France?"

"It is."

"And aren't the French like heads and tails above us in
terms of cuisine?"

"In some respects, that's true, but—"

"I'm sorry, but I won't apologize for being here at the top
of the food chain." Evvie felt for the millionth time that she
would really like to get out of the world immediately, then

remembered that she actually loved the world, and drew in a deep breath. "We don't need you to *apologize* for anything of the sort, but you might want to consider what our responsibility is to those who have no voice."

Now a balding man in a long tweed coat stood beside her. They made a handsome pair, but handsome in a way that was so dependent on money it just looked depressingly ephemeral.

"I do admire your conviction," the woman said. "Really."

And she had such a sincere expression in her eyes.

The man said, with probable tongue in cheek, "We really appreciate you educating us"—steering the woman inside the restaurant—"but maybe you should care about all the starving people first, huh?"

"But we're all connected, everything and everyone," Evvie said, but quietly. "Best thing you can do for starving people is stop eating meat," she added, almost whispering. She knew when to give up. She knew when to stand still and take a deep breath.

"HEY, EVVIE?"

Ben was standing across the street in his long dark coat with a newspaper tucked under his arm. For a moment the image of him seemed like something she'd conjured up. She almost felt shy, seeing his beautiful singularity, his form so intensely and deeply known it was painful. She'd been missing him all day and hadn't even known it.

"Evvie?" he called again.

"Ben!" Happiness flooded her body with warmth. She saw him as she sometimes did, especially in autumn or winter, when his memories were with him like ghosts, watching as his father married the fourth-grade phonics teacher, Miss Burns, whom Ben and his siblings had been required to call Mom, even before the divorce was legal. "Mom's no dummy," Ben's father had liked to say about her. "She wears a lot of hats."

And that was literally true too, Ben told Evvie. His new "mom" wore berets, and sometimes a cowboy hat, smoked clove cigarettes, and said things like "If I have to teach phonics to fourth-grade dwarves for the rest of my life, can someone please shoot me now?" He'd preferred his mother's house next to the old-age home, where once he and June had sung Christmas carols, all by themselves, since their friends had not shown up.

Evvie froze for a moment—she wanted to rush across the street and embrace Ben the man and Ben the boy, even if he did, as he moved a few steps closer, look like an impatient boss with a bone to pick. Had she left the stove on or something? She finally walked over to him, crossing the dim street. The few remaining duck liberators agreed it was almost time to call it a night, and she bid them farewell.

"Hi!" She threw her arms around Ben, nuzzled her head into his collarbone, and then stopped. His body was rigid.

"What's wrong? Did I do something?"

"We have to talk."

"Did something happen? Did someone die?"

"No. I have to talk—"

"Something about Kline?"

"No, no."

He steered her down the street, with what she began to perceive as a terrifying mixture of sadness and distance. She had a feeling in her spine now, electric with ineffable presentiment. But she walked beside him.

"I have to leave you, Evvie."

"Where are you going? Stupid business trip?"

"I need to be out of this marriage."

A wild hiccup of a laugh escaped her and the landscape tilted. She placed her hand over her mouth for a moment. Then she began to talk loudly with great enthusiasm.

"This fat man tonight got about *two* inches from my face and started *shouting* at me that if I *loved* geese I should go clean up the *shit* they leave all over the park near his house, and then I should have sex with them if I think they're as important as humans. He goes, 'Why don't you just *fuck* those geese, lady? You know that's what you want!' This guy was amazing, Ben. The worst I've seen since Mr. Personality last year. Cedric couldn't take it, he just walked home alone. That's because Cedric has good sense. Remember how you loved those imitations of Mr. Personality I used to do? Back then? Remember how ballistic I—?" She was out of breath.

She stopped and sat down on the curb, her head bowed down into her hands. She had told him a lie. No man had done that tonight. A man had done that last week to another duck liberator in Omaha, and she'd read about it on the Internet.

He sat beside her in his fine woolen coat. She despised that coat. She missed his old parka. Green, dill green, with an orange lining, and big pockets twice repaired (by her) where once he'd loved to hold things for her—keys, books, the old lists she used to make, with all those exclamation points.

1. *Get rid of crap!!!!!*
2. *Go running!!!!*

3. *Buy guinea pig food!!!!!!!!!!!!!!!!!!!!!!!!!*
4. *Call Mom!!!*
5. *Get rid of more crap!!!*

She had stopped making those lists. Everything got worse after she stopped making those lists.

His new coat, the long black coat, was alive. It had captured him. She took a gulp of black air and then another and looked up at the dark clouds sailing across the moon.

"This is just a stage you're going through, Ben. Some midlife crisis thing. Just don't panic." She tried to sling her arm around him, but her arm wouldn't move. Her arm was now made of iron. She managed to stand up on wobbly legs that were not her own. "Let us go home."

Let us go home. It rang in her head.

The two walked to Ben's car, somehow, in silence. Evvie watched her black sneakers moving across the cement. She hummed. *Let us go home.* She sat beside him in silence, watching the darting snow like stitches try to mend the gaping dark.

WHEN THEY ENTERED their front hall, Evvie flicked on the light. "Really, Ben, people go through these *stages*. Whole books are written about it. Apparently it's human. Obviously." She swallowed down a thick stone of terror.

"Please don't say that."

"Why?"

"It's the hardest thing I've ever done in my life, and you dismissing me by calling it a stage, Evvie—you need to hear me. You can stay in the house and I'll keep paying the rent for a while. You won't be poor—I'll see to that. You can go back to teaching. And you should charge Cedric more rent."

"Poor? I won't be poor? Are you insane? Back to teaching? I was never a teacher!"

"You said you wanted to work with those kids at the wildlife center again."

"I did not!"

"You can have whatever you want. And I'll move and you'll stay in the house."

"The house," she said, stupefied so that for a moment she literally saw stars. "But it's a houseboat. The house turned into a boat. We're going overboard." She reached out for his arm. "We're at sea! We're out at sea, Ben! You and me! Stop it!"

"Evvie."

"Man overboard!" she cried. Her jaw trembled. She put her forehead against the wall and talked to the floor. "When did you make this decision? And why wasn't I *included*? Why did you not bother to include me, Ben? You're my best friend! You're all I have!" Her voice was all wrong. She wanted to plug her ears. She couldn't look at him.

"That's part of the problem. Don't you see? We've been strangling each other for years."

"No, Ben, I'm sorry! Ben, I'm sorry! I'm so sorry for everything! I'll calm down, I'll change, I'll go on meds, I'll go to a marriage counselor, a therapist, whatever you want, I promise!"

"Evvie, please."

"I'll take salsa dancing lessons! We both will! Or go to China! Whatever! Shake things up!"

"Please, Evvie." He pinched the bridge of his nose.

"Please what?"

"I grew, Evvie. I grew in unexpected ways. I wasn't even trying to."

"Grew? That's what you call this? Grew?"

"Yes!"

"All you have to do is wait, and I'll grow too. I can grow! I like growing! Whatever you need, whatever you want, just—let me grow! Maybe I just need some help but I can *definitely* grow!"

"Please don't make this harder."

How could she possibly make this harder? This was so hard she could not believe it was happening.

She walked to the closet and searched for his old parka. She put it on. It still smelled faintly of his body. The smell of her real home. The only real home she'd ever had! Didn't he understand that?

She ran outside and sat on the front stoop. The skin of her arms was melting. Melting right off the bones. Her face was melting too, like in a horror movie. She buried her hot face in the parka and held the skin of her cheeks tightly to hold it in place. He opened the door and stood there behind her. "I really didn't want this to be so dramatic," he said, coolly, a refined stranger with a well-modulated voice. "I wanted to talk like two adults facing down a really difficult situation."

What the?

She was quiet. And then, after a while, she spoke in a thick southern accent. *"I don't know about you, but I want my chicken to be cut in the throat, hung upside down and bled to death, that's just how we do things here in America."* She was impressed with how authentic she sounded. She started to laugh.

"Evvie, stop! Come inside. Please."

"You goddamn animal rights people are worser terrorists

than those goddamn al-Qaeda folks. It's unbelievable!" She was shouting. A woman across the street, Peg, an ex-cop who had once asked Ben, "Is your wife a little different?" offered a worried wave before slipping into her Chevy.

He yanked her inside. She resisted for a moment, then went limp. He steered her upstairs, pulling her by the hand. Upstairs he laid her down in bed, covered her up. She shook as if with fever, held her eyes wide open. Besides the shock a strange spirit of inevitability was already making itself known. He sat with her and held her hand, his profile set in anger even as his hands had been soft, and his voice the softest she'd ever heard it.

"I'm really, really sorry, Evvie."

She looked up at him. She wanted a thermometer. She wanted to throw up.

"It's because I couldn't have a baby," she said. "Admit it."

"No! That's not it."

"You're lying!"

"I swear to God the baby isn't it."

"We should've adopted! A little girl like in my dream. She'd be in first grade now. Or a boy. Or both! We could still have both!"

"Stop, Evvie, it's not about that."

"Then why? What are you doing? Really, Ben, what are you doing?"

"We just grew apart. It's not that *unusual*."

"That's the problem! You want to be *usual*? Is that the goal? And what about going to a marriage counselor?"

"I'm sorry, I'm so sorry, I never planned this." His eyes *were* sorry. They terrified her.

"Aren't you attracted to me anymore? You just fell out of love?"

"It's not that simple."

"Maybe it is. Aren't you? Attracted to me? Anymore?"

"It has nothing to do with that."

"Nothing?"

His voice was different. He was a different Ben. She faced it now. She had imagined his changes belonged to the world of surfaces—the job demanding a certain attire, a boost to the ego. He had to put behind him the pushcart guy, the musician, the self that had relished being on the margins, the perspective this had afforded them, or so she'd imagined. He had stepped into conventional, manly success, and conventional, manly success had stepped into him.

But she had trusted the soul could survive the changes the personality endured. Trusted the soul.

And she was right to trust, she saw, looking up at him now. His anger had abandoned him. His face had been left naked. He was Ben and nobody but Ben. In his dark eyes she saw his love, and for a moment she smiled; it didn't matter that this love was dependent on his sorrow, on his ensuing freedom from her, his guilty relief that he'd finally said the words he must have been carrying inside him for months.

Her heart was big and opening, breaking in half like a drawbridge.

She looked at his face. Now that he had crossed this radical, irreparable line, he loved her again, the way you love your old town as the train pulls out of the station.

She sat up and pressed her head against his as hard as she

could, as if she could make their two heads into one. They'd
done this when they'd first gotten together.

"Sleep with me," she said.

"I can't."

"You have to say *good-bye* to me as a lover or I won't believe
any of this."

"I can't do that. That would be cruel."

"It's terrible! The last time we made love I didn't even know
it was the last time! And you did! You said *good-bye* without me
knowing it was good-bye?"

She turned on her side, away from him. She curled into a ball.

"I didn't know, either," he said. "I didn't know anything."
His voice was tired, defeated.

"Where will you live?" she said.

"I've rented an apartment."

"Oh. Did you fall in love with someone else?"

"No."

"There's nobody else?"

"No."

"Where's this apartment?"

"Bloomfield."

"Bloomfield? Why Bloomfield? And why are you leaving?
Tell me again?"

"Because I've changed. I need different things. I don't want
to drag this out and get bitter."

"Changed. Different things. Drag this out." She sounded
like a shell-shocked parrot.

"People get bitter when they drag things out."

"It's a good thing this is all just a dream, partner," she said, suddenly deeply exhausted. "And why am I so tired? Did you slip me a drug of some kind? Have you tried to murder me to make your getaway easier?" She smiled; her face felt strangely lit from within for a moment, as if it could serve as a night-light if need be.

"We'll separate for a bit," she said. "People do that. But it won't be forever. I can feel it. We'll be finding our way back together even as we're moving apart. Happens all the time. Remember those people in Boston? What were their names? Finnolis?"

He narrowed his eyes, looked toward the window, the moon, and she felt his enormous sadness and how heavy it made him feel.

"That Barb Finnoli went around the bend one year, then came right back the next. And then they were so happy. And they realized it was mostly the stress of their life that split them up. It wasn't that they didn't love each other."

He kept looking at the moon.

"Can't you just change your mind?" she said. "And then I'll do whatever you need me to do."

He sneezed and got up and went into the bathroom and blew his nose. He almost never got colds.

"The stress is breaking you down. I could make you something. Soup."

"Please don't."

"I think I'll get plastic surgery."

"Jesus, Evvie, stop that. It's nothing to do with how you look. You look great."

"I think I'll get implants. And a new face. I think I'll charge it on my new Visa. I could be a real knockout."

"What the hell. Evvie, come on!"

Ruth walked into the room and jumped on the bed, stretched out by Evvie's side, and laid her head between her paws, looking at her. "Ruth, tell him we're mixed like cement. Tell him we're a family and this can't happen."

Silence.

"Your words. Mixed like cement," she said. She was burning like a child with a high fever and shivering. She looked at the black-and-white poster of an old carousel in Paris that hung like a portal on the wall; Ben could slip through. He could go anywhere. Find a young lover and head for France and ride that carousel forever.

"Did I just get to be too much?" Evvie said.

"It's not you at all. It's me."

"Don't say that! Feel my head. I'm burning up."

He put his hand on her forehead and she closed her eyes. His hand was cool and light, and then it lifted. She opened her eyes.

"Maybe I'm coming down with something," she said.

"You don't feel that hot to me."

"I'm burning up."

She thought of her mother. Even when her mother was hungover and wore a terrible back brace, whenever any of the kids had a fever, she would fold a cool cloth on their foreheads. She took her cell phone out of her pocket and dialed her mother's number now, but got the answering machine. *Howdy, folks. Why don't ya go right ahead and leave us a message*, her mother's voice said, more like someone ready to hop on a horse than a seventy-four-year-old in a Philadelphia row house. This had been on their machine for years, but Evvie heard her mother's voice as if for the first time. She tried, but couldn't speak.

Her mouth was filled, as if with newly settled ash.

"It'll be OK, Evvie," Ben said. She looked at him.

BEN

BEN MOVED INTO the second-floor apartment of a stately old brick house on a tree-lined street, in walking distance to all the stores and restaurants on Liberty. The wooden floors and slanted wooden pine ceiling were beautiful, honey colored, and the windows were broad. But it wasn't well heated, and in the apartment below him, a couple fought terribly at night. The first night he'd moved in, he'd opened his window and leaned out, thinking he could touch the branches of a giant pine. He'd sucked in the cold air while below him a woman's voice screamed, "You fucking threw a gallon of milk on me? Did that really happen? You fucking threw a gallon of milk on me?" But the milk had not doused the flames of that fight. They'd gone on into the night while Ben lay in his bed, near the window, watching the tree's branches lift in the wind, thinking he'd find another apartment in the morning, fighting a feeling of despair. He'd wanted peace and quiet more than anything.

But the next day, the couple had emerged from their door arm and arm, smiling and wishing him a great day after telling him about the pancakes they were headed to eat at Pamela's in Squirrel Hill. "You could totally join us," the young woman said, and Ben said no, thanks, but marveled at her wide-open

expression, how her eyes were washed clean of the night before, how neither one of them looked especially tired or broken.
He and Evvie had rarely fought like that, but when they had,
the next day they'd barely been able to function. They'd moved
like zombies, wept with pity as they apologized to each other,
lost their appetites, called off work. Finally they'd drink too
much wine to celebrate how the echoes of the fight were fading.
Neither one of them had been built for conflict.

HE'D LEFT EVVIE almost everything, taking only his clothing,
some music, some books, and the single mattress. It was like
being in college again, only you were haunted—your expectations mostly collapsed and in need of serious, and probably impossible, restoration—and yet there were moments when part
of him took flight, through a set of heavy doors that opened to
a whole new life.

Other times he'd be standing at the sink and find himself
suddenly weeping.

The simplicity of the space was both soothing and jarring.
He missed Evvie, in moments. Missed Ruth too, and in one of
his dreams the dog could talk on the phone and told him to get
his ass back home. A few times he'd driven back to the house,
parked a block away, walked toward the old front door, and almost knocked, but then at the last minute had turned away and
walked across the street to see the river below in the dusk, a
view he'd taken for granted when living there.

He'd played guitar for hours tonight and was happy not
to have Evvie in the other room wondering when he'd stop.
Happy not to feel her need so thick in the air it had been hard to
breathe in that house for the past year or more.

On the answering machine was Evvie's voice, as always. It had been two months already and she showed no signs of accepting what had happened. His patience was beginning to wear thin.

Hiya, Ben, just wanted to say hi. You all right? Call me. Cedric says hi, he misses you. Not to mention Ruth. I guess she can come stay with you next week. If you want. She seems a little down. The vet was thinking she should go on some kind of Prozac, and I was like, no way.

He always called her back—the first forty times he'd been kind—and now with reluctance that bordered on anger. "I'm fine," he said, emphatically.

"How is that possible?"

Her voice was childlike. She had been stripped right down to the bone. She was not angry, but bereft and confused. It was not easy to hear. It hurt him. He braced himself against it and, like Cedric, reminded himself that there was far worse agony in the world; plenty of things were worse than a broken heart.

Soon cultivated anger would shift in his gut like tectonic plates.

"Did you read about Saviour?" she said, barely audible. Was she holding the receiver away from her mouth or just pretending to be catatonic?

"No. Can you speak up?" Night in the window was filled with wind and rain. He didn't want to picture her in the old house or ask if the roof was leaking. He knew it was leaking.

"In Nairobi this stray dog, Saviour, found a newborn baby girl in the woods. She was in a bag, and the dog dragged her across a busy road through a barbed-wire fence and into a shed where her puppies slept. The dog laid the baby girl down next to the puppies. The baby's picture is on the front page of the paper, and so is the dog's."

"That's a nice story."

"The baby's just fine. It's a *great* story. So come back home! I'm *dying* here without you. So is Ruth. I'm *hallucinating*. Please. Just come over and watch a movie with us. I'll make popcorn. You can still be my *friend*, right?"

"I *can't*, Ev, at this point. Not yet."

"I don't get it! *Why not?*"

She needed to have him repeat things a hundred times. It was as if she had no brain anymore, no comprehension.

"It's not good for you to talk to me like this. It just keeps you attached." He walked with the phone into the kitchen, and opened the door. The night was wild and cold, and wind washed over his face as he closed his eyes. "It keeps you thinking like we're still married."

"We are still married!"

"We're separated."

"Maybe you are!"

"That's my point."

A silence fell.

"Remember that other story about that crazy kid in the Bronx who started hearing voices coming out of his meat?"

"Yeah." He opened his eyes to the low moon, the torn purple clouds.

"Well, I'm going to the Bronx to find that kid and I'm bringing him home. That kid should be mine."

"OK."

"OK? Just like that?"

He stepped back, and closed the door. "You're an adult, and

a free citizen. If you want to go abscond with a psychiatric patient in the Bronx and get arrested and go to jail, you should. By all means you should do what you want."

"Are you trying to be funny?"

"Maybe."

"You don't even care that I'm going crazy?"

"I care deeply. I think you know that. But I'm not the one to help you. The more I try to help, the worse it gets. You end up passed out in a bar, remember?"

"You're the *only* one who can help. I'm coming over."

She hung up.

Then called back. "I wouldn't come over there if we were getting nuked and you had the last fucking bomb shelter on Earth."

"OK."

"Oh. Isn't it sweet to have all the power in the world, Ben? Especially on a night like this, when we're getting a tornado?"

"*Sweet* wouldn't be the first word that came to mind. And we're not getting a tornado."

"I really don't like how calm you sound. I really don't. You can sit there and think how *crazy* I am, Ben, how glad you are that you put me in the Dumpster, and then you'll hang the phone up and forget about me within five minutes! You haven't even bothered to check in and say hi to Cedric at Giant Eagle! And what about Ruth? We're the discarded, I guess. On with your new life. Trading us all in like a good American. It's become the national sport, so why not join in?"

She slammed the phone down.

For the first time, she was really angry, and he was grateful. It meant she might be halfway normal after all.

LATE THE NEXT night she managed to climb into his window. Using all her strength, she'd hoisted a ladder (their landlord's ladder, which he'd used to paint their top shutters last year) against the side of the house, climbed up to the second-story apartment, whistling no less, and pushed the slightly open window up as high as it would go. He watched from his mattress as she did this. "This is not happening," he chanted. He watched as she climbed in through the window dressed in his old coat, his old high school football helmet!, and flannel pajamas. No doubt she wore the helmet to protect her head in case she fell from the ladder, but she looked insane, and now she was singing Lou Reed's "Coney Island Baby," a song they'd both loved.

Had to play football for the coach . . .

"What the fuck are you—"

He sat up. It was true. This was happening. Inside his room, she stood in the middle of the floor, hands on hips, singing. Then stopped herself. In an almost eerily odd voice, a voice that recalled *The Wizard of Oz*, like a mix between the good and bad witches, she said, "What have we here?"

"Evvie! What the fuck are you doing!"

For a moment he believed she really *was* crazy and had come to kill him. She breathed heavily, stood looking at him. Did she have a gun in the coat? Was he really asking himself this?

"This is not a dream, my friend," she said, whispering, as if someone might be overhearing all this. "This is not just the glory of love." Then she took off her coat, dropped it to the floor. "This is, how you say? Real life." She spoke in a Russian accent of sorts. She took off her pajama top and stood topless, hands back on hips. A laugh escaped her.

"I have not come to collect money," she said, and now the accent changed. "Because you do not have it *een* you to care for the neeglected ones standing at the door of death. Indeed, they remain numbers to you. Perhaps the universe can forgeev us all thees how you say? Thees lack of under-stand-ing."

She paused, breathing. She crossed her arms over her breasts.

"This is called breaking and entering," he said. "I think you should climb back out now."

"Ha! In fact it's *pitiable* that you've turned your heart into a piece of black ice." Now the accent was as Australian as that crocodile guy's on TV she didn't like, but some of the words were slurred.

"Black ice being the most dangerous sort, the kind a person can't see on the road. The killer ice, it's been called."

Was she drunk? He thought he could smell alcohol on her. She could never handle drinking. But always it had unleashed the performer in her. She took off the flannel pajama pants, kicking them high in the air, laughing a little. "Introducing. My first striptease." She had lost so much weight she looked ill. Ribs. The endless limbs. Finally she removed his football helmet. Then stood naked, stepping into a streak of light from a streetlamp. She made a microphone with her fist and spoke into it in yet another accent.

"Iss so good to be here wiz you! I know you're awake, Meester Benjameen. And I know you want to laugh, so laugh, laugh!"

For one moment his heart ached for her.

"Jesus, Ev. I wish you could see—"

She was walking toward him, and kneeling down by his

mattress, her cold, trembling hand stroking his head. He didn't move. "Ben, I can't *do* this," she said, a penitent with a desperate prayer. "You don't understand. I can't *do* this anymore. You can't just *disappear* like this. You're not a monster, Ben. Move over—I'll sleep beside you."

He sat up. She sat down next to him, and he held her. "Ev, this is beyond crazy now. You need to get ahold of yourself. I keep telling you! I sound like a broken record but you're not listening. I really want you to reach out to people who can help."

He was shocked at how unfamiliar her body felt, how Lauren's body had rendered Evvie's the strange one. She kissed his cheek, and thanked him.

"Don't thank me. Evvie. I'd be glad to—"

"I love you."

"But if you love me, you shouldn't have broken into my place!" he said, anger obliterating pity for a moment.

"Shhh, you're too loud. Let's just be quiet," she said, nuzzling into his chest.

"Please get dressed, Evvie. And please, get out. Immediately." He let go of her and stood up.

"What?"

"Get dressed and get out," he said. "I really need you to do that. This is called breaking and entering. I'm trying here to establish—"

"So who is it, Ben? Your new secretary?" She stood up. "When can I meet her? Is she good in bed? A real acrobat?"

Watching her get dressed, he said nothing. He didn't even have a secretary, but to say so was futile.

"Are you on *drugs*?" she said. "Is that what happened?"

"Could you just leave without saying another word?"

"Really?"

"Really."

"Really?"

"Leave, or I'll call the police."

She laughed. "You just said that, didn't you? You actually just said you'd *call the police*. I'm gonna quote you on that when we get back together. And please. Call the cops in right now, because I can curl up here on the floor like the, like a dog. Like the queen of the dog-wives, and when they come to get me I'll run to the window and howl at the moon and then turn around so I can bite the shit out of their ankles."

But when he turned on the overhead light, she looked at him with terror in her eyes, and shame. He had to look away. "Ben!" she said. "Stop this!" He couldn't look at her. "Did you ever love me, Ben? Was I living life in a state of delusion or what?"

"Of course I loved you!"

"Loved?"

The past tense clanged like a prison door shutting, and changed everything; the room itself was transformed by it, the bed, the dresser, the bare floor, the window, all seeming to step back while absorbing the word's singular power.

She finished dressing and quietly began to climb out the window. She was almost nimble. She made her way down the ladder. She'd left the helmet behind.

"OH MY GOD! She did what?" Lauren said.

"She basically got a ladder and climbed in the window and watched me sleep." He couldn't tell her about the naked display, the Lou Reed rendition, the football helmet, the whole performance.

"That's such an *invasion*, Ben!"

"I *know*."

"I mean, weren't you shocked?"

"I was really surprised."

Then, in Lauren's blue eyes he saw a sense of amazement and appreciation of this so-called invasion. Or was she merely amused? He felt a little wave of protection for Evvie move through him.

"Was she always nuts?"

"I don't know." He shrugged. "Maybe. Not really. I guess she was a little. Let's talk about something else." He pulled her close. Kissed the side of her head. He did not want to further betray Evvie by disclosing what made her unusual. Moreover, he wanted to protect the boundaries of this new life with this beautiful woman, who loved to have sex with him, who was planning to teach him how to garden when summer came. This woman who radiated a calm that seemed rooted in wisdom she'd be too humble to own. He breathed in the scent of her shampoo.

"I could never live with a vegan," she said. "They all tend to be so judgmental. You must be a really tolerant person."

He didn't take the bait except to sigh. "Not really."

THEY WERE WALKING under a lavender evening sky, down a narrow street in Erie, near where Ben had grown up. They'd come back to visit his father and stepmother, to introduce Lauren to them. His father had been mildly saddened when he told them about his separation, even though both he and his stepmother had never particularly loved Evvie. Both of them had their old-time Protestant (though they were atheists) distrust of

Catholics; they knew that Evvie descended from people who played bingo in church basements, drank obscene amounts of liquor, prayed rosaries in front of statues, and crippled people with guilt. Evvie, a supposed agnostic, had one night, years ago, exploded at the dinner table when Ben's stepmother had said something innocuously offensive about a parade for Saint Anthony where people taped dollars onto the life-size statue of the saint before he was hauled through the streets of Pittsburgh. They'd never seen that explosive side of Evvie, and it eclipsed all the selves she'd displayed to them before and after. She'd become the crazy Catholic, even though she'd apologized, welling up with tears that made things worse. She'd explained that when she was a little girl, parades for Saint Anthony were some of the best times of her life, since she got to be with her grandmother, who was called an honorary Italian by her Italian neighbors because she was so nice and loved to eat the homemade pasta and listen to Luigi Tenco.

"Don't worry, dear," his stepmother had said, and his father had winked, but nothing, according to Evvie, was ever the same after this.

Then, two years ago, when Evvie had started preaching about factory farms, she'd lost considerable favor again, not because they loved meat so much, or even because they disagreed that corporate farms were hell-worlds, but her delivery was so off, her voice trembling as it rose, that they both suspected something deeply *personal* overshadowed her conviction, making it suspect. "She should ask herself when *she* felt slaughtered. She's got a deep identification with these animals, which points to something pretty dark," his father suggested.

So Ben was surprised when his father, hearing the news,

said, "I'm so sorry, Ben. I guess I figured you and Evvie would always be together."

"I did too," he remembers saying.

"SO SHALL WE go meet them?" he said to Lauren. They'd been walking the streets for nearly an hour; his palms were damp with anxiety. It was Sunday, quiet and empty. *Dead* would be the word. They'd seen only two human beings: a fat-faced child on a bike who shouted "beep beep" and a cop on the corner talking on a cell phone. Lauren wore a snug blue cap, faded jeans, and a dark red jacket, black boots with heels that clicked on the sidewalk. Every so often she did a little step-dance. Her small nose was red with cold, and her eyes brightened each time they met his.

"You doing OK?" he asked her.

"Maybe I'm a little nervous."

"They're pretty easygoing," he said. *Unless you know them.*

He took her hand and steered her down one street and up another, until they stood on top of a low, stone wall with a view of the lake, a block from the unadorned but newly repointed half-time brick home of his last years of childhood, a place he'd mostly avoided as an adult. He held no serious grievances anymore against any of his parents, just a discomfort in their presence he preferred to avoid.

A green metal chair sat alone on the front porch.

A similar chair used to adorn the back porch; early on with Evvie, the two of them once sat there in the middle of the night, feverishly draped around each other under a blanket. A huge deer, a buck with full antlers, had approached them in the moonlight, and everything went still. The deer had come so close, and this had been so thrilling, that both of them had tears in their eyes by the time the deer turned to walk back to the woods.

"Hey there, look who the wind blew in!"

His stepmother had short dyed red hair now, and bright bluish eyes that seemed never to move in their sockets. If she wished to look to the left or right, she turned her whole head, as if injured. Her smile was broad and inviting as usual, if devoid of intimacy. The fourth-grade teacher she'd once been was nowhere to be seen, even as her face had changed little.

"Hi, Mom, so . . . this is Lauren."

Mom grasped Lauren's hands, squeezed once, then let go, as was her habit. "Pleased to meet you, Lauren," she said. The front hall was beautiful with flowers and shining wood.

"Place looks great," Ben said.

"That's because I shined it up for your visit, Ben. Lauren, come sit down. Let me get you kids a Coke." She looked at him with detached curiosity, as if after all these years, she still couldn't figure him out.

"Maybe we can all have a beer," Ben suggested. "Where's Dad?"

"He was out back tinkering with something. Let me go call him."

"Dad's tinkering?" Ben called. "Since when?"

Lauren and Ben sat in the living room, facing each other like schoolchildren suddenly seized by giddiness; Lauren laughed out loud for no reason, then clapped her hand across her mouth. "Is that you?" she said, pointing to a photograph of a strapping six-year-old batter squinting into the sun.

" 'Fraid so."

"Pretty cute!"

Evvie had held that picture, practically fallen into it, and said, *This picture destroys me.*

Tell me everything you can remember and I'll tell you every-thing I can remember. Even irrelevant stuff, like how you drank a glass of milk one day in front of the window when some guy across the street was cutting the grass and he stopped to wipe his brow with a handkerchief.

"Hey, Ben!"

He got up to embrace his father, who stiffly clapped his son on the back three times in lieu of a hug. His father was com-pletely bald now, and his glasses were thicker, but he was still strong despite a potbelly making itself known under his striped polo shirt. "You'll stay the night?" he asked, hopefully, and Lauren spoke up and said, "Yes," before Ben could explain they had to get back in a few hours.

"You must be Lauren," his father said, smiling, and Lauren stood up.

"So nice to meet you," Lauren said. And then, strangely, his father and Lauren embraced as if they'd known one another forever, as if his father weren't suspicious of such displays of unearned affection. Lauren's direct warmth could be like a high beam of blinding light; a person couldn't see clearly in that light, basically forgot who they were.

"So do we have beer?" Ben said.

His father had remembered himself, and now looked con-fused. "Beer?" he said, blinking.

"We always have beer," said Mom. "Oh yes, we do, can't live without our beer around here," she added, in an abrasive singsong that implied perhaps someone liked beer a little too much around here. He guessed his father was drinking more these days.

"I'll get them," Ben said. He left the room and first walked into the backyard to shake his head, rid himself of Evvie. When she first loved him, she'd wanted to come to Erie so as to inhabit every childhood haunt he'd known, to draw closer to the boy he'd been. He'd taken her to the tiny house beside the nursing home, and she'd looked into all the windows, a detective working a crucial and endlessly mysterious case. It gave him a pang to remember how young and alive she'd been back then, how seemingly happy, with that walk she used to have, leaning forward on her toes—*Evvie walks like someone headed through a parking lot to hear their favorite band in concert*, his friend Paul had said. This girl in her twenties, the person she'd been—did she survive inside of the woman who'd broken into his place and said his heart was black ice?

He stood in the kitchen and tried to shake it all out of his head, like a dog shakes water out of its coat, though his resistance to thinking of her, he knew from experience, only intensified the memories. He would drink a beer and make small talk, his parents peppering their conversation with names of friends Ben had never met and couldn't keep track of.

They would eat roast beef and nobody would really miss Evvie, not exactly, not consciously, though Ben would try to hear the echo of one of her old cow-abuse lectures to remind himself of how her presence could darken a table, to puncture the strange and unwieldy grief rising in him. Evvie had somehow protected him here in this house, with these parents, in a way that Lauren could not. Not yet.

———

"IT'S SAD," LAUREN whispered.

"What's sad?"

"This is your home, and you're like a stranger here."

His stepmother had beautifully arranged the guest room for them. She was, on some practical level, a hospitable soul. Because Lauren was this way too, it allowed him a new appreciation for all of it: The quilts on the mahogany sleigh bed were hand-sewn heirlooms beautifully softened with age, the sheer curtains were embroidered with butterflies. She'd arranged fresh blue towels on a rack, and the sheets, they saw now, climbing naked into the old bed, were the softest, whitest dream-sheets, like silk against their skin as they turned to each other in the dim orange glow of the night-light.

"A stranger?" He was immensely grateful for the surprise of her perception. She'd seemed quietly oblivious at the table, and afterward, when they'd all taken a walk to the lake.

"Don't you think?"

She rubbed his shoulders, introducing him to the tension he must've felt all evening long. They made love, quietly, and the silence of the room deepened around them. He squeezed her hand. "That was nice."

"Nice? You're amazing," she said.

"Really?"

"You're really surprised? Your wife never let you in on that little secret?"

"Don't call it little."

She laughed.

He was still not completely at ease with her, which made him feel like a pedestrian lover, too considerate, too careful. He suspected her of flattery.

"So should I never mention her? Like she never existed? If so, that's cool."

He considered this for a moment. "You can mention her."

"Someday I'd like to get to know her."

"Stranger things have happened."

"You could meet Carter if you wanted."

"No, thanks."

"Really? No curiosity?"

"I think I'll just let Carter be Carter in Carterville."

"OK."

A silence fell. He tried steering his mind to more neutral territory. The morning. They could head to a bakery before leaving town. Eclairs. Espresso. And then a long drive down 79 with some music.

"I'd like to meet your mom."

"Soon."

"Are you a stranger there too?"

"No. I mean no more than any grown-up child is a stranger in their parent's house. My mom knows how to watch football and get high on Pepsi. She lives on a llama farm with a guy who used to be the mayor of Indiana, Pennsylvania, and she takes life as it comes."

"Wow. A llama farm? And you never bothered to mention this?"

"She's only been with the mayor for three years."

"And she's happy?"

"She can spend ten hours in a tomato garden. Sort of happy no matter what. And I don't understand it, since her father was horrible." He could never think of his mother without thinking of his grandfather, but he stopped himself before saying more.

He'd found out who his grandfather was when he was seven years old, staying with his grandparents while his parents went to Niagara Falls for a long weekend. His grandfather had beaten him with a belt one night, in a mudroom where the sound of the whirring dryer muffled the sound of his grandfather's voice as it ordered him to strip naked. He'd tried to run out of the room, and this had enraged the man. "I have to take you down a peg or two," he'd confided, twisting Ben's arm, "for your own sake."

Ben had been black and blue afterward, and stunned, a different person altogether, and his grandmother had sat him at the kitchen table while she moved around in heeled slippers humming her denial and baking a cake. A clock hung high on the wall, and a small totem pole sat on the sill above the sink next to a glass frog. He couldn't drink his milk. "Go on and play, then."

"Your grandpa was just trying to teach you a lesson," she'd said later that night, outside of the bedroom door where he lay awake in the dark, her voice hoarse. "Maybe all that carrying on at the breakfast table," she half explained, leaving him to deduce that he shouldn't have told her riddles, shouldn't have told the story about his friend at school who went to SeaWorld, should have stayed quiet. She didn't come into the room, but he felt she'd wanted to, and hated her for those moments, feeling both her desire to snatch him up and drive him to someplace far away, and her reverent fear of the man that would allow for almost anything to happen in that house.

He'd never beaten Ben's mother or her sister Grace. He didn't believe in beating the weaker sex. He'd beaten the shit out of his own son, Jimmy, who'd moved to Nevada when he was seventeen years old, never to be seen again, except for the one time Ben's mother and Grace had taken Ben and the twins and their cousins on a road trip when Ben was ten. Jimmy was a tall, thin man with a head that seemed too heavy for his neck, a wide face, slicked-down black hair, and large hands that held tightly to each other or pulled on the opposite hand's fingers. He managed a diner and took them there that first night of the visit. It was late, they were road weary, the diner was decorated for Christmas in July, but Ben was wide-eyed and fascinated by this uncle who barely spoke, holding his body stiffly, laughing too loudly when one of the customers, smoking in a booth, said, "About time you took a day off!" His outburst of laughter was so awkward his mother and aunt exchanged a long, sad, meaningful glance. Then they all sat down and ate rice pudding "on the house!," Uncle Jimmy boomed, though until then he'd been unusually soft-spoken. He sat up too straight in the booth, not knowing how to ask the usual adult questions such as "How's school?" and "How old are you now?" but simply staring at all of them with widely held hazel eyes, as if he'd never seen children before. Then said to Ben, "Do you know what Rufus Youngblood, the Secret Service man who fell on Johnson when Kennedy was shot, said?"

Ben shook his head.

"Rufus Youngblood said had it been Nixon, he would've fallen the other way."

Ben's mother and aunt Grace tried to help him. "So, Jimmy, the kids love your state! Right, kids?" And June said, "Nevada's cool," and Russell echoed her, but Ben nodded and sat there thinking about Rufus Youngblood, whose name would resound in his head, repeating itself for days as he thought of his uncle's face and how it had looked in the diner.

Before they left the next morning, after an awkward good-bye that was strange for its brevity, given that his sisters hadn't seen him in all those years and would probably not see him again for a long, long time, he ran out to their car—just as they were getting ready to get into it—and bent down to sob in Ben's arms. Everyone watched this. Why Ben? Why sob in the arms of a ten-year-old boy? Ben was terrified. He stood there, paralyzed, waiting for it to end, on the verge of sobbing himself.

"Jesus Christ! Leave the kid alone! You belong in an institution, Jimmy!"

"Grace! Stop it!" said Ben's mother.

"I think you've done us a favor by pretending we don't exist!" Grace persisted. Jimmy had let go of Ben, taken a step back, and put his arm over his eyes. "I don't understand myself anymore," he said.

"Jimmy, don't listen to Grace. She's a wreck from traveling," said Ben's mother, so different from both of her siblings, possessed of kindness that seemed to him, in those years before the divorce, unshakeable.

HE WONDERED WHY he had no urge to tell Lauren this story. Would their lives together exclude their darkest memories, allowing them to fade? He tried to imagine that, tried to envision how carefree they might be someday. Maybe he'd tell her everything eventually, but now, here at the beginning, he'd tell her what was best.

The story of his grandfather and more lived inside of Evvie.

Evvie who'd *had to know everything.* If he ever forgot anything, he could consult her, his personal archives.

LAUREN HAD BEEN raised by a stepmother, an elegant, brainy woman named Lillian Ross who died six years ago in a car crash while visiting her sister outside of Chicago. Lauren carried a picture of Lillian Ross in her wallet. Her father lived in Seattle, but she rarely saw him. She had yet to tell Ben what had happened to her biological mother. "Oh, someday I'll get into all of that. A bit of a downer." It was as if she were talking about somebody else, and yet he'd known not to press. "Think drugs," she'd added.

HE WANTED TO see Lauren happy. Really happy, without the brakes on. Once, when he was fourteen, he'd found his mother weeping on the phone, but the tears had been happy ones. He'd stood watching her in the kitchen doorway; she'd been over near the sink. "Who was that?" he wanted to ask, later. But something had held him back. It was as if he hadn't wanted the source of those tears to be particularized. Often he remembered her face as it had looked that day, as if the memory were an amulet clenched in his hand. She'd wept with a joy—he was certain of this—that was stranger and deeper than anything he'd known, though he'd craved it at fourteen and even before that, maybe as long as he'd known what craving was.

He'd wept with joy like that sometimes with Evvie, and tonight, suddenly it seemed it was something he'd not know again. This love was different. This love was solid and of the earth. Was it more reliable because Lauren wasn't dying to escape the confines of her own body, as Evvie had been? This calm of Lauren's, what was the source?

"Lauren?" He sat next to her. "Lauren?"

He got back in bed, and her warm body turned toward him. He felt a keen desire for her that eradicated his fear. Of course he would weep with joy again. "Lauren?"

"Hmm?" she said.

"I was thinking we could drive to the lake. I think the moon is full." This wasn't like him at all. This was him being Evvie in one of her semi-manic states.

"It's too cold," she murmured. "Stay here."

He waited. "You like lakes?"

Lauren nestled her head into the crook of his arm. "Yes. And I love the ocean. We should go this summer. Or sooner."

His heart sunk. "I prefer lakes." He wanted to stay away from the ocean for a while—Evvie's favorite landscape. For years they'd rented a room in the Dew Drop Inn, a motel in Wildwood that took dogs. All the most passionate dog lovers came, and the rooms smelled like shedding dogs and the people all traded endless dog stories, and everyone loved Ruth and some even sent her Christmas cards signed with the pawprints of their own dogs. Evvie had always brought a boom box on those vacations, mostly so *The Wild, the Innocent & the E Street Shuffle* could provide the sound track for the days. She wanted to believe there might be boys from the casino dancing like Latin lovers on the shore. She had memorized "Sandy" when she was thirteen and prided herself on sounding a lot like Springsteen when she sang it from start to finish. She'd loved the boardwalk—playing games where she'd win gigantic homely stuffed animals, riding the roller coaster and eating fries soaked in vinegar, watching the parade of humanity in the night light while a small train ran back and forth on the boards. *Watch the tram car, please!* a loud voice said over and over again, as much a part of the atmosphere as the salt air and screeching gulls. (In the winter, Ben had sometimes whispered into Evvie's ear, *Watch the tram car, please!*) Always there seemed to be some skinny, ravaged kid with a guitar whom Evvie would listen to and befriend, including the heroin addict who later had come to their room and robbed them.

He'd never felt completely *included* in her enthusiasms, even when he'd most admired them. He'd had to pretend, but part of him hung back like a chaperone. He was tired of that role, which seemed, at times, the only role he'd ever known how to play. That was part of what he'd grown tired of in Jersey, especially those last two years. Tired of being a spectator to Evvie's excitement while feeling bad about his secret weariness, and guilty, and unable to talk about it because there was something inside of Evvie that played like a constant song whose lyrics demanded that he never hurt her. He heard that song playing even in his dreams. He would not have to go to Wildwood this year. That was both a source of relief and surprising pain. He reminded himself now that he'd grown tired of the smell of mold in the room, the wretched, creaky bed, the painting over the bed of Santa Claus holding a basket of adorable puppies, the way she lined up ordinary seashells on the sandy bureau, arranging and rearranging them like a kid, the way she was perfectly satisfied with their annual return, and said things that drove him nuts such as "Doesn't get any better than this," when they were sitting with cheap beers on itchy beach chairs on the concrete floor outside their measly room with no view of the water while the sun set and other people's dogs came by to lick their sunburned feet. Just two years ago he'd suffered a fit of jealousy because a young history professor with a chocolate lab had flirted with Evvie, praising her way with dogs. *You're magnetic*, he'd said. *It's beautiful.* It was true; all the dogs were crazy about Evvie. Ben had sometimes envied her this. But last summer he'd watched her with adoring dogs and wondered what it was they sensed about her that he'd lost track of or couldn't believe anymore.

Meanwhile their friends were jetting off to the Canary Islands or Rome or Brazil.

"Lauren?"

"Mmmm?"

"Do you like lakes at all?"

"Sure. Love lakes. But I'm really an ocean girl. When I was ten, I was like two feet from a dolphin."

"Wow. Nice. Well, I love lakes. I really prefer lakes. Not so much Lake Erie. But Lake Ontario. Lake Michigan. Actually, Erie's great too. Any lake."

"OK. Got it. I'm registering your love of lakes."

He laughed. "You a good swimmer?"

"I was a lifeguard when I was seventeen."

"Really. And every boy in the pool pretended to drown so you'd save him."

"Not every boy. But one of them did that. Repeatedly. And he was hilarious. His name was Harvey the Basket Case." She laughed. "I kind of miss Harvey the Basket Case."

"I'll bet you do."

She fell back to sleep, and he lay there in the dark, for a

long time. He knew, on some level, that his remembering the beach and boardwalk with Evvie was at least partly false. He'd loved Evvie by the ocean. He'd loved her on the boardwalk. He hadn't really minded the sunburn and itchy chairs and dogs that much until last year. And he'd been the one to find batteries for the boom box so they could hear Springsteen most years. The pleasure he'd known being with her in salt air, sitting on a bench at night and watching the parade of humanity—couldn't he let the simple truth of that survive? Did he have to take the pain of the present and inject it into the past so that all memory was rendered suspect?

ALWAYS WITH EVVIE he'd been the one to fall asleep first, the one to sink down into a well while she talked on and on like someone on speed. He held a lock of Lauren's hair between his fingers, his eyes wide open, and something caught inside his throat, some lump of pain that he tried swallowing down. He breathed and swallowed and breathed, and imagined, as Evvie had once taught him to do, that he was an entire field of incredibly harmless cows, dissolving into even more incredibly harmless particles of light. It struck him how strange this was—to imagine being not just a cow, but a whole field of cows. On the back of one of the cows, she'd add, is a crow that can count to six. And if anyone tries to hurt the cow, the crow knows how to say, fuck off. And the crow has several thousand night-roosting friends who will join him if need be.

He buried his face in Lauren's hair. Coconut. Soft curls, color of autumn. He breathed it in as deeply as he could.

EVVIE

EVVIE HAD WORKED at the Frame Shop for more than a year. She'd learned how to frame just about anything, and also to help the do-it-yourselfers frame whatever they brought in. It was fairly low stress. But sometimes Evvie was unsure how the place managed to stay in business. Hours would go by and nobody would venture in off the street.

Today a grandma in red sneakers and wild white hair who'd brought in her grandson's painting of what appeared to be a mad elf saying, "I am Jesus," had told Evvie her whole life story. And why not? They both had all the time in the world. But it was such a sad life story Evvie had had to work not to turn away from the woman, who'd been twice widowed, battled breast cancer, and was even homeless for a month back in the early 1990s when she was too proud to knock on her daughter's door. "She had her own problems. Everyone does. So I slept on a bench in the park, and let me tell you something, sister, you don't want to end up there. But if you do end up there, if that's the way life goes for you, just tell yourself *all of this is a dream.* The good and the bad, it's all a dream. And someday we'll wake up and find some peace."

Afterward Evvie had cried in the bathroom. But then the

hours had gone by more quickly, thanks to lots of customers. Near the end of the day, Evvie's coworker Joseph handed her a book called *Time to Marry Yourself*. He eagerly flipped through it with her, up at the counter before they closed shop. The chapters had titles like "Coming Home to You," and "You're the Best Thing That Ever Happened to You." The last chapter was all about *the wedding*. It was crazy—you stood up and took vows to stay with yourself in sickness and health, 'til death do you part. You threw a great reception and even, if you wanted, had people pummel you with rice as you ran alone to your honeymoon car. (Evvie could picture this far too vividly.) But you were never really alone, said the book, because you had yourself! The most important relationship of your life.

Joseph said he thought this was a great idea for Evvie. He had been at such a wedding before, at the Nuin Center, and people cried.

Evvie wanted to cry just thinking about this.

But now on the bus she held the book on her lap, and was moved, remembering the love and concern in her coworker's face.

A MAN ON the bus called from a few seats behind, "Miss, can we ask you a question?" Somehow she knew she was the miss. He had a voice like warm gravel, and she turned around without apprehension. It was as if she'd rehearsed these moments, as if she'd heard the voice before, and her spine tingled. A longer than usual sense of déjà vu consumed her for several moments, and she knew she'd been on this very bus before, that she'd known this particular dim dusk of earliest spring, that she'd long ago ridden beside the very same delicate Indian girl in her red anklet socks and tiny pearl bracelets, a backpack heavy on her narrow lap, and yes, she'd seen the face she turned to now, a face that for a moment made everyone else on the bus a blur.

He had bright blue eyes, a trace of silver in his brown side-parted hair, a boyish face she liked immediately for its quality of wakefulness. His eyebrows raised up high so that his forehead became a series of lines that recalled to Evvie the I Ching hexagram she liked best. "Well? Are you ready?" he seemed to be saying, and for a moment she couldn't look away. It was not just the almost shocking blue in his eyes, though that was part of it. He wore a dark blue wool jacket with small wooden buttons, the sort of coat her mother had called "a car coat," for reasons Evvie hadn't bothered to learn. A bus coat, she thought.

The blue-eyed man sat next to a stocky balding man in sunglasses whose pasty complexion and amused smile recalled a man her father had boxed in Philly. He introduced himself as Bruno, and the blue-eyed man beside him as Rocky. Bruno and Rocky? For real?

"Hi, Bruno. Hi, Rocky," she said, liking the sound of it. She turned back around, leaning her head against the window. The dusk was cold and gray and people hurried down sidewalks, each one with their own full life. Déjà vu vanished, and she felt unprotected in the wake of its mystery.

The next thing she knew, the Indian girl was rising, then stepping down off the bus. Evvie watched her move down the sidewalk on nimble legs that set off a yearning to be that young, a kid whose biggest mistakes were still far off in the future. Bruno was taking the girl's seat, and Evvie stiffened. She watched the girl begin to skip, then finally turned away from the window.

Bruno wore a khaki raincoat, heavy black shoes, and white socks. "We run a business unlike any other business in the world," he said.

She looked down at her own folded hands. "That's good." A woman across the aisle talking on her cell told someone, *"You gotta be shittin' me!"* and a man several seats back was having a coughing episode.

"We happen to reunite lovers with a ninety-eight percent success rate." He spoke confidentially, the voice barely audible.

"Uh-huh." Why was he telling *her?* Were they computer hackers?

"Ninety-*nine*," Rocky called.

"No offense, but why should I care?" Was she that obvious? Did brokenhearted people give off a certain scent? She wanted to put her head down in her hands.

"You've got the perfect look, darlin'. The Rock knows how to spot it. And your kind is always the kind we work for. Out of the goodness of our hearts, believe it or not. We work for the ladies and the men, but we prefer the ladies. The good ladies who are *lost unto this world*. Like our own mothers." He crossed himself. A Catholic?

"Good ones," Rocky echoed. "The good ones are *often* lost unto this world."

"What are you talking about? Did you get into my e-mail or something?" Evvie's heart had begun to pound.

"Nobody got into nobody's e-mail. We're not the scum of the earth," Bruno said, shifting in his seat, offended by her presumption.

He reached into his coat pocket and brought out an

impressive-looking flyer. She was drawn to the colors. Deep purple and gold, a sunset, but something odd about it.

"Who took this picture?"

Bruno turned around to Rocky. "Who took the picture of the sun?"

"The Internet." Rocky crossed his eyes like a clowning kid in school. She laughed in spite of how disconcerting this was, and he winked.

"It's lovely," she said, using a word she never used. Under the sun were the words "Don't Give Up. Let us help you walk the long and winding road back to Love."

She couldn't help staring at the sun, the words, the sun, the words, the sun.

The bus stopped and some people got off, allowing Rocky to move up and sit across from Evvie and Bruno. They had the back of the bus to themselves except for one old woman in a raincoat carrying several plastic bags. Evvie kept turning around to look at her.

"My stop is the next stop," Evvie said, but this was a lie. Rocky smelled like her father's cologne. Aqua Velva. A pang shot through her.

"What we do is, get you and the ex in a room *together*," Rocky said in his raspy voice (she did love it) that was just above a whisper. "We hold you *pretend-hostage*," he continued. "We get the two of you in a room, and we have a gun, *no bullets*, nothing dangerous, and your husband, or boyfriend or sigother or your what-have-you, *he* thinks you might be about to be killed. It's all innocent, since of course you aren't about to be killed. There's nothing dangerous going on at all. All on the up-and-up. It's theater. But what goes down—in ninety-four percent of cases—is the ex begins to feel the love."

"Ninety-six!" said Bruno.

"OK. Right. And the love comes shining through like what, Bruno? Like a surprise at the track? That horse you bet on all your life and finally there it is, against all the odds, the most unlikely winner of our time. That horse everyone said was too old, too tired. That loser horse that nobody liked but you, since *you're* for the underdog."

"How do you know what I'm for?" She couldn't help smiling at their strangeness.

"I'm perceptive verging on psychic," Rocky said, "but in your case I don't need to be. You wear it all on your sleeve, baby." Rocky said this softly while peering straight ahead, up the aisle, where passengers were rising to disembark. "You're a babe with your heart on your sleeve," he said. "And it's killing me."

"Killing you?"

"I'm an empath."

"OK, Empath."

He smiled.

"So there you are, in a locked room, thinking maybe one or both of you will die. It's like going to the movies," Bruno said, talking out of the side of his mouth.

"No, the theater," corrected Rocky. He pronounced it *thee-ate-her.* "It's like going to the theater. Believe me. I myself was in the theater a long time ago," he added. "I was the Lord High Executioner in *The Mikado.*"

Evvie nodded. She tried to imagine this. "When?"

"Long time ago. I was a talented boy. Head full of dreams." He paused to knock himself in the temple and smile. "They all wanted to send me on to Hollywood, but next stop was Vietnam."

"Oh. That's too bad." So the guy was in his fifties. He looked younger.

"We all of us have our qualities that don't get properly developed. I bet you're no exception." He raised an eyebrow.

She turned the sunset over, and on the back, in white letters against a red background, were several quotes from past customers.

> *Not only does it work, it returns you to a love as fresh as morning dew. I am grateful, grateful, grateful.*
>
> —SANDRA B.
> *Minneapolis*

> *This is professional match-making on steroids! Reunited and it feels so good!*   —RICHARD AND LEONA FROM PHILLY
> *(in our hot tub)*

> *I'll tell you one thing. You are in good hands with Rocky and Bruno. They're magic, they're professionals, and this works, and just do it.*   —TOM LOVES BETTY IN PITTSBURGH!

> *When my husband realized he might really lose me in the grand scheme of things, he said he saw my heart was a perfect rose unfolding and all the chakras were totally vibrating in alignment with what is meant to be. On our journey back home to the casa we built with our own hands, I knew I was having a real mystical vision like in the days of old. And now, now to have the one you love waking up beside you each day is to know you are winning life's biggest lottery.*
>
> —NAME WITHHELD
> *Pittsburgh*

It was Evvie's stop for real now.

"You call us," Rocky said, and lips tight, she nodded, taking the flyer, shoving it into her pocket before she walked home in the dark, the faces of Bruno and Rocky inscribing themselves, shining in the dead center of her mind like the moon.

She smiled. She couldn't stop smiling. When had she last smiled like this? What she really wanted was to call Ben and tell him all about it and laugh. He would *love* the story of these guys. Or she could go over there and tell him about it. And laugh.

In bed.

A dark feeling swept through her. She had to get out of this dreamworld. They would not be laughing together in bed, ever again. *Ever*, she told herself, *you stupid bitch*, she added. *It's over.*

Unfortunately, on some level, she didn't believe that for a minute. It began to rain. She was going to get soaked.

She went home drenched, and even before drying off she e-mailed Celia about the guys. Celia was someone she'd known for two years in high school but had been out of touch with for twenty years. At this point, she hardly knew Celia, but somehow she'd become quite the anchor on e-mail. In high school, they each had had radar for the other, since they were both surviving fairly severe family chaos, and successfully abusing drugs. After smoking Colombian in Celia's garage, they'd go to South Street together for onion rings and strawberry shakes, and after several of these meetings, Celia had finally confessed how embarrassing it was to have a father who worked as a clown. Everyone hates clowns, she'd explained, fourteen and dying of self-consciousness. "It makes me feel really bad."

"I don't hate clowns," Evvie lied. "I like them."

Celia smiled. "Really?"

"Yeah. They're good people."

"Well, he's a clown who's been in *prison*." Because they were high, they fell out of their seats, laughing at this. Then grew silent again, in the booth.

"I like people who've been to prison," Evvie said, and she'd meant this. Her father the boxer had always said that half of those who should be in prison were walking around free, that serious criminals were ruling the world. The few times prisoners managed to escape, he would follow the story on TV, and root for them. She told Celia this that night at Burger King.

They'd lost touch until out of the blue, in a surprise e-mail, Celia had reminded Evvie of all this.

YOU PROBABLY DON'T REMEMBER ME, she'd written, which made Evvie feel as if Celia had never known her at all: had she *known* her, she would have realized Evvie was incapable of forgetting a girl whose father was a clown/prisoner.

I THINK I'VE HEARD OF SOMETHING LIKE THAT BEFORE, Celia wrote back the next day, referring to Rocky and Bruno's business. YOU SHOULD TRY IT. I'M PRETTY SURE THE ROOTS OF THIS KIND OF THING ARE IN ANCIENT GREECE.

YOU SAY THAT ABOUT EVERYTHING, Evvie wrote back.

NO, I DON'T. THE GREEKS BELIEVED THAT FEAR COULD BE A CATALYST FOR A GREAT AWAKENING. I THINK YOU CAN FIND THIS IN CONFUCIUS TOO. OR WHAT'S HIS NAME MARCUS AURELIUS. FEAR CAN SEND PEOPLE RIGHT ON THROUGH TO THE OTHER SIDE.

MAYBE YOU'RE OUT OF YOUR MIND, CELIA, BUT I'M NOT, Evvie wrote back, then wrote a second message saying the same thing, adding an exclamation point. Celia shot back: THINK

ABOUT THAT PHRASE "OUT OF YOUR MIND." WHY'S THAT A BAD
THING? WHY DO WE WANT TO BE STUCK IN OUR MINDS? OF ALL
PLACES!

In good times, Celia felt like a friend. But now she felt like a
disembodied voice that was getting stranger every day.

REMEMBER, AMATEURS BUILT THE ARK. PROFESSIONALS BUILT
THE TITANIC, she wrote. Evvie had no idea what this had to do
with anything.

"Ruth?"

The dog came up the steps. She'd been watching TV. She
was so smart she'd leave the room when any kind of violence
came on. Ruth stood in the doorway, with her square head
cocked to the left. She might as well have said: "You called?"

"Ruth, if you weren't here, I couldn't take it."

The dog walked over to her. Sat down.

"Come with me to brush my teeth," Evvie said. Ruth was
the type of dog who understood this request, and who gladly
complied, with a spirit of equanimity that was sometimes, at
least before Ben left, supremely contagious. Evvie brushed
while looking at Ruth. "You're so good, Ruth. Thank you for
being so good."

SHE SLEPT IN her clothes these days. It seemed a waste of energy to put on pajamas, or even to strip down to underwear.
She slipped under the blankets in the dark room. She and Ben
had always gone to bed at the same time. They'd had their
best talks in the darkness. Long and rambling. They'd joked
around in the middle of the night sometimes, half awake from
some dream, then fallen back to sleep. Even with Ruth, Evvie
felt like an amputee, lying there, the best part of her missing.

———

AFTER WORK THAT day Evvie had spent hours making a vegetable lasagna for Neil and Nora Kline and their kids, then delivered it along with flowers, thinking she would leave both on the front stoop with a card, but Nora had come out the side door with a bag of trash to put on the curb. "Evvie!" she'd said, dropping the trash and rushing to embrace her. Nora had reported that Kline (they all called Neil *Kline*, even his kids) was doing really well. She had him on this organic diet, all fresh juices, no meat. Really responded well to the chemo with an attitude they should bottle and sell. He was definitely going to beat this. And you, Evvie, how are *you*?

"Me? Oh, pretty good." The brick house was tall and narrow. All the windows were lit. Evvie kept expecting a thin bald Kline to appear in one of them.

"You don't have to put on an act with me," Nora said, and placed her hand on Evvie's tense shoulder. "I know what it is to be brokenhearted."

"You do?" Evvie couldn't imagine anyone breaking Nora's heart.

"Oh yeah. I was *catatonic* for a year when this Italian guy broke up with me. I would pretty much drive around in my roommate's car, hoping someone would hit me." She had lowered her voice to a near whisper. "I didn't eat, I didn't sleep, I was like anorexic and calling him every day and feeling suicidal."

"Really?"

"You feel like an infant on the side of the road screaming and all the cars are going past!"

"Exactly." Evvie was hugely relieved to hear someone put this into words.

"Sometime I'll tell you the whole insane Alberto *six-and-a-half-year* saga."

"Alberto." Evvie was trying to take this in. Nora was in slippers, a nightgown, and a winter coat. It gave her an old-fashioned look. She smiled and said, "Now I think back and see he looked like a lounge singer. What'd you bring?"

"Lasagna."

"Oh my God!" She nearly shouted this. "So did Ben! Yesterday evening. It's like you guys are still in synch. That's what I said to Kline, I said, *those* two will work it out. Those two are peas in a pod. They're just taking a break."

Evvie's heart pounded and rose up in her chest. "That's how you see it? Really?" Evvie's mouth stretched out as wide as it could. Not a smile, but a stretching, as if a great reluctance to believe this thing she wanted most to believe was preventing the real smile.

"Definitely!" Nora said. "I've actually always admired you guys. I mean, you've always been the best-friends type, right?"

"We have. At least I thought so."

"And you crack each other up, right?"

Evvie thought about this. "We used to."

"A lot you used to! I always envied that. Let me tell you a story, Evvie. About three or four years ago, I saw you guys at Kennywood. The kids were babies, and my mother had them on the merry-go-round, and Kline and I sat on a bench together, eating fries in the dark. It was a good enough time, even though we were always exhausted in those days and really didn't have a lot to say to each other. Anyhow, I saw you and Ben together that night. You probably don't even remember. But the two of you walked by with your arms around each other, and you'd just been on the Jack Rabbit. You'd been laughing really hard about something. I saw you laughing as you approached us, before you stopped and talked to us—"

"I remember," Evvie said. "It was right around the Fourth of July."

"And you looked so in love, I felt a serious pang of envy. The way you glowed and the way you looked at each other. All that passion. I mean, it was so obvious that night. And suddenly I was afraid that I didn't have that kind of love, that I never had, that I never would."

Evvie was deeply moved by the surprising confession. "But I think you do," she said, stupidly. "Have that kind of love."

Nora widened her eyes and looked up at the night sky for a moment. "I have something. Some kind of love. And it's all right. Whatever it is." Then she looked back at Evvie, leaning in. "What I'm trying to say is I know someday you guys will be cracking each other up again."

"You know?" Evvie smiled.

"Come on, you don't really think this is for good, do you?"

"What did Kline say when you said you thought it would work out?"

"Kline said he wasn't sure. So I said, close your eyes, can you see them canning peaches together when they're eighty? Because that's what his parents do—and they have a great marriage. And he closed his eyes and said he sort of could see you guys canning peaches together when you're eighty."

Evvie swallowed. She was salivating. She could hardly bear this good news. "Do they have peach trees?"

"Come on inside—it's cold. They get the peaches from the farmers' market."

"The farmers' market!" Evvie followed Nora into the house. "I love the farmers' market!" *And I love you, Nora.* The front hall was dark, except for a small lit candle on a table underneath a painting one of their children had done of what looked like a huge, deranged moose.

Upstairs she could hear the voices of the children. That night at Kennywood, Evvie had watched tiny kids in Kiddieland riding the miniature Whip and Ferris wheel, Ben beside her agreeing that when they had their own child, they'd come to Kennywood all the time. *But part of me doesn't want to share you*, he'd said. *I mean, kids are so demanding they change everything.* A ripple of panic rolled through her, a collision of feelings she steeled herself against.

"Kids, get out of the tub!" Nora called up. "Put on *Little Bear*, and I'll be up in a few minutes."

"Is Kline here?"

"Uh, no. He's not here much these days."

"What?"

"He's taking classes at night. He's trying to stay really busy, even though he feels like shit. And he doesn't like being around the house much for some reason."

"Oh. I'm—"

"It's OK. It'll pass. He's freaking out a little. Stay for tea."

"OK."

The kitchen was a generous yellow and warmly lit, with a round table in the center, wooden chairs, and white curtains framing a long window above the sink.

Nora put the teapot on, then a basket on the table filled with apples and grapes. The kids' art adorned one of the cabinets.

The ceiling was low, the teacups the color of raisins, the honey in a little brown pot with a lid that said GET SWEET.

"It's decaf," Nora said, pouring from a flowered pot. She sat down across from Evvie.

"The prognosis is good," Evvie said, "right? I mean, Ben said it was good."

"Oh yeah. It's great. But even so, you get cancer, you start to see things differently." She looked down. "I'm supportive of whatever he wants right now. He wants to take art classes. So fine. His parents gave us a bunch of money to make this time easier."

"That's great."

"Yeah. They just had their fiftieth anniversary, and all *seven* of their kids and twenty grandkids came. Kline had tears in his eyes when he watched them dance. And they can actually *dance*, the way people used to. They somehow still see the mystery in each other. At least that's how it seems."

"Wow."

"People forget that another *person* is a complete mystery." Nora looked up, her eyes narrowed as she sipped her tea.

"I guess day after day after day things starts to—"

"People start figuring each other out, solving them like a puzzle, then getting mad or bored. I mean, people should never be *solved*. Alberto totally *solved* me. Or so he thought."

"Sounds like an idiot to me," Evvie said, and Nora laughed, but then sighed, as if suddenly too tired to be having this conversation. She kept going anyway. "Kline's parents are the types to understand life's *short*, even when it *feels* long. Besides, that generation understood the value of standing by each other. I mean, they didn't see loyalty as some kind of sentimental *imposition*. They weren't so selfish. Want an English muffin or something?"

"No, thanks. I agree. Loyalty's just kind of disappeared. It's not really a value people talk about."

"It's harder now. Our generation's a bunch of *option* nuts."

"Exactly," said Evvie. "A bunch of option nuts." She wished she could do more than echo this back, but what could you say about all this that hadn't been said before?

A silence fell. Evvie took a breath.

"This could all just be a midlife thing, Evvie. They say after a certain age, everyone's a cliché. I mean, he could just need some time away. It just becomes part of a longer story and one day looks like a *blip*. I believe that. I can't stand thinking otherwise. *Four* couples we know have busted up in the last two years! I really think divorce is contagious and stupid."

"That makes sense. I mean, everything's contagious on some level."

"It affects everyone. I mean, how are you supposed to have a *community*? People break up and move away or get so pissed off they might as well move away. And then you don't have them over anymore. My parents had the same friends their whole life long. Didn't yours?"

Evvie shrugged. "Sort of, yeah." Those couples her parents had called friends had mostly been alcoholics and addicts, or ex-boxers like her father. Well-meaning, big-spirited people who'd often end up passed out cold in Evvie's parents' living room. Catholics, they'd stayed married in that generation. Two had died before age fifty. A memory came to Evvie. One night, drunk, her mother walked into a bar and somehow got into a fight with a man named Harry Chiakowski, who'd cheated on his wife, Beverly. She'd decked him. "She's the real boxer in the family!" people said later. She tried to imagine telling Nora some of this, and couldn't. Few people on earth were the proper kinds of listeners for such stories.

"Kline's really lucky, Nora," Evvie said. "To have you. Is there anything I can do?"

"You did it. You made a meal so I don't have to cook."

"Anything else I can do, please just call me."

Evvie got up to leave. Nora rose too. Evvie hoped she hadn't overstayed her welcome. They walked down the candlelit hall toward the door and a kid called down, "Mom?"

"Coming! Look, Evvie. Call me sometime. We'll have lunch," Nora said. She said it so easily. Evvie could hear the echo of all the hundreds of times she'd said it before. What must it be like, to move in the world with ultimate ease? She was a person who'd had hundreds of wonderful lunches. Why shouldn't Evvie have lunch with Nora?

"I'd love to have lunch," Evvie said. "Anytime." Her heart slammed up against her chest. She hoped she deserved this potential lunch with this good person whose face at the door was lit from within by something quiet and mysterious that Evvie wished she could photograph. "Thanks, Nora."

SHE STOPPED BY Ben's apartment "on her way" home that night, after stopping at the store to buy some yellow roses, along with lipstick, blush, and eye shadow, which she applied in the car after brushing her hair. An omen of a song had come on: *Get up offa that thing!* She looked good, at least in the dim car light. The yellow rose of friendship, she'd explain. Just staying in touch, bud. Here in the world that's going to hell we might as well. The window was lit. She stood below that large square of light and hurled pebbles at the glass until he appeared in a blue shirt, scratching the side of his head. She held the yellow roses high in the darkness. He waved her up. He wasn't wearing his glasses, and it was quite possible that he waved her up thinking she was someone else, but so what.

"Did you know both Kline and Nora think we'll get back together? Since we're the best-friend type who crack each other up?" She was out of breath. "And that Nora has always envied us? And can see us canning peaches when we're eighty?"

"People think things."

"Ah, yeah, they do."

"People like to stand on the sidelines with their theories. I've done it myself. It's mostly bullshit."

"But sometimes on the sidelines you can see better than if you're playing the game. Sometimes you have a vision of two old happy people canning peaches, and you trust it."

"I really have to get some work done. Ev."

"I know. Just came by to give you these."

She handed the roses over, and backed away, slowly, hoping for a miracle moment to shift the atmosphere, to shift his expression.

He stood there, not looking at her, waiting like someone counting inside their head.

"Enjoy," she said.

"Thanks. And you should really start eating more."

"Why don't you lend me your appetite? Nothing tastes good anymore."

"You're going to disappear if you keep this up."

"Oh, believe me, I've already disappeared."

Ben sighed. "Eat some yogurt. Just force-feed yourself! You'll get sick if—"

"Why don't you feed me?"

"Evvie, do you hear yourself? Do you hear what you just said?" He grabbed one of her arms, held it tightly, and looked at her in the eyes, the closest he'd come since he'd left. She froze, relishing the proximity and the fire in his eyes, but also scared of his anger.

"I was just kidding," she tried. A nervous smile flitted across her face; she couldn't control it.

"You're killing me." He let go. "There has to be some end to this!"

She turned to leave.

"Evvie?"

She kept on walking. He called her name again. She didn't turn back. This would've felt good, had it not felt so awful.

AT HOME, CEDRIC must have been asleep. She'd wanted to sit at the table and eat ice cream with him. Now she lay in bed, listening to "Living in the Now," a lecture by a man with a German accent who insisted pain did not exist in the moment. She liked his tortured laugh, which made its way through what he called *the pain body*. He claimed that if you could stay with the moment, there was no pain. Pain came only when people told themselves stories. Well, that was easy to say, Evvie said to Ruth, but wasn't man the so-called storytelling animal?

Last week she'd seen this kid walking down the street yelling, "Hey Morris, your pants is on fire"—to the air—no Morris anywhere to be seen, and no fire, and the kid looked happy.

She'd called and tried to leave this story on Ben's answering machine but had stopped herself halfway, saying, "Never mind."

He didn't like it anymore—the part of her that brought home stories like a cat brings home birds. "Ruth, he doesn't want the bird anymore. Maybe he never did."

That was the problem with being put in the Dumpster. Your whole history was up for grabs. It turned you into a mad detective combing over the past for clues, trying to figure out when the first time was that Ben said to himself, Maybe I'll leave her. Or, She's so hard to live with. Or, Do I still love her?

She imagined she had at least one clue. Once, half a year before he left, they had sat in a Taco Bell in the Midwest, on the way to his aunt's funeral. She'd torn her burrito into pieces before eating it. She looked up and saw his face. Mild disgust that deepened into something impatient and cold. "What?" she said.

"Why do you attack your burrito that way?"

She had no answer for him. "Uh, because I'm a burrito attacker?" He hadn't laughed, but almost winced. The memory seemed revelatory and shaming. At the time, though a chill had gone through her, she'd paid it no mind, gotten back into the car, and rested her head on his shoulder all the way to the funeral.

SHE TURNED OFF the cassette tape, and the room was silent. It was clear that sleep was not coming tonight. She put on a coat and boots and decided to walk Ruth around the block. But when she stepped outside, she decided she couldn't. Ruth didn't seem to care, so they walked up to the attic, but Cedric was snoring the room in half.

In the kitchen, she tried to eat. No appetite. The phone was there on the wall, black and heavy and old-fashioned. She couldn't resist. She called Ben. No answer.

An hour later, tried again.

"So where were you tonight?" she asked him.

After a long hesitation: "That's really none of your business."

"Oh," she said. It was like being punched in the stomach so hard she had to sit down and bend over to catch her breath. Her eyes watered, her face blazed. "Did you see the stuff about cluster bombs?" she said. "We're blitzing *residential* areas in Fallujah."

"I know. It's a nightmare. I'm sorry. I shouldn't have said it was none of your business. I'm just—"

"Hundreds of thousands of refugees walking out of there now." She looked out the kitchen window, as if they might be walking through her backyard. "And where you spend your nights really *is* none of my business."

She waited for him to disagree, but a silence had fallen.

"Look," he said, "try to get some sleep."

"Yeah. You too."

SHE HARDLY SLEPT at all for the next three days. Each day she felt a little more unhinged. In certain moments, she was like a tightrope walker, the one who never should've been in that business, the one who falls down and looks back up at the rope and thinks, No way. Never again. I'm staying right here for the rest of my life. And then climbs back up.

EVVIE

WHAT WAS THE racket downstairs? Under the electric blanket she slammed her eyes shut against it.

"Evvie?" Cedric stood in the hallway. She got out of bed and opened the door.

"What?"

"I told some guys to come over and have a party and meet you. But then too many came. Like friends of friends of friends." His jaw trembled the way it did when life was too much. He was still in his green Giant Eagle shirt. "Sorry."

She got dressed and walked downstairs. Fifteen or twenty people, mostly men but a small cadre of women, one of them old, were crammed into the kitchen. "Jesus!" a woman was practically screaming to a rotund younger woman who appeared to be half asleep on her feet.

Evvie stood in the doorway and watched Cedric move through the crowd to stand by the door that led out to the porch, his face blanching, his hand on the doorknob, as if at any moment he might escape. "Dude!" a sheet-white man in glasses said to Cedric. "Where's the rest of the beer?"

"I'm about to get it!" Cedric lowered his head, pinching his nose. "This is a situation."

She made her way through the crowd, some of them nodding and smiling to her, and one man saying, "Did you lose some weight?" He was a bubbly and harmless evangelical, and whenever Evvie visited Cedric at work, he'd try to talk with her, saying curious things such as, "God told me to tell you he loves you like you're the only person in the whole world."

Another man, who had Down syndrome and whom Evvie knew as a bagger from the store, had his usual faraway smile in his eyes, and his arms crossed over his Giant Eagle jacket.

Evvie walked up to Cedric. "What were you thinking?" She couldn't be mad at him when he looked so scared.

"I invited only *four* people. Then I guess maybe they invited some other people who I don't even know. They all like to party, so I—"

"Can you please tell them to leave?"

"What? You can't do that!" He looked off into the room. "Everyone! Quiet! OK, OK. For those who don't know, this is my sister, known as Evvie!"

The cramped kitchen settled a bit and everyone looked at Evvie. A freckled, oddly attractive woman with red hair who had to be six feet tall bent her head to the side in sympathy. "Sorry 'bout the big D," she said.

"The what?" Evvie looked at Cedric as if he might translate.

"The big D," the woman repeated. "The *d-i-v-o-r-c-e*."

"We're not divorced. We're just having a trial separation." She stared at Cedric again.

"Oh. Then the big S. Sorry about the big S." She tilted her head to the side.

"Thanks." Evvie tried to stare a hole through Cedric's

head, but his eyes were innocent. "Brianna likes Fine Young Cannibals too," he explained.

"What?"

"I'm a *huge* Fine Young Cannibals fan," Brianna said. Evvie hadn't even thought about Fine Young Cannibals in ten years or more and was amazed that they were having this conversation. "You can have a good time and stop being so sad," Cedric added. He didn't know how to modulate his voice. The whole kitchen had heard this, and someone said, "Aw . . . that's so nice."

"Cedric sweet," said a deep voice from the other room.

It was true. As usual, the purity of Cedric's intention made it impossible to stay angry. He had never thrown a party before, nor had he ever wanted to. He'd never even gone to other people's parties. He endured the family get-togethers, but even they could be too much, and sometimes Evvie would find him hiding out back on a stoop, recovering from the noise and the chaos. Crowds, even small ones, more than challenged him, but this one was all for her. The least she could do was get drunk. Suddenly this seemed like a very good idea. She had a real fondness for alcohol, which was why she mostly refused it, but just for one night, one night here in their own house with all these people, why not opt for partial oblivion. Even the hangover might be nice—the headache a distraction from heartache. She went into the living room and pushed a lot of things into the corner—mostly boxes of pamphlets, and books. She hunted for the Fine Young Cannibals. Ben must have taken them. She put on another old CD, and blared it. It was a Ben favorite, the Talking Heads song called "Creatures of Love," and Evvie downed two whole beers before it was over.

The old song was making her happy. She loved the phrase

"sleep of reason." She'd like to hear "Burning Down the House" next. She'd like to sing it at the top of her lungs. The music was bringing it all back. David Byrne's big suits and apocalyptic voice. How they'd blared that record in the morning to start the day. She and Ben and their old now-divorced Russian friends had roof parties and shout-sang "Burning Down the House" under the night sky one summer. The young man, Kostya, had worn platform shoes from the seventies and danced wildly. His wife had told them stories about seeing her dead grandfather making sandwiches in the kitchen at night. They'd had almost nothing in common with the couple, who'd pursued them aggressively and provided a lot of humor. The memory filled Evvie with warmth and hope and an urge to call Ben, but she managed to resist.

She walked upstairs and found Ruth on the bed, kissed her, grabbed forty dollars from her money box, and went back down. She gave the cash to the man with the beefy arm, and requested that he go buy some more beer around the corner. "Party 'til you're homeless!" he hollered into the room. He was no more than thirty but wore a plastic necklace around his neck with tiny frames featuring pictures of his three children. He lifted the pictures off of his chest and looked down at the kids and said he hadn't seen them in two years; they'd been *abducted by Mom*, words delivered as if he were just explaining that they'd all gone out for an ice-cream soda.

"God, I'm sorry," Evvie said.

"Someday the cops will stop eating donuts and find them."

The tall red-haired woman with the big teeth was standing next to Evvie now, draping a long, heavy arm around her shoulder. "I don't trust anyone," she said. She had the weight of someone who'd been drinking for hours. She bent down and whispered into Evvie's ear, so that she could feel the woman's hot breath and a tinge of her wet lips, "This is how life should be." Then backed away and looked at Evvie with bright, beaming eyes. "Well? Am I right?"

"You're right," Evvie said, opening another beer. In the other room David Byrne had begun to sing about the city in his mind.

Evvie took a long swig of delicious beer and smiled.

NOBODY HAD BURNED down the house, exactly, though there had been a substantial kitchen fire when a young man named Linwood attempted to cook crepes while his hungry audience rapped along with Tupac. (Evvie had been right by the counter, urging Linwood on until the flames burst.) Linwood's exuberant girlfriend, no more than twenty years old, had called the fire department, and even though the fire was mostly out by the time they arrived, the firemen came in with their hoses and masks and overalls. And everything was nicely soaked, and beer had been spilled all over the hall carpets, and when Frank came in—Frank Grubbs the landlord who'd been a nice enough guy for the past seven years—Evvie was still hungover, two days after the party had ended.

Frank the landlord walked inside, paced around from room to room, and said not a word. "Want a cup of tea?" Evvie asked. He shook his head and grimaced at her boy's striped pajamas, the silence surrounding him dark and portentous. "I'll pay for new carpets," Evvie said, "and get a professional cleaner in here too, obviously!" She followed him around the rooms. "I'm still interested in the option to buy someday. Aren't you? Interested in getting the place off your back? It's a real headache, isn't it, Frank? A disaster ready to happen? Like you were always saying?"

She tried to get some eye contact out of Frank. But Frank, in his plaid shirt, his thin body except for the long, protruding stomach, his square glasses, and his Steelers cap, had nothing to say. Only his hand in his pocket, jingling coins, made a sound as he walked down the hall toward the front door in black businessman shoes. She'd followed him out through the gently falling rain in her stockinged feet. "Frank, can you just say one word?" and he'd finally looked at her with flat blue eyes and said, "One word," then opened the car door and drove away while she stood there in the snow with her hands on her hips and her mouth, as they say, agape.

So it should have been no surprise to find they'd been evicted.

"WE'VE BEEN LATE with the rent only once in all these years!" Evvie shouted on the phone. "I offered to pay for the damage! You're just like all the other fat-cat landlords after all, aren't you, Frankie? Even though you pretended to be our friend!" He let her rant some more and then hung up, but not before saying, "I'll give you two weeks."

She slammed down the phone. Called him back with her heart racing and pounding. She was becoming a certain kind of person, the kind who screams at the landlord. "Are you sure you want to be a complete and total fat-cat *asshole*, Frank?"

"I'm sure."

BUT HE GAVE them three months.

Cedric hated the idea of moving even more than Evvie did. His routines were all thrown off. He was a wreck when Evvie told him the news, talking out loud to himself about how he had no right to be a wreck.

"This is all my fault. I'm an idiot," he added, his face blotchy with nerves.

"No, Cedric, it's my fault for getting so drunk. You were trying to help, and I monitored nothing and nobody, not even myself. I'm the fuck-up here."

"Maybe we're both the fuck-up."

"Wonderful."

They were up in the attic that night, eating caramel corn and watching *Law & Order* on the floor, leaning back against Cedric's unmade bed. It was snowing again, and Evvie kept looking away from the courtroom and into the night. She had called Ben and told him what had happened, more than half expecting him to say, "Just come here, at least until you find a place." Instead he'd said, "Bummer."

Bummer? He'd never said that word in his entire life.

She'd stayed quiet.

"I'm sorry to hear it, Ev, but maybe it's good to get a fresh start somewhere. You told me the memories in that house were hounding you."

"They are, but it's not like they won't be coming with me. Maybe you can shake them, but I can't."

"I don't even *want* to shake them, Evvie."

She'd held the receiver up in the air, shocked. Shocked and grateful beyond words for this. She mouthed to an invisible audience, "Did I hear that right?" And then, pulling the receiver back to her ear, said to Ben, "You don't?" Her heart raced.

"Of course not. I want to remember *everything*. It's a huge chunk of my life."

Silence. She said nothing. She had this gem, and would not allow it to be tarnished.

"Think maybe I'll go visit my parents. They don't even know we're separated."

Silence. She refrained from asking him how he could imagine never seeing her parents again. How did a person do that? Just cut themselves off from people they'd visited for all those years of holidays and claimed to have loved? She missed his mother and her llama farm and was plotting a visit.

It struck her that wanting to *remember* their life was really wanting to render it history. Something to preserve, but not something that was still alive.

"I have to go, Evvie. Listen. Good luck. I somehow think moving might be for the best."

"Yeah. I think so too."

"And Ruth's good?"

"Yep."

She slipped on her coat and took Ruth out for a short walk in the cold, taking deep breaths, admiring the moon, the black trees shuddering in the wind, the sound of a train in the distance. She was history. For moments, a person could disappear. A person could turn into what felt like an immaculate spirit of appreciation. It was easy in such moments to see the world pressing in as if it desired to be seen and heard and loved as it really was. Unclouded, untainted, unmarred by the distortions of the mind. All you had to do was leave your mind on the side of the road. Set that burden down. Leave your heart and mind on the side of the road, and walk on without them, looking at the world.

This must be the key to happiness, Evvie thought, walking behind Ruth in the dark. Below her in the lamplight the sidewalk glittered, and when she bent down to pick up a lone gray stone, she was amazed to feel how cold and soft it was. She ran it along the side of her face, closing her eyes, the wind rushing through the trees like dark water.

BEN

IN THE SQUIRREL Cage, Ben sat in a booth with Paul, who was home from Chicago for a week, staying with his mother. Paul, in a black sweater, his head shaved, his skin ruddier, and his large, dark eyes calmer than they used to be, sat drinking his nonalcoholic beer. He'd told Ben about getting fired from the prison where he'd been head of a choir, the venture he'd been most proud of in his life. A guard had decided he was gay and began to hound him, poking him in the chest whenever he could, asking him all kinds of profane questions, demanding answers, until one day, after a month of this harassment, Paul punched him in the face, and that was that. "I hadn't punched anyone since I was a kid. And I'd never punched anyone in the face. And the guy was a lot smaller than me."

"And this happened?"

"Last month." Paul sighed. His eyes traveled around the bar for a moment. "I miss those guys. Prisoners can sing like nobody else."

Ben sat digesting this story. It was strange how big his friend's life was now, that something like this could happen and take its place alongside other events—who knows what they were—and not be worthy of mention in a phone call to

Ben. For years they'd spoken on the phone at least a few times a month, but life had changed. Paul had a large circle of recovering addict friends out in Chicago, and their bond surpassed, Ben imagined, Paul's bond with him.

"You seeing anyone?" Ben asked, changing the subject to banish a wave of jealousy, a feeling of being suddenly stranded.

"I'm seeing someone. But it's so new I don't want to say much."

"What's her name?"

Paul shook his head. "Not yet." Ben would normally enjoy this display; he understood Paul's need to be mysterious, to guard what still felt fragile, but right now he felt strangely bereft.

"All right. Linda. Her first name is Linda."

"OK. Linda. How'd you meet her?"

"She's the sister of one of the prisoners. The sister of the guy who had the best voice. Sang like, I don't know, Al Green. But I won't be hearing him anymore. Thanks to an asshole I'd like to kill. But I'm called to forgive that asshole. And I'm going to." Paul smiled like a maniac.

"Impressive," Ben said. "I don't think I'd have it in me."

"It won't be me doing the forgiving. It'll be him." He pointed up to the ceiling. "He works with anyone."

Ben recoiled, having had enough God talk. A dull anger rose to the surface. "I was surprised you came to town and visited Evvie first, Paul. That stung me."

"I'm sorry. I didn't mean to sting you. It's just, she's the one who's devastated." Paul's long fingers spread out against the table now. "I've been devastated three times before, as you know. I know where she's at. And you, luckily, do not."

"I just hope you know where I am too. I've tried to tell you. If you think this is easy—"

"But you seem to be doing really well, dude. And you look great. Better than ever."

Paul's eyes held a complex expression that changed before Ben could say what it was.

"It's not been a joyride. Believe me. It's not like that."

"I know. I'm sorry. Anyhow, I like Lauren," Paul said.

"You met her for only ten seconds. How can you like her?"

"I got a good feel. You know that's how I am. I either get a good feel, or I don't. Lauren's solid. I can see that. And obviously loves you. I mean, really. And very pretty. What's not to like?" Paul drummed the edge of the table with his index fingers. His legs were moving up and down too.

"It's still incredibly hard." Ben looked out of the booth toward the bar, where an old man sat alone with his head in his hands. "I don't recommend the experience at all," he said, and wanted to be out of the booth now. Wanted to be as alone as he felt. Taking a walk somewhere. Paul had never had to leave anyone; he'd never understand this pain, how heavy it could be, how entwined with guilt and confusion.

"I'm sorry. I'm not unsympathetic," Paul said. "Maybe I'm even a little jealous."

"But you've met someone."

"You know how that goes. I'll fuck it up. Give me a month or two."

"That was the old you. You're no longer Eeyore on a binge, pal. This is you meeting someone as a sober guy who has all this hope at your disposal. You have a life."

"I hope so. I hope I have hope."

Ben softened. He was lucky to have this friend of twenty years.

"I'm sorry it's been hard, Ben. I don't mean—"

"I know you don't."

"Why do you think that guard thought I was gay?"

"Uh, because you're nicer than most men? And better looking?"

"That's exactly what Evvie said. Anyhow, it wasn't a great visit with her. I got her to sit down with me at the computer to check out Match dot com. I was trying to do you a favor and convince her that the world was teeming with great guys and that she really needed to move on. But it was a bad Match dot com night or something. We kept coming up with guys named Beefcake and Hornytoad. Guys who forgot to put their shirts on."

Ben laughed, but this gave him a pang. "God."

"Evvie was going right down the tubes, and I kept saying, 'Wait! Stay with me here. We'll find a gentleman or two. You gotta weed through frogs on Match.' First I put on the Byrds to protect us from despair."

"Good thinking."

"I cranked up 'Eight Miles High.' She loved it."

"Good."

"Then we sat on the floor with her laptop and zeroed in on Made4luv. And Sugar-man. And Lance No Pants, and The Abomination. What kind of guy would call himself The Abomination? We got hysterical laughing. It was great, actually, we were laughing so hard. Finally I found Keith, who looked sort of like he was freaked out by the whole game, but Keith, who liked sitting by the fire, long walks on the beach, was spiritual, not religious, and was looking for hot babes in their forties, had to go and list his favorite foods." Paul paused, his eyebrows raised before he delivered the verdict. "Rocky Mountain oysters and cow tongue."

Ben laughed. "You're making that up."

"Evvie laughed so hard she cried."

Ben laughed a tight laugh, his chest constricted.

"I was trying to make it easier for you, dude. If she could meet someone, someone she really liked, everything would settle down, and you'd be off the hook."

Ben ordered another beer. "Here's to Rocky Mountain oysters," he said.

"And cow tongue," Paul added.

A silence fell into the booth as Paul peeled the label off of his bottle. He had long, strong piano-player fingers. His eyes were narrowed, as if the peeling took all his concentration.

"You know," he said, when he looked up, "I tried to tell Evvie she'd made you into an idol. That nobody should come before God. That she has all this ability for ecstatic love, but only God deserves it."

"OK. And what'd she say to that?"

"She said that would probably ring true if only she could believe in God."

"She's still claiming she doesn't believe?"

"She doesn't."

"Sure she does. She's just in some kind of holding pattern."

Paul looked at him, confused, then raised his bottle. "Someday you'll believe, brother."

"Maybe in hell."

"Here's to one very befuddling life, my friend." Paul set the bottle down. "Did I mention that nonalcoholic beer is another name for horseshit?"

"I thought meeting in the bar was a bad idea. We should go out and walk."

"It's a way to get stronger, Ben. If I can be sober here, I can be sober anywhere."

But Paul's face was shadowed by a sudden exhaustion that made him seem, for the first time, seriously middle-aged.

ON THE WAY home from the bar, Ben saw Evvie and Ruth out front of the mini-mart gas station. He pulled his car over alongside the air pump, turned off his lights, and watched Evvie walk with Ruth toward the door of the convenience store. She told Ruth to stay put and entered the place. Ben got out of the car and ran toward Ruth. Maybe it was the beer, but he felt he could sob, just seeing the dog. Ruth jumped up the way she hadn't in years, and licked his face. Ben needed to get some joint custody deal going soon. He hadn't had the heart for it yet.

Evvie was looking better. He stood by the door, petting Ruth, watching her move around under the assault of soul-sucking lights, loud colors, and abundant junk food. The place was a little sickening. He watched her like she was the star of this show. A peculiarly compelling actress. He almost knocked on the glass.

She had her video camera with her. She was probably here to get some footage of the convenience store saint, as she'd once called him. Was it that Indian guy behind the counter?

Evvie walked over to where a plastic case of cinnamon buns sat next to the coffee and grabbed herself a snack. Ben watched her approach the guy at the counter, who smiled in his cage of bulletproof glass. Then Ben went and opened the door to the store, just a crack, so he could hear what she was saying. He stood there in the dark, waiting, but she said nothing at all.

And then, "So, you're the star of my next movie. I'm a documentarian."

The clerk took a step back, and an exaggerated look of shock spread over his face. "Who, me?" He'd spoken into a mike. He was already acting! Evvie knew how to pick 'em. Ben watched the clerk step forward, one arm across his waist. "And what is this movie's name?"

"*The Man Behind the Counter*, or maybe, *The Counter Man.*"

He laughed. It was both a soft and full-bodied laugh, unexpectedly rich. Evvie loved people with rich laughs. A customer behind Evvie said he wanted a lottery ticket; he was gruff, with a bashed-in-looking face under a green cap, and he pushed Evvie to the side. This pissed Ben off, an old habit that made him want to walk into the place and tell the man off, but he steeled himself. Then Evvie must have sensed him. There she was, looking right at him. But somehow, she didn't see him. She looked right through the glass, in his direction, and didn't see him at all.

A shudder went through him; he was invisible to her out here in the dark. Ben put his face down into Ruth's head, breathed the scent of her coat, and turned to go.

Ruth barked in protest, but he told her to stay, and she stayed.

RANJEEV

THE WOMAN CALLED Evvie has visited a few times before, the last time explaining that she is interested in filming the people of the community, especially him. He had been wondering about her. Now it's two in the morning, and other than Boris, his coworker, they have the store to themselves. Even the gas pumps outside are unused, the empty lot made emptier by the metallic light raining down. And she has her video camera with her again. She takes it out of the case and holds it.

"We could start."

"Oh." He flashes his smile, then looks down. She always reminds him of someone. He can't say who.

"Is that OK?"

"It's OK." He steals another look at her face, looks down again. She may be drunk. Or maybe it's just insomnia making her a wreck.

"Do they really call you Apu?"

"Oh yes. For two years, I am Apu."

"Do you watch *The Simpsons*?"

"Five times I am watching *The Simpsons*."

Ranjeev didn't really talk like this. He was imitating Apu. People liked it. A way to please the customers. Certainly this woman, Evvie, liked it. She couldn't get the smile off her face.

"Can you tell me what's hard about this job? I mean, can we start there? Because you're a pro. You're the guy who makes everyone want to come in out of the rain."

He smiles, shaking his head; he knew how to transmit a drastic humility.

"You are!" she says. "You're like a magnet! Is it some kind of mystical thing? Never mind, let's slow down. I'm sorry. I'm sort of exhausted. Have you ever not slept much for a long time? Your mind starts to go." She makes loops around her head. "You start to think you're someone else. And maybe you are. Anyhow! So."

Her dark eyes are both soft and somehow penetrating, but she makes no sense. This evening she is wearing a black coat and her face is too pale.

He himself is in a sky-blue jacket with a satin sheen to it. A customer said this is like something a greaser in a gang would wear in the 1950s. He'd had to stop himself from telling the customer to fuck off, because the jacket had belonged to his favorite uncle. He was glad when another customer said, That ain't no greaser coat.

"You don't mind me filming you like this? Just a little?"

"If you must," he says, with a sweep of his hand and a smile he intends to be encouraging. He feels a strong urge to help. If he can help by being in her movie, this is fine. He will be Apu for her. Why not? It's the least he can do. She's got something in her face, some sort of beauty

She pulls out her camera.

"The way you're looking at the camera right now," she says, "it's like you feel completely at ease. Am I right?"

He widens his eyes. Is she right? Is this easy? Ease, he wants to say, is relative and hard to come by. He feels at ease compared to what he felt when his mother had cancer. At ease compared to what he felt when he watched a kid die on Rippey Street, thirteen and shot in the head. At ease compared to what he feels when he stops to consider the nature of the world.

"You are right," he tells the camera, and the woman named Evvie. "I am at ease."

"What's the secret to your happiness?"

"Who is saying I am happy?" Then regrets saying it, because the woman looks nervous.

"I'm sorry," she says. "I don't mean to assume that. But you seem happy."

"For me, it is privilege, to serve the people coming in and going out. I am seeing humanity. All the humanity is coming for candy, tobacco, the lottery ticket. I am thinking when I look at them, they are sometimes forgetting who they are. Many have their eyes bloodshot. Still, for me, it is privilege. Sometimes they are hating me! Hating life! Still, it is privilege."

He isn't sure these words are complete bullshit. Saying them, they start to feel true. He would like to say them again.

"That's beautiful," she says. "People must feel that."

He smiles at her. It is hard to resist smiling at this woman who seems to love him. For no reason. This woman who sometimes comes with her beautiful dog. This woman who one night last week was drunk and told him she liked his missing tooth because it's like a tiny dark door that makes her imagine herself as a tiny person, an almost invisible person who could walk through the door in that mouth and disappear inside of him. He laughed when she said that, even as it was nuts. She laughed too. He walked her home. She said she was sorry. She lived in a room. She said he could come in. He thought that was a very bad idea. She said she thought he was a saint. He said she was drunk and needed to sleep and good luck in the morning when she remembered telling him she wanted to walk through the door of his missing tooth. And she laughed and laughed.

SHE THINKS SHE is making a movie. Maybe she thinks she is some kind of Hollywood director. He isn't sure she is 100 percent crazy (like some of the customers are—one man thinks he's a horse), but she is also not quite right. But is there harm, he asks himself, in pretending to be a director? He sometimes enjoys pretending to be her star.

A WEEK LATER she is back. She's out there with her camera. He leaves Boris the coworker on the cash register and quietly steps outside for a moment, then leans back against the wall in the darkness, spying on her. He is fairly certain she's aware of his presence. He can't say how. It's as if he can feel her sixth sense attending to him there. She seems not to mind. Her sixth sense seems to be the happiest of all her senses tonight.

SHE ASKS A boy, "Do you have any connection at all to the man you just bought those chips from? You seemed to talk to him for a long time. I'm working for a local TV station on a story about clerks in the city."

The tall boy is wearing long shorts and enormous white sneakers that are not tied. His black chest is strong and narrow, and his face, handsome atop an unusually long neck, seems to hover above his body. It is a face ready to detach and float up into the dusk like a balloon.

"Channel what?" the boy wants to know.

"Twelve," she almost shouts.

"OK. That dude who works in there," says the boy. "I seen him throwing bottles against a wall one night. Dude dresses like a frackin' freak."

Ranjeev wants to leave his position against the wall and defend himself. The boy is wrong. He never threw bottles. And he doesn't dress like a frackin' freak. The boy's the one who dresses like a freak.

"I don't think so" is all the woman, Evvie, the director, can say.

The boy laughs. He has great presence. He throws his shoulders back. His upper body does a sinuous, subtle dance as he speaks. "Dude's a Hindu or a Muslim. You hear all that music he plays? That be some Hindu shit or some Muslim shit. Put *that* in your movie."

The boy winks. Nods. Walks off.

"Where were you breaking bottles against a wall?" Evvie calls, and looks over at him with a smile. She is sometimes beautiful, and stops time.

"He is mistaken."

"I believe you."

Ranjeev laughs. "You believe me. That's good."

"Why is that funny?"

He doesn't know why it's funny. He doesn't know why she'd inspired him to come out and lean against the wall, or why for one moment he thinks of holding her head in his hands like a lover in spring. It is spring.

"I am going back inside," he says.

MANY HAVE COME to know Evvie as the strange woman with the video camera. Some have started avoiding her, taking wide circles so they don't have to pass by her. Ranjeev sees this. But always he'll talk with her. Something is irresistible in her face. Maybe it's just how happy she looks when she sees him.

"How you doing tonight, Ranjeev?"

It's late. She wears a Steelers cap. Her eyes are sleepy black beneath the rim. Almost as dark as his sister's eyes. His mother's. But her skin looks ghost white. She is too thin, and she looks exhausted.

She repeats the question. "How are you tonight, Counter Man?" Her long fingers cover her mouth.

"Happy." He could add "to see you," but no. He mulls this over for a moment, rocking back on his heels, but now must attend to a very hungry customer who wants to know what the *fuck* Evvie has a movie camera in here for. She doesn't answer him because she can't see his eyes; he's wearing sunglasses. She slinks out the glass door and sits in her car over by pump 8. Ranjeev tells the man, "She is professional." His heart is pounding. He can see Evvie is looking up at what he assumes is a good bright moon.

"SO, DO YOU know the man behind the counter?"

The woman Evvie's approached is middle-aged in thick glasses and drinking a large coffee on her way back to her car.

Ranjeev again is spying on a slow, gray-skied evening at the end of April. Someone in the distance is slamming on the brakes, screeching to a halt.

"He's a beautiful fellow. For insomniacs such as myself, he's someone to count on."

"Why is it you have insomnia?"

"I don't know, but if I did, I wouldn't tell it to a stranger with a camera. I don't even know who you are."

"I work for a cable TV station and I'm making a film called *The Man Behind the Counter*. Are you an artist? Not to pry, but you look—"

"Honey, good luck to you. You're going to need it."

Ranjeev shakes his head. People were always in such a fucking hurry. And not so very nice to the director.

"Sir, I'm making a movie about convenience store clerks. Would you mind telling me what you think of the man behind the counter?"

The young man shrugs, eyes downcast.

"Does he seem especially kind to you?"

Shrugs again, staring into the camera. His white face is scarred with acne, his hair hangs down like a dude in an old-time rock band. He emits the don't-come-near-me spirit that Evvie ignores. Ranjeev wants to call out, *Leave him alone.*

"Anyhow, any words about the man behind the counter?"

"He's from Islam."

"He's from Islam? Where's Islam?"

"Fuck you."

Ok, sorry to bother you.

"Evvie," Ranjeev calls, "come over here."

She pretends she is surprised to see him outside. He

pretends, to himself, that he isn't worried about her, and mystified by his own deepening affection.

"You should ask only the friendly people," he says.

She laughs. "Hard to tell who's friendly until you talk to them."

"I don't want you to get hurt."

His words hover in the air.

BEN

EARLY MAY, AND with it an explosion of blossoming trees, clouds of pink and white lining the streets, and the sun shining in the blue. Ben stood at his window, talking on the phone, eyes closed to the light streaming in. Four months had gone by, and Evvie still thought he was unattached. She'd requested that they keep wearing their wedding rings as "friendship rings," and Ben had complied. But soon he'd take the simple gold band off, put it in a box, and close the lid for good. Or toss it. He should have never agreed to keep it on anyway. How willfully naive he'd been, imagining you could smoothly transition from husband and wife to friends. That she could be appeased, slowly but surely, by empty little gestures.

"You should tell her the truth soon," said his cousin Murphy, his one confidant these days outside of Lauren and occasionally Paul. (He couldn't talk to Kline—Kline was doing chemo and radiation. That put things into a perspective Ben could only imagine. Twice Ben had dropped off meals that Lauren made, leaving them on the step, saying he was there if they needed him.)

Murphy lived in Philly with his second wife, Neeni, and several kids—his, hers, and theirs. He was a man who regularly hid in his own bathroom. He had no discernible wisdom, but at least he had been through hell and back a few times.

"I don't want Evvie to feel like Lauren is to blame for it all. That will only confuse the issue."

"Right," Murphy said. "I remember thinking that way."

"And?"

"I'm not sure it matters. When you break a heart, you break a heart. Might as well be honest."

"But it's not Lauren that's the problem. It really isn't. I don't want Evvie imagining it is."

Yes, he loved Lauren. Yes, he was moved by her smile, her low expectations of others that lent her a strange peace, and how beauty seemed to follow her around so that any room she entered looked brighter. Yes, it was great to make love to Lauren and then listen to her talk, even as the room was still occasionally haunted, and his dreams were surreal; one night Evvie's head fell through the window and onto the floor. He hadn't slept at all after that. Even when he was awake, there were moments when her face seemed to float in the darkness just beyond the window.

But even before Lauren, he reminded himself, he'd looked across the table that last year with Evvie, as if she were light-years away. He'd been dying of loneliness and now said as much to Murphy.

"I know the feeling," Murphy said. "But don't think you can cure that with another woman. Not gonna happen."

Ben started to pace in protest. "I think I absolutely *can* cure that with another woman. I happen to be in the process of doing so."

"Uh-huh."

"Are you telling me you're lonely in your marriage to Neeni too?"

"Let's just say I feel like most of me is shelved away at least half of the time. Maybe more. But that's life! We got kids. They're demanding as hell! Even when I was with Danielle, before kids, we had the stress of shitty jobs. Basically what happens, unless you're rich as hell, is you just pour yourself into making it through the days. The days zap you, and you can't expect to come home to some kind of love nest, since the days are zapping her too."

"Oh. Well, I'm sorry to hear that, Murph. I really am. And by the way, people who are rich as hell don't look so happy to me, either."

"Let's just say I feel like we all have to be who we are, no matter who we're with. That it doesn't much matter in the end. You get zapped. You think one woman's not the right one, so you go shopping for another, and for a while she'll seem like a lucky charm. You get a lot of action, you get some sweet talk over coffee in the morning. But then it goes back to just getting by. And one day you say to yourself, whether I'm here or there, whether it's this woman or that woman, my balls will eventually be kicked, and I'll still be the man in the mirror."

"Sorry you see it that way."

"Talk to me in a few years."

Ben considered saying good-bye and hanging up. Instead he took a deep breath, waited, then said, "Murphy, you should really talk to Neeni about this. You shouldn't just go through the years feeling lonely."

Murphy laughed. "Who said? Who said that wasn't exactly

what most people do, whether they're married or not? Ever hear of the human condition?"

"This is where romanticizing your pain gets you, Murph. You're a guy who hides in your bathroom."

"I love my bathroom. It has everything I need." Murphy laughed. "When we hang up, I get to sit on my throne with *Calvin and Hobbes*. The door is locked. This is the secret to happiness, brother."

Ben laughed, with a sinking sensation, since part of him suspected this might be true. "Later, Murph."

SOMETIMES BEING WITH Lauren was like being on a mountain. He could look down and survey the life he'd left behind. A combination of sadness and exhilaration would overtake him. He could almost see Evvie down there, walking around in a strange town without him. She would find her way. It all made him want to write some music, something he hadn't wanted to do in a long time.

You just left so you could have a festival with your feelings! Evvie had said once. And in part, that was true. Somehow marriage had domesticated his feelings out of existence, and now they were back with a vengeance.

He knew a wild, almost frightening joy, at times. Like when he looked across the table at Lauren in a restaurant and thought, *We have years. We have years together. You're my traveling companion.* Lauren wanted to go to Spain sometime, and they were saving up. She was collecting Barcelona information. He would lean across the table and kiss her.

Other times, alone in his apartment, his stomach hurt, as

if his guts had been taken out, mixed up, then put back inside of him.

He hated to keep lying to Evvie, but someday he wanted to be *friends* with her, and if Evvie knew that he and Lauren had been together for months now, she would be in the position of having to hate Lauren, and any friendship would be impossible. He had to protect their future.

LAUREN, WHO TASTED like sweetened cinnamon. It wasn't just Ben who thought so. Her ex-husband and several guys before that had all commented on this. Ben was vaguely jealous of her past and did not enjoy how often she mentioned some of her ex-lovers, but at forty-three, he knew how to curb emotions that had once nearly sabotaged him, including with Evvie, whose ex-boyfriend had played minor league baseball and had shown up in Ben's dreams for years, shirtless in the sun, even though he'd never laid eyes on the guy. Maybe that guy was someone Evvie would eventually look up, Ben thought. The faintest tinge of jealousy came and went like a sneeze. He tried to believe that after this transition, Evvie would find someone who would make her truly happy. Someone who shared her vision of things. Maybe an animal rights person. Or was she going to end up a woman surrounded by cats in a crumbling house? She'd told him years ago she'd always feared that.

She'd sent him poems in the mail recently. The latest was the last stanza of Matthew Arnold's "Dover Beach."

> *Ah, love, let us be true*
> *To one another! For the world, which seems*

To lie before us like a land of dreams,
So various, so beautiful, so new,
Hath really neither joy, nor love, nor light
Nor certitude, nor peace, nor help for pain;
And we are here as on a darkling plain
Swept with confused alarms of struggle and flight
Where ignorant armies clash by night.

He wanted to write back, "*We* are the ignorant armies clashing by night, Evvie."

SHE SENT A long letter explaining to him that *love played hide-and-seek*, that when it was hiding you didn't just *quit* playing the game, and that she was already changing and that she missed his mother. The letter's tone was restrained (for Evvie) but had a PS saying she'd give years of her life just to have one more night with him. Didn't she recognize this as a brand of insanity? He'd read once that a certain kind of grief *was* insanity. She sent him a poem every day, for two weeks. Pablo Neruda. Dickinson. Shakespeare.

He dreaded putting his hand into the mailbox, but one small part of him—he was barely conscious of this—remained fascinated and oddly grateful for her persistence.

"LET'S TAKE A break," Lauren said. "Let's walk over there by the flowers."

Lauren wore short faded red gym shorts with white blouses on the tennis court, where he couldn't stop watching her. Her brand of compact grace and coordination had eluded him all his life—not just in his own body, but also in the bodies of those he'd loved. For years Evvie had tried to teach herself to do a simple cartwheel. Finally she gave up. She was the sort of person who fell down steps at least once a year, walked into tree branches, and bumped her head on doors. "I can't help it if I was born with impaired proprioception!" She'd been on crutches three times in sixteen years. A mere transient in her body—a neon JUST VISITING sign might easily have flashed across her chest—whereas Lauren truly inhabited her skin, as if long ago she had decided to settle there for the duration. This, he imagined, was the source of her happiness.

They took a break. In the shade he noticed her sky-colored eyes. "We have to pick up Ramona from Scouts in twenty minutes."

He shrugged. "Sure."

"She's starting to get attached to you."

"I don't know about that."

"She's always asking if you'll be coming over!"

"That's nice. But maybe she's just asking so she can be prepared."

Lauren looked at him, thinking. She never had a knee-jerk response. She listened to others, mulled over their words, and then spoke her answer, simply, rarely stumbling. The more he was with her, the greater his respect for this quality grew.

"Maybe she *is* trying to prepare herself. I hadn't thought of that." She smiled, meaning to compliment him, and he received it like warm water down his spine, and loved her heart-shaped face as it turned away toward the whoosh of wind in the shuddering tree beside them, all the leaves turning over, their shimmering undersides silver in the light. "I love spring," she said. She put on some glamorous sunglasses; smiling, she managed to look like a kid playing dress-up.

"I do too."

RAMONA GOT INTO the backseat in her Brownie uniform, carrying a yellow seat cushion she'd made herself. She had a milk mustache. In the car she complained that a Brownie named Brenda Kehoe had said, "Move your *a-s-s*."

Lauren, driving, looked at her in the rearview. "She spelled it?"

"No, she said it. I'm spelling it."

"Good."

"And she also took five cookies and we're only supposed to take two. And when I tried to tell Mrs. Kasper she said, 'Brownies don't tattle on their neighbors.'"

"Mrs. Kasper's a little overwhelmed. Her husband rides a motorcycle."

"Yeah, well, maybe I don't want to be a Brownie."

Lauren turned from the wheel to look at Ben. "She says this every week. Then she's always dying to go back."

Ramona hung her head out the window like a dog and screamed something. Lauren explained to Ben that Ramona loved how the rushing air shredded her words. "It's a little science experiment. Sometimes I think she'll go *in* to science, the way she always investigates stuff. When she was little, she'd hang out with the plumber when he worked in our bathroom. She wanted to know about the pipes!"

Ben smiled. "Cool." But she'd told him this before. It surprised him. He knew he was incapable of repeating himself to Lauren at this point; he was still too cautious, weighing his words and delivery, wanting to impress and taking nothing about her for granted, remembering and savoring all she said and all her responses to what he said.

"And she loved bugs. I'd take her and this little friend of hers to the Natural History museum when they were tiny, and Ramona would sit and look at bugs under the microscope, and talk to them like they were old friends. It was almost impossible to get her to leave that place." He hadn't heard about this before.

"Wow. Does she still like bugs?"

Ramona still had her head out the window but was no longer howling. The car in front of them, an SUV, sported a bumper sticker: IF YOU BURN THE FLAG, MAKE SURE TO WRAP YOURSELF IN IT FIRST. The country had lost its mind.

"Look at that bumper sticker!" Ben said.

"I've seen those before."

"It's embarrassing."

"Well, yeah, it is. Anyhow, then when she was only four, she went on this kick where she got really interested in natural disasters, and we had to read tornado and tsunami books constantly."

"Were you like that?"

"I don't remember. Like I've said, early childhood's a blur for me."

"You don't remember anything?"

"No. Not like that. I remember stuff that doesn't mean much. Like I remember this lady in a red dress sitting at a table by herself in a restaurant."

"Odd."

"She comes into my mind, and I'm like, oh, you again. You

can leave now, miss! Because I have no idea why she's there! Freaks me out!"

"Maybe she was beautiful and she smiled at you?"

"No. I was a few tables away. She didn't even know I existed. And meanwhile, I don't even know who was sitting at the table with me! Probably good ole Mom and Dad."

He gave her leg a squeeze. "That's the way it goes sometimes." She rarely mentioned Good ole Mom and Dad. He took this as an opportunity to ask for more.

"So tell me about how you—"

"Ole Dad was a heroin addict who left me in a King's Family Restaurant one day." She turned from the wheel and smiled at him, but her eyes were hidden behind the sunglasses. "But he's cool now. He's in Seattle trying to stop smoking."

"Left you?"

"Strapped in to one of those booster seats, the story goes. By that time my mom was already out of the picture. The manager of King's had to call the cops."

Ramona had gone back to shredding her words in the wind.

"I think she gets high on this," Lauren said, and laughed a little.

Ben sat quiet, a feeling of sorrow and reverence colliding in his chest. Lauren fiddled with the radio, found a song, turned it up. "Please don't think too hard about all that stuff," she told him. "It was a long, long time ago. Dad lives in Seattle with a woman who looks just like Carol Burnett."

Somehow, imagining Lauren as a child abandoned in a family restaurant set him wondering if he and Lauren would ever have a child, a girl who might look just like Lauren. He remembered shooting Evvie with needles of something called

Pergonal—was it made from horse piss or did he make that up?—shooting her in the hip years ago with long sharp needles that supposedly would make it easier to get pregnant. Nobody could find anything wrong with Evvie, or with him. It was an unsolved mystery. And he'd not really minded; it had been Evvie who had wanted a baby.

"You know what's weird?" Lauren said. She had beads of sweat glistening on the top of her forehead.

"What's weird?"

"Ramona looks more like you than she does her father."

He was surprised to feel happy about this, and when Ramona stopped screaming her words into the shredding wind, and ducked back into the car for good, flushed and bright eyed, he turned all the way around in his seat and told her, "I used to do that when I was your age," which was a lie.

She flashed him an unguarded smile. She had pigtails sticking out of the sides of her head. And around her neck, a plastic magnifying glass.

She was a great kid. She could be a great big sister. Suddenly he wanted that.

How would he push a baby in a stroller and risk running into Evvie in the park? What would he say, "Hi, how are you?"

Anger cut through his body like a single strike of lightning. He was tired of the prison of his old affection. The guilt. He would not live beholden. He turned up the radio. He would not be paralyzed by memory. Fuck that! If he was supposed to have a baby, he would have one, with Lauren, and if they needed to move to another city, they could do that too. He squeezed Lauren's thigh.

He imagined opening his head and hosing out his brain.

"Can we go to Taco Bell?" Ramona said.

"My treat," Ben said.

"Yay," Ramona finally said. "Yay Ben!"

"Yay Ben!" said Lauren.

EVVIE'S MOTHER HAD called him on the phone two nights ago. "Ben?"

He loved his mother-in-law, despite or because of her brokenness.

"Hi, Mom." Could he still call her that?

"What do you think about Evvie?"

"Not sure what you mean, Mom." The last he knew, Evvie hadn't told her anything.

"I mean, do you think she's going to be OK?"

"I do."

"Cedric told me there's trouble in paradise."

"Well—"

"I'm sure it's temporary, Ben."

He took a breath. "How are you?"

"I was thinking you should come for a backyard picnic in June. Like last year. Not to push anything. But we did miss you two at Easter. Next Door came over and cut the ham, then invited himself to the table. What was I going to say? Cut the ham and go home?" She laughed, and so did Ben. Next Door was the neighbor, Charlie, an old-school Italian man who still said things like "I don't believe in the women's lib." He tried courting Evvie's aunt after his wife died, but she'd understood that what he wanted was a maid. Next Door missed home-cooked meals, clean sheets, sparkling linoleum. Those things were like his wife's attributes, he'd explained to Ben one day.

"After some long years you can't distinguish between what the person does and who the person is."

That narrowing of what one was to what one did was something Ben had always resisted, wanting to believe in a self that could hang back, like a hovering soul, intact, with qualities that had nothing to do with its action in the world. Suddenly he'd seen that was absurd.

"So will you come? For a picnic? You know who would love to see you is Berenice."

Evvie's morbidly obese aunt with the eyes like raisins in dough and the bright schnauzer named Hackie, whom she liked to introduce as her husband. A sweet woman with a good sense of humor, but it hurt to watch her try to get out of a chair.

"I'd like to see her too." He would. Evvie's extended family had been his own. "And Uncle Carl," he added. Uncle Carl had a dummy named Augustine.

"I'm afraid he's on my *s-h-i-t* list right now."

"Oh."

"Not that I don't feel bad for him. But he and that dummy of his gambled away Sissy's inheritance, then apologized with roses, and Sissy wouldn't forgive him. So Carl says, or rather *Augustine* says, 'Fine, then you won't get the car I bought you either.' And he drives off into the distance like he's never even worked the steps."

"God. That's crazy."

"That's Carl. He'll be back too. That's the real problem."

Ben laughed. It was easier to laugh, now that he was free of a lifetime of obligations to them.

"Anyhow, maybe some Saturday in June, you'll come. Just a family thing. I'll make you a steak. And Evvie can eat her oats and hay like a pony, and we can all have ice cream and toast marshmallows on the grill. Just come say hello. Because boy, did we miss you at Easter."

"I missed you too." He winced. He didn't, couldn't add, *I can't come in June. This isn't temporary. I'm in love with somebody else.*

"So with any luck, we'll see you in June."

"I'll definitely try my best."

THE NEXT DAY he sat through two long meetings in a windowless room. The lights buzzed and turned everyone green. At least he had lunch breaks where he could walk on Carson Street, listening to music on his CD player. He had been listening to Erik Satie, the mystery of simplicity, glancing at the faces of passersby, amazed to see how each face seemed completely deserving of their own feature-length film. Each face was the center of the world. He understood that this perception was a cliché, but that didn't matter. He'd been moved.

He wanted to call Evvie on the phone after that walk, to tell her this. It was the first time he'd felt an irresistible urge to do so. But no. He shouldn't. He really should be telling her about his need for a divorce.

He'd called Lauren instead, to tell her how each face had looked like the center of the world. She'd listened carefully, as was her way.

"That's so cool," she said, yet he felt vaguely that she hadn't understood.

"I love you," he told Lauren, missing Evvie, looking at the sky. It was the end of spring, but the purple clouds looked autumnal, the kind of weather that sent him back to the pushcart days, and suddenly he sensed all their old customers, regulars who'd required nicknames. The Freelance Mortician, Miss Informed, The Man Who Required You Love His Dog as Much as He Did, Our Lady of the Terrible News, To Sir with Love, Peppermint Patty, The Laughing Poet, all the customers lining up, waiting for their hummus and tabbouleh in the autumn, Evvie making the change in her old blue sweater. . . .

"I love you too," Lauren said.

Evvie had named one phlegmatic old woman Bubbles, blurting out, "Thanks, Bubbles," one day as she handed over her change, and the old woman walked away in the cloud of knowing there was no explanation for this moniker, but a smile played upon her lips nonetheless. They called her Bubbles all the time after that and watched her personality change, as if the name had called forth hidden joy beneath the surface of her dour face, and eventually she'd shown up wearing kid sneakers with blinking lights in the soles.

"More each day," Lauren added.

"We're going to have a lot of good years together," he said, a pressure in his chest rising into his throat. "A lot of good years." He wished they would hurry up, those years, and get behind him and Lauren. A history to lean on. Filled with memories of rooms where they'd made love, or cried, or laughed until they cried. They hadn't done that yet—laughed until they cried. They needed more rooms.

EVVIE

EVVIE TOOK A train to Philly, thinking she would visit her parents, but after she disembarked, caught the subway, and walked the long blocks to their house, she began to feel she had no skin. For these visits home, Ben had been her skin. Ben had understood that the house of childhood cast a spell, gave her a form of multiple personality disorder, rendered her all the ages she had ever been inside of its walls. Without him, how was she to navigate the collision of selves? He'd seemed to love those selves, had lifted photographs out of an album and taken them for his own possessions: a picture of her when she was a fat, bald baby; her second-grade school picture where she'd tried to look like she had extreme buckteeth like her friend Kenny Walters, who kept white mice in a Barbie castle; and a photograph of her fourteen-year-old self in black cowboy boots, holding her pet rabbit, Zorro. Ben had framed this last one. Now it seemed to her he'd rejected not just the self she was now, but all those other people too. The ones whose ghosts still haunted the old house. She wasn't sure she could actually make this visit.

He'd loved her old bedroom with the light-switch plate of Jesus, Mary, and Joseph, the faded flowered wallpaper, the white plastic radio that looked so quaint, it seemed ancient songs like "Hooked on a Feeling" or "Gypsies, Tramps, and Thieves" were about to come out of it. The gray-and-pink flannel sheets printed with poodles from 1970 were his favorites. And he'd known every important story that had taken place in that room, that house.

Now all of it seemed wrong and broken, warped and tedious.

She found herself walking quickly right by her house as if it were any other house on the narrow street.

Then, at the very end of the street, she sat on the curb, put her head down in her hands, and asked herself, "What are you doing?"

She rose and walked the city streets, walked as if in a dream, then circled back to her parents' house in early dusk, sidling up to the side wall like a spy. In the kitchen window her mother was on the phone, seated at the table in a T-shirt that read, IF THERE'S NO CHOCOLATE IN HEAVEN, THEN I AIN'T GOIN'. Her mother laughed and looked up at the ceiling, then got up and started to walk toward the sink, and Evvie ducked out of sight. Her mother was looking good with her strawberry blond hair and extra pounds. Since her father had been to rehab nine years ago, her mother didn't drink either. She'd quit cold turkey, to accompany her husband, just as she'd always accompanied him drinking. Nine years' sobriety had returned a youthful expression to her face that always surprised Evvie.

SHE STILL HADN'T told her parents what had happened. Apparently Cedric had mentioned that she and Ben were "going through a rough patch," because their mother had asked and

Cedric was incapable of outright lying. Evvie had imagined this trip would be an occasion for confession, but now that seemed unlikely. It was not only Evvie's desire to protect her parents from bad news, but how she knew that telling them would make the whole thing suddenly seem too real. And besides, they'd had enough trouble for one lifetime.

Also, she didn't want their AA-slogan-riddled pep talk right now.

Their favorite by far: *If God's far away, who moved?*

SHE REMEMBERED QUOTING "Desiderata" to them when she was ten, pacing in that living room like a campaigning politician as they drank themselves into oblivion at night. If she just kept reciting "Desiderata," things were bound to improve. They had a right to be here. They really weren't less than the trees and the stars. Ben had liked that story above all others. Now the ridiculous child she'd been on those nights seemed for a stark moment, suddenly alive, unsponsored. She could not bear the memory without the refuge of his listening.

She turned from the window, from the view of her mother leaving the kitchen, and leaned against the house, then stepped back and looked up at her old bedroom window. It faced what had been the bedroom window of her next-door neighbor Donnie Olivetti, who'd come back from Vietnam without a leg when Evvie was eleven. He would sit in the dark and listen to Motown or the Byrds, and Evvie would listen too, across from him in the dark of her own bedroom, kneeling by the window, imagining they were in communion of some kind. She had loved him since she was six years old. Once that year she'd worked up the nerve to call out to him, in a silence that fell after "Ballad of Easy Rider."

"Donnie!" She hadn't meant it to be such an obvious cry of the heart.

He'd come right up to the screen. "Hey, Evvie. How you doing over there?"

She'd hesitated. She'd wanted to tell him something profound that spring night. She'd wanted to speak of a great loneliness. And to somehow tell him nothing else in her life could compare to him. But how impossible that would have been. He might have guessed she'd had a schoolgirl crush, a terrible diminishment of what she'd felt then.

His old window was curtained now, and seemed smaller than she remembered.

It struck her now that the love she'd had for Donnie had somehow paved the way for the love she had for Ben.

SHE STARTED TO walk around to her parents' back door. If it was open, she could slip inside and surprise them. She could visit without saying a word about what was going on with Ben. If they mentioned anything, she could wave the subject away as if the trouble had passed. That was the solution. She could sit and have a cup of tea at the table and enjoy some small talk.

The back door was locked. She knocked. She knocked harder. Maybe her mother had gone upstairs. She gave up and walked around to the front door. Knocked and rang the bell. No answer. Rang and rang. Was it broken? She walked around to the other side of the house and looked into the living room. Photographs of her and her siblings all over the walls. Sears portraits. Her mother's collection of ceramic birds. Her father's amateur boxing trophies on the mantel sharing space with a blue-robed Virgin Mary, all of this barely visible in the dim light cast from the dining room. She knocked on the window without hope. Maybe her mother had gone up to sleep and her father was out at a meeting. Maybe they were both home, and losing their hearing. Or they had heard the knock and imagined an unwanted visitor. For a split second she considered that maybe they'd actually seen her approach, and had rushed to hide from her. "What's wrong with me? Am I that far gone that I'd entertain such a thought?" She spoke this to the darkness, and a shiver went through her.

She missed Ruth.

SHE HAD A problem now. Where to sleep? She could get on a Greyhound and head back to Pittsburgh and sleep all night long with the road rushing beneath her. Or she could go see Frances Trudnack's parents. Frances Trudnack had been her best friend in grade school and was now a surgeon. Her parents still lived two blocks over, as far as Evvie knew. She started walking there. The route was so deeply familiar it felt like walking into the past.

Frances and Evvie had been the sorts to talk about "life" up on top of the jungle gym throughout grade school. What was life? Why was there such a thing as life? Why had they been born? Metaphysical speculation so fresh it was a wound that sent them into a kind of hysterics up there on those bars, under the sky. They'd hang upside down and scream.

She hadn't seen Frances in years, but her parents had always liked Evvie, and Evvie had once considered their house a second home. But the house was dark, she saw now, and closed for the night, or maybe even empty. Or maybe they'd finally moved, like everyone else.

Her long friendship with Frances had seemed indestructible, until a girl named Moira Bangs moved to town in seventh grade with her fishnet stockings and her great idea to have a Little Prince club. Evvie had loved *The Little Prince*, but had not loved how Moira claimed Frances for her best friend, as if Evvie didn't exist. Rather than fight for Frances, Evvie had retreated entirely, reading books about the astronauts. Now she felt a fresh humiliation remembering how badly she'd wanted Frances to drag her away from outer space and back to the world. Why did any of this matter now? Why did old wounds still seem present in the body, in the way that happiness did not? Why couldn't happiness leave the same deep traces? And where was she going to sleep tonight? She sat down on what had been the front stoop of the Trudnack house.

After a while, an old man stood on his front porch next door.

"Hello, sir. Would you mind if I used your phone?" Evvie asked him, standing up.

He didn't answer. He just looked at her.

"Just for a quick moment. I'd like to call my parents."

"Where you come from?"

"I was raised two blocks from here."

"Uh-huh. OK. Come on."

Evvie followed him into the narrow house, which smelled of split pea soup and newspapers. A loud television was tuned into a rerun of *I Love Lucy*. Evvie stopped and watched for a second. "Love this show," she said, turning to the man, but he was not in the mood to chat. He pointed her to an old rotary phone on a table by an armchair. "Sit on down and make your call," he said. She sank into the old chair and picked up the heavy receiver. The old man hovered over her, watching closely as she dialed, as if making sure it wasn't long distance.

The phone rang and rang. Just as she was ready to give up, her father answered.

"Hey, Dad!" Tears of relief filled her eyes.

After a short hesitation, her father said, "Pittsburgh!" He called all of his children by the names of their adopted hometowns, including Louise, who lived in Saint Paul. "What's new with you, Pittsburgh?"

"Actually, I'm in town for business, and I thought I'd spend the night with you guys."

"Business?"

"You know, animal stuff."

"Right, right. Well, sure, come right on over!"

"Be there soon." Evvie smiled and hung up the phone. "Thank you so much," she told the old man, who followed close behind her as she made her way back to the night. She would be a pleasant guest for her parents, full of small talk. She would eat, sleep, and get back on the train.

HER FATHER GREETED her at the door with what might be called a hug. They hadn't been a family of huggers until Evvie's sister Mary brought a hugging, hippie fiancé into the mix years ago. The hippie hadn't lasted the year; the hugging habit stayed. But it still wasn't all that natural to the family.

Evvie wondered why her father was dangling car keys and why the house was so dark.

Her mother, as it turned out, was out doing karaoke. "She's

quite the karaoke junkie," her father said, smiling at Evvie. "Two, three times a week now. You gotta come hear."

"OK. Great."

"How you doing?" he said now, walking her to the car. "Keepin' it simple, are ya?"

"Oh yeah," she agreed. She loved him and usually softened in his presence, but felt strangely absent now.

"Good, good. Ya keep it simple and you got it in the bag, kid."

"Easy does it," Evvie agreed.

"Your mom wishes you'd call home more often these days," he said, as they got into the car.

"I will, I will. Just really busy."

"We know all you kids have lives. That's a good thing."

HE DROVE HER to the Greek restaurant, where they sat in a high-backed wooden booth drinking Cokes while a guy who looked like Moe from the Three Stooges sang a fascinating version of "You Shook Me All Night Long," followed by a young woman in eight-inch heels who belted out "Hit Me with Your Best Shot." Evvie's mother was up front with her karaoke friends at a long table. The plan was to wait and surprise her, give her a standing ovation after she sang.

Between the next two songs, both Rolling Stones numbers sung by what appeared to be a biker couple, Evvie's father asked her about the Steelers. Did she think Troy Polamalo would be the backbone again next year?

"Troy and Hines Ward." Evvie nodded, her eyes on her mother, who was rising from her seat now.

"She's up next," her father said. "The lady is up and rarin' to go. Watch out, America."

Evvie's heart quickened. Her mother wore a red dress and had a strange kind of star appeal for a hefty woman in her seventies. Soon she was up there singing "Sweet Caroline" like a pro whose life had placed some salty, scratchy, beautiful resistance in her notes. Evvie, listening, felt both proud and protective. It was easy to love her mother from this distance, as part of a friendly audience in the dark. Evvie looked over at her father, whose face registered a complex mixture of love and fear. It was good to be here, Evvie told herself. Everything's going to work out fine, eventually. Bad times come and bad times go, and people survive and go forward. And now she stood for the standing ovation, and her mother, seeing her there with her father, waved and smiled, her face lighting up, then settling into confusion.

Evvie smiled broadly to let her know that everything was all right, while the audience asked for an encore. "Come on, Gracie, one more! Knock it outta the park!"

Her mother didn't need to be coaxed. She began singing "Total Eclipse of the Heart" and her friends went wild. Evvie watched her father watching her mother, and for a few stark moments, he looked suddenly old, like a stranger. Then he was himself again. The love in his face, born of the pain and effort of a lifelong marriage, was exquisite. She steeled herself against the sadness rising in her chest, and kept her eyes on her singing mother. Then rose for another standing ovation.

EVVIE

JUST AFTER CEDRIC moved out to live in a house of Russian professionals in Greenfield, Evvie walked down Forbes Avenue one Saturday afternoon, eating a bagel, and ran into a landlady whom she had rented from over fifteen years before. Tessie did not appear to have aged much since then. She was still a tanklike woman in a thin cotton dress and black tie shoes, still had the odd habit of talking out of the side of her mouth, still accepted animals—even a big dog like Ruth was OK—and still loved the great saint Padre Pio. In fact, when Evvie asked her, "Do you still have a devotion to Padre Pio?" Tessie's bright eyes widened, as if it were severely sacrilege to suggest that such devotion could ever fade. "You bet I do!" And yes, she had a room available.

The room was right across from the old room she had lived in the summer she'd met Ben. That old room had been small and white, with a wooden floor, a single mattress, and a boom box. She'd owned almost nothing then and was happy that way, making minimum wage in a record store that had long since closed, waiting tables in a Chinese restaurant on the South Side, and sometimes singing in a band—mostly punk bands that formed and broke apart every few months.

No matter where she worked, it had been good to come home to such an exquisitely empty room, knowing there were other people in the other rooms, most of them older and all of them friendly and strange. She bought a broom and liked the daily habit of sweeping the wooden floor. She remembered thinking that summer, this is who I was meant to be. Someone who lives in simplicity in a boardinghouse with old people. Someone who sweeps the wooden floor in the morning. She had not been aware then that her happiness was dependent on a sense of infinite possibility, that the view from that room was a wide-open future, a yellow-brick road with no end in sight.

Then she met Ben and her little empty room seemed suddenly irrelevant, except that it was a container now, for all her longing, and for what soon became a transfiguring love. Ben brought his cassettes of Jimmy Cliff and Joan Armatrading and Leonard Cohen and the Smiths and the Stranglers and a hundred others. Then he brought two guinea pigs, Lou and Marlene, in a big cage.

And his guitar and the stories of his life. Summer of endless revelation, childhood grief still fresh under their skin, they talked through the nights and cried when they made love, and sometimes Rudy the magician, who lived downstairs, woke them in the middle of the night to tell them, "You think I'm just Rudy from Baltimore, when really I'm the Messiah!" And Rudy's friend Mrs. May, a sixty-year-old woman on the third floor, kept chinchillas and made whiskey Popsicles, and *agreed* that Rudy was the Messiah. It was that kind of place, that kind of beginning for Ben and Evvie. Now it was strange to be back in the house, which in the new century had a new spirit, filled up with college students, except for Diligence Chung, who Tessie had said was "a little Chinese Jesus freak," when really she was a pale, thin Korean missionary who wore a purple wool hat and long skirt, no matter the weather. She liked to sing God songs to Evvie.

"PEOPLE WHO WORK near me at the Frame Shop, including the real estate people in the office next door, don't understand why I can't just get over it," Evvie told Tessie one hot August night. They sat on the front porch. "And one of the lawyers across the street, this young woman in a suit, says to me, 'You just need to get laid. Then maybe you'll get your appetite back and cheer up. I mean, I wouldn't want to get divorced,' she said, 'but if it happened, I'd seriously think about all the people I could suddenly sleep with. I mean, can't you look at this as a little get-out-of-jail-free card?'"

Evvie was drinking Tessie's brother's homemade Italian wine and feeling pretty good tonight.

"People got no respect," Tessie said. "They all lost the compass." She'd bent over to take her black tie shoes off, and now her bare feet sat planted resolutely on the cement of the front porch. In her white metal chair, she leaned forward toward the street, mildly wary of whoever passed by, her eyes following them until they were out of sight.

"Divorce is so common people think it's no big deal," Evvie continued. "You know, all the *stars* are doing it, all the neighbors are doing it, all the politicians are doing it—it's like some kind of dance where you just change partners, and life goes on. But really it's *death*. It rends the soul." Evvie took a swig of wine, then held it up to the sinking sun. "I feel like warning the whole world. Not that they'd listen."

"It's terrible, what you're going through. All you young people. In my day, you got married, you stayed married, that was that. My husband and I didn't expect life should be so fun. Now it's everybody has to have their fun." She sipped her own glass of wine, which was leaving a purple mustache on her face. "And all the rush, rush, rush. Where do the people think they're going?"

Evvie took another sip and sighed. "I don't know."

"Six feet under."

Tessie never rushed around. She made tomato sauce and ate dinner and collected rent and fed the dog and cats or rode around with her brother Robert and his wife, Carla, in an old Cadillac, slowly, as if she had all the time in the world. Around her neck Padre Pio's handsome, bearded face was framed in a gold locket. Tessie had told Evvie that the saint had stopped the Americans from bombing San Giovanni Rotondo during the Second World War by appearing in his brown robes up in the sky before the enemy planes. This was a documented miracle, and besides, her late husband had seen it with his own eyes. Evvie dimly recalled learning about the saint in third grade, how he'd had the stigmata, and how the nun had instructed them all to pray that the wounds of Jesus showed up in their own bodies, and how one kid, Eddie McKeever, had shouted *No!* from the back row.

"Mr. McKeever, you can step out into the hallway now," the nun said, horrified.

"Prayer is the oxygen of the heart," Tessie said now. "I would be dead without this man." She held the medal up and closed her eyes. Then opened them. Behind where Tessie sat, Diligence Chung stepped out of the house in her long skirt and purple hat. She had a beautiful face, a quietly certain expression. Evvie liked Diligence, though wished she didn't sing in such high octaves. "Do you mind if I sing to Jesus the Christ?" she'd asked when they first met. "Not at all." And Diligence bent down to pet Ruth. "I love you, dog," she'd said.

"Where you headed tonight?" Tessie asked her now.

"To services," Diligence practically whispered, then took a little bow and floated out toward the sidewalk. They watched her go in silence.

Tessie invited Evvie to take a ride in the Cadillac with her brother and sister-in-law. Going out for a ride was still a form of entertainment for them. Tonight they were headed out to the airport to watch the planes take off. "Come on, it lifts the spirit to watch those big jets getting away like that," Tessie said. Evvie declined, thanking Tessie for the wine, and then walked into the evening.

Maybe it was the silky warmth of the air, or more likely the wine, that made Evvie feel like something good was going to happen. Some nights in summer are this way. Like the sky itself is holding its secret breath in anticipation of something utterly surprising, and the moon looks wet as ripe fruit, unusually present, and glad to be a part of things. She took great big steps, willing herself to give the world a chance, because it was a great, great world.

She began to sing, and found herself walking up the steps of Saint Paul Cathedral. She slipped inside and sat in the very last dark oak pew. The smell transported her straight back to childhood. Her eyes stung with tears. She'd *believed*. In second grade she'd even been in the May procession, walking right

beside the girl who'd been chosen to crown Mary—the girl
tiny and stunned in a white gown, lifted up in the light as two
hundred children sang, *Hail, Holy Queen Enthroned Above!*
Oh, Ma-ria! Hail Queen of Mercy and of Love, Oh, Ma-ria! Always, every year, tears had come into Evvie's eyes—*Those are*
Mary's tears, her grandmother had told her once. Tonight the
stained glass was possessed of a radiance she felt throbbing in
her chest like something about to shatter. She looked up at the
altar, where Christ hung on the cross. She still loved him. Her
first love, born of sorrow and pity in childhood, while saying
the Stations of the Cross. No matter that she'd lost faith, the
love could not be shaken. At least not here, not now. Nor the
sense that she had greatly disappointed him. Failed with flying
colors. And yes, there was probably a God. But this God had
to be held accountable for this world, right? With its hideous
suffering that could never be explained? Suffering she couldn't
even imagine? And so Evvie closed her eyes and crossed her
arms and sat in rigid silence, and then got up and left.

An old priest stood on the stone steps just outside the heavy
red doors. "Good evening, Father." She liked his face. He was
good-looking in a shipwrecked way. He was a man who wore
the heart of his profound weariness on his sleeve, and yet his
face was so kind she couldn't stop looking at him. She asked
him if he knew Saint Basil. She'd become enamored with Basil
when someone from Mercy For Animals had quoted him in a
talk in Cleveland.

"Never met him. He was a little before my time."

She laughed. "Did you know Saint Basil was a vegetarian,
loved and respected animals, and wrote a beautiful prayer?"

"Well, let's hear it," the priest said, looking off into the distance as if the ocean's horizon were at the end of the wide street.

Evvie hoped she remembered. "God, enlarge within us the sense of fellowship with all living things, our brothers and sisters the animals to whom thou gavest the earth as their home in common with us." She paused. The priest turned from the traffic to look at her. She said the next line of the prayer looking into his eyes, and those moments were more intimate than any she'd had in a long time. The priest looked away. She took a breath and finished. "We remember in shame that in the past we have exercised the high dominion of man with ruthless cruelty so that the voice of earth, which should have gone up to thee in song, has been a groan of travail."

The priest nodded. "Very nice. Really. By the way, you don't smoke, do you?"

"No."

"Good. Then I can't ask you for a cigarette. I'm quitting at the age of seventy-one." He smiled. His eyes lit up.

"You can do it," she said.

"Maybe. So when did Saint Basil come out with that prayer?"

"Third century."

"That's right. So you like your animals," the priest said. "I bet you don't know about Saint Guinefort. The dog saint. I mean, Saint Guinefort was a dog. Venerated in the Middle Ages for saving his master's child from an attacking snake. A beautiful greyhound. All the people in France were praying to Guinefort the greyhound."

Evvie smiled. A dog saint! She'd never heard of it. "Here's

a picture of my dog," she said, opening her cell phone. "She's pretty saintly herself."

Maybe she would come to Mass here just for old times' sake, and to be close to the old priest.

"Did you know a dog saved Saint Rocco's life by bringing him food when he was starving in the woods? You should go to the procession they have over in Morningside this summer. They still carry Rocco through the streets."

"Maybe I will sometime."

"I have to go in now." He looked at her, then after a long hesitation, stepped into the church.

SHE WALKED TO Forbes, thinking of the priest and the dog saint and Basil and Tessie's Padre Pio devotion, and how it had felt to sit in the church. It was somehow more of a home to her than anywhere else on earth, but could not be home, not really, because she could not abide its bigotries. But could she find a way in again if an old priest like that talked to her every day in the shade of the cathedral? Did the priest even believe? What did he think of the scandal of all those pedophile priests that were suddenly all over the news? Did he walk around feeling guilt by association? She hoped not.

She was buying a slice of pizza she didn't want when she spotted Cedric, in the passenger seat of a beat-up car, hanging out the window calling her name. The car pulled over to the curb, and she ran to it, pizza in hand.

"Get in."

Cedric was in the backseat, a young couple was in the front. The seats were brown velour and had the comfort of an old,

sunken couch. They were all going to the movies. Cedric almost never went to the movies and rarely went anywhere with
other people.

"How did you three end up together?" she had to know.

Cedric shrugged. "They nabbed me at Mickey D's."

The girl in the front turned around. "Your brother's a *doll*."
She had misty eyes at half-mast, probably stoned out of her
mind, and big 1980s Pittsburgh hair. Otherwise she was tiny
with bitten-down green nails. Her boyfriend at the wheel was a
flabby man in a Black Sabbath T-shirt and sunglasses. "We're
going to see *Lord of the Rings*," he said. "You can come if you
like a long-ass movie and you've got eight bucks."

Evvie shrugged. "Sure," she said. It was a summer night and
it would be good to be together with Cedric and these people,
and it was always soothing to sit in the dark with strangers and
let the screen take over one's life. She had gone to only one
movie since Ben left—*The Station Agent*, about a dwarf who
lives in a train station. Big mistake. She'd sobbed through the
film, for the dwarf and his friend—a woman who'd lost a child.
Evvie had wanted to walk through the screen, introduce herself, and sit around a table with them.

In some ways she had never felt so loved as when she'd gone
to the movies with Ben, who'd had the habit, up until a year or
so ago, of leaning forward in his seat to look over at her face,
checking out her reactions, as if her experience of the movie
was more important to him than his own. That had touched
her deeply, but now she wondered if her very presence had
usurped his enjoyment.

You looked back and all that you'd imagined was so good
were things whose meanings now were entirely up for grabs.

"How do you guys know Cedric?" she said to the young couple.

"We don't, really. We live near Giant Eagle. We heard him talking to himself one day out at the Dumpster, right, Ced?" The misty-eyed waif turned and smiled demurely. Evvie wanted to tell her she had cascading hair.

The car was not a low-rider but felt like one, since the seats were so sunken down.

"I wish we were going to a drive-in," Evvie said. "Do they still have drive-ins?"

Nobody answered this question.

WHEN EVVIE CAUGHT sight of the back of Ben by the glass concessions counter at the multiplex, her heart jumped like some small creature atop a skyscraper, then plummeted head-first down onto the concrete and exploded. He was handing a small bucket of popcorn to a curly-haired woman. Evvie's face burned and no sound emerged from her parched throat, though her mouth hung open, stupidly, heavily. The curly-haired woman was dressed in tight black straight-legged pants and wore heels.

"Uh," Evvie finally managed.

Cedric's friend with the big hair was asking her what her favorite candy was. Couldn't the girl see Evvie's face was hot enough to cook a meal on? Evvie excused herself and went to the bathroom and almost threw up. Then splashed water on her face. She walked back into the lobby, and across the way, Ben was holding the water fountain for the woman. Like they were in grade school. Wasn't that cute?

She lined herself behind a pillar, burning as they passed by (not holding hands, not draped around each other, maybe they were just friends—please, *please*). She noted that they were going to see *Frida*, so when Cedric appeared, his arms filled with popcorn and Cokes, she told him she would be seeing that instead of *Lord of the Rings*.

SHE'D ALWAYS KNOWN she was a masochist. Had always just barely kept that streak in check. Not now. Now she was enjoying every fiery masochistic bone in her body, or perhaps what she enjoyed was that feeling of having no choice. When you have no choice, anxiety vanishes. In the throes of necessity, you become undivided. She sat there five rows behind them and watched the back of their heads.

During the previews she moved up to sit two rows directly behind them, both because she had to make sure she wasn't seeing things (it appeared that the woman was eating her popcorn with chopsticks), and because Ben pulled Evvie forward like an outsize magnet pulls a tin can. Evvie sat stiff in her seat and strained her eyes in the dark to make positively sure that chopsticks were being used by the small-handed woman. It made no sense, but it was happening: she was gently lifting one popped kernel after another into her mouth.

That's really sad, Evvie mouthed to herself. That's really, really sad.

But it wasn't the most interesting thing. The most interesting thing was how they didn't touch each other. Their heads didn't incline toward the other's. They didn't whisper or laugh to each other. They didn't even slouch. They were possessed by a certain formality that made Evvie's heart race with hope;

this could be a young medical equipment salesperson who needed a mentor.

Until Ben draped his arm around the curly head, and gave her a peck on the cheek.

"That's sad," Evvie said, only this time the words were audible, shot into the dark with considerable force. She saw Ben freeze, and then his head turned, and his eye widened, and she knew he saw her. But he simply turned back around to face the screen. He was playing "this isn't happening." He made himself sink like a scuba diver, down into the rich world of his interior life, a world she'd navigated for so many years. She could feel him swimming around, willfully keeping his mask on, the flippers kicking gently, the bubbles of breath a kind of music. He would stay down there forever if he had to.

"Pathetic!" Evvie nearly shouted, then got up out of her seat and marched up the dark aisle and into the lobby. She was aware that everyone was staring at her. In the lobby she put her face in freezing water at the fountain. Then walked out onto the street.

SHE WALKED AND thought about the factory farm in Idaho that produced 1.2 million hogs every year and more waste than the entire city of Los Angeles. She thought about the suffering of those hogs that went on day and night, trapped in concrete and metal, covered in their own excrement with broken legs from trying to escape or just to turn in their cages, covered with festering sores, ulcers, tumors, and most people believing it meant nothing on the grand scale of things, since the hogs didn't write books of philosophy, though if they did, Evvie thought, crossing at the red light in the dark, the books would do more good than all the books of philosophy produced by the humans, and now the Dutch hogs would possibly end up in enormous sky-scraping hog hotels, since the Dutch were running out of land, and Oh yes, Evvie said, talking quietly to herself as she headed up the hill past the Saturday-night couples and hordes of young bare-legged girls, one of whom practically shouted, "Excuse me, m'am!" when she bumped into her, oh yes, it makes sense to spend several million dollars on a hog hotel, go ahead, Dutchmen, do it, I admit it's an ingenious improvement, let's have hog bellboys and hog desk clerks and maintenance hogs and hog maids too, in uniform. Why not?

She started singing the old song "War." She was loud, but who cares. This was within the realm of reason. People were entitled to walk in the streets and sing a song they hadn't thought of in thirty years. A song they'd known in childhood when their neighbor went to war.

Once a lady was vacationing in Erie with her pet pig, and the lady had a heart attack and fell down in the cottage. The pig went out on the road, lay down, stopped traffic, and made mournful noises, trying to communicate. People just drove around the pig. Then finally someone stopped, and the pig led him back down the driveway and into the cottage. The man took the woman to the hospital, and the pig rode in the car with him, crying. That's one of the animals we're torturing, that's the animal that's jammed into a metal cage so small it can't move, the one who doesn't see sunlight until the day they push her into the truck for the slaughterhouse.

She found a huge box behind a store where she'd wandered just to catch her breath. A box so huge, she moved in for a while. She sat there, cross-legged, and remembered the boxes of childhood. How at Christmas, a big box was better than the gift that came inside it. She would sit in the box, quietly, and think, holding a stuffed animal and a bowl of water.

But even then, she'd been herself. No refuge to be taken in memory, because all memory was laced with that old anxiety that apparently came with being herself, *Evvie.* Chewing on the paw of the stuffed dog, chewing on her hair, on the sleeve of her shirt until it was sopping wet. No wonder she'd been a disappointment to that fucked-up family. No wonder. *"Piece of shit kid! Fucking piece of shit!"* She was shouting. She took a chunk of her own hair and yanked it like the nuns had yanked it way back when. Then sat back farther in the box. Took a deep breath.

Once when Cedric was only two they got him an enormous foam dinosaur. The box it came in sat next to the dinosaur in the basement, and she and Cedric slept in the box for a whole week or so. Evvie remembered waking up in the middle of the night and seeing the spindly white dinosaur that Cedric named Roberto, after the great baseball player. She looked out at Roberto that night and he'd seemed alive with a great spirit of protectiveness, a perfectly benign creature who was glad to hover over them forever.

To be alone in this box behind a string of stores, on a summer night, after leaving the movie theater like that, was different, but the box was a shelter that offered a frame for the sky, that hid her body from the eyes of others, and allowed her to lie down and close her eyes.

She dreamed she was an old woman in a rocker, looking at someone's photographs. Every picture was interesting, but they were all strangers. Strangers having birthday parties, strangers wading in creeks, strangers dancing at weddings. She wanted to say she didn't know any of the people, she wanted to scream and wake herself up, but then a voice said, "This is your life, Evvie," and she froze in the rocking chair and understood that her life had happened without her. She had somehow lived the life but had not been present for any of it, and now it was over. She rocked in grief that could not be contained by her body. It spread into the landscape of the dream where cows were eating yellow hay against a silver sky. "Where're Ruth and Ben?" she said, her old neck craning back to ask the invisible person who stood near the window by her chair. "I want Ben when I die," she explained. And the invisible person began to laugh.

She sprung up. She took her shoe off and rubbed her foot, her heart pounding.

THE MOON LOOKED so far away and incidental, someone's tossed hat. She used her cell phone to call Celia.

"Your voice is all shaky. I *really* think you need an antidepressant."

"You were right about—"

"About what?"

"Ben's seeing someone."

"Of course he is. I told you that."

"I never thought he would lie. It feels like I'm being repeatedly stabbed."

"Yes, that's the way it feels."

"He's seeing someone who eats popcorn at the movies with chopsticks."

"What does she look like? Is she young?"

"I don't know, Celia. And I don't even know who you are. Good-bye."

Then called right back to apologize.

"Why did you do that?" Celia said.

"I don't know. Maybe because it doesn't matter what she looks like. Maybe that seems like idle curiosity to me. And who cares if she's young!"

"I don't know. Maybe you're right," Celia said. "Maybe you don't know me, and I don't know you. Maybe this whole relationship we have is a fraud."

"No! No, it's not! Please, Celia, I'm sorry."

"Fine. But you better pull yourself together. I'm worried about you, Ev! If I was rich, I'd hop on a plane."

This stilled Evvie; tears came to her eyes.

"Don't you know what they say about living well is the best revenge? Make yourself look like a million bucks and go out with some rich, handsome dude and walk by Ben on the street like you never saw him before! Take up some cool new hobby, like rowing—it makes you buff."

Celia's saying "buff" made Evvie want to curl up and go to sleep again.

"Seriously, Evvie, lots of guys would go for you. Just date someone who looks good, and make sure you run into Ben."

Bad advice, but offered in a voice filled with love.

"Thanks, Celia."

"There's nothing wrong with you."

"Thanks, Celia."

She went home and grabbed her camera and walked down to the convenience store. Even though the summer thunder was rolling in.

THE GAS PUMPS were packed. Loud rap blared from a red Jeep. A beautiful woman stood by an old mustard-colored Mustang, pumping gas in jeweled sunglasses, dressed like a fashion model, staring off into the distance and emanating a disdainful, full-throttle tolerance, as if nothing about the present scene could interest her. Evvie slipped by her quietly, glancing at her face. She had the same curly hair as Ben's chopstick person.

Evvie walked to the door of the convenience store and saw Ranjeev's face light up for his customer. She walked in and nodded to him, and he returned the nod, but this was a far more restrained welcome than he usually gave her. Was something wrong?

She pretended to look at some gum. It humbled her to hear his sincere *thank you*, or *Many thanks* spoken as if the words came from the very center of his heart, *Thank you, dear one, for being my perfect customer this very evening that will never come again*, he might have said.

Now, way back in the corner of the store, she pretended to look at magazines, peering over the top of *Newsweek*. She saw him look at her once, then look away. No smile. Something told her not to pull out the camera tonight.

"Why they out of Juicy Fruit?" said a black girl in a yellow sweater. She stood on one elegant leg in a flamingo pose, speaking to the row of gum as if one of the packs might answer. Then she walked over and asked Ranjeev.

"Is Juicy Fruit your favorite?" he said.

When the girl answered him after a long pause, her voice had changed dramatically. The accusation in it was gone. It was soft and musical. "It's not my favorite—it's my mom's favorite."

"Oh, so you come here and get your mother's favorite gum, and then take it back home to her." The way he said this made it seem like the little favor had its source in a splendid, even heroic divinity.

"Yeah."

"That's very good." Pronounced *veddy* good.

"I also get her favorite chips," the girl said, slowly, trying to prolong this contact, the way Evvie noticed so many did.

"And do you get something for yourself?"

"Sometime."

"That's veddy good too." The bright smile, soft, arresting, and strange, as if it didn't quite belong to his face tonight. As if it might hover there in the air without him were he suddenly to vanish.

The girl stood there, saying nothing. She pulled on the sleeve of her yellow sweater; she began to hum; she kept looking at him and looking at him until a customer came up and said, "Excuse me. I'd like three lottery tickets, please."

"Three lottery tickets are coming right up, sir," he said.

"I like the way you say that," the old man said. "Where are you from?"

"I live on Flotilla Way."

" Flotilla Way. What country?"

"Right here. Pittsburgh, America."

"Before that?"

"Goa."

"Goa?"

"That's right."

The man nodded.

Just like the girl, the man in the red cap stood hesitating before the window.

FLOTILLA WAY. TWENTY years ago, Evvie cleaned a duplex on Flotilla Way every Thursday for a year. At the end of Flotilla Way sat the aluminum-sided three-story home of Norm the playboy dentist. She and her coworker, a girl named Bonnie Rent, who never left town but wanted everything to be like *On the Road*, had sucked in nitrous oxide from a tank after making the place shine one day, and the playboy dentist had come home to find them laughing on the floor.

The Juicy Fruit girl walked outside and Evvie followed her, not looking at Ranjeev.

"Hey!" she called. "Can I talk to you?"

The girl just looked at her, her chin tucking.

"I'm making a movie. Wanna be in it?"

Still the girl said nothing. She smiled a little.

"It's about Apu. From the store." Evvie nodded in his direction. The girl took a step forward, and Evvie started filming.

"So what do you think of the man who works in the store back there? The man they call Apu?"

The girl ignored the question and started dancing. She was really good. No, she was exceptional, an obvious student of Michael Jackson.

"Come here often?" Evvie tried, filming the great dance.

"Do I, do I, do I come here often?" the girl sang, fist a microphone. Evvie zeroed in on her face. She was beautiful.

"Mrs. Lipton call Apu Mister Sweetie Pie Jesus Face," the girl said, down on her haunches.

"Who's Mrs. Lipton?"

"She givin' all dis money out. She be here tonight."

"Do you think Apu's like Jesus?"

"I don't know," she sang, walking backward, smiling, then turning, then galloping on down the street.

EVVIE WAS SUDDENLY exhausted. The exhaustion flirted with the edge of nihilism, that small but sinister part of being alive. Hadn't she always identified with Dorothy and her three friends lying down in the field of poppies when their destination loomed so close?

A large woman with red lips and dough-white skin exited the store whistling Stevie Wonder's "You are the Sunshine of My Life." (There it was *again*—Evvie had heard this old song three times in *one* week and each time was reminded of her father, who'd never bought records but had bought this one, and played it late one night, sitting alone, drinking in the dark, and Evvie had come halfway down the steps and watched him, not wanting to disturb him, not wanting to leave him alone. She'd been frozen there, watching him listen to the song, light from the street falling in through the window by his chair, leaving him half lit, so she could see how he closed his eyes, and how tired and baffled by his life he seemed. She'd felt a desperate and inexplicable love for him then, and only when the song ended did she manage to turn and head back up the stairs.)

The woman made her way over to the gas pump in tiny high heels. She had crammed her feet into the heels, and God only knew how she was walking; Evvie admired the effort. "Excuse me, miss?" The enormous woman turned around to face Evvie. Her bright green eyes looked directly into Evvie's.

"Can I ask you a question?" Evvie said.

"If I can pump gas when I answer."

"Oh, certainly."

Evvie offered to pump the woman's gas, and the woman was charmed and amused by this, and leaned back against her car to apply some lipstick. "So what's the question?" the woman asked. "What can I help you with?"

Evvie watched the numbers race by as she filled the tank. "That man in there, the one behind the glass, do you know him?"

"Nope."

"Never had any contact?"

"No, I pay here at the pump."

"Will you do me a favor?"

"What is it, honey?" the woman said, already losing patience.

"Walk in there and buy something from that man, then come back out and tell me what you think of him. I'm making a movie. And you might be in it, if that appeals to you."

The woman barked out a skyward laugh. "A movie," she said, narrowing her eyes and turning to Evvie. "How would you ever do a thing like that?"

"I make movies. It's what I do." Evvie straightened her posture and cleared her throat. "I was the writer, director, and producer of *The Urgent Child's Pig.*"

The woman squinted and said it didn't sound familiar.

"So will you go on in there? Just go in and buy a candy bar or something. My treat."

"Don't be silly," said the woman, and she walked toward the store. Evvie waited, leaning on the shiny green car, her eye on a pale moon that floated toward one of the city's many boarded-up churches across the road.

She would not exploit anyone. People would not be obscured by irony run amok. The audience would not have their superiority confirmed. Somehow they would feel like everyone was in it together.

Now the woman was back, arms hanging by her sides. "Alrighty, he's a mensch," she said. "Now, what's up with your movie?"

"What do you mean, 'he's a mensch'?"

"Just what I said. A good guy. A sweetheart. A genuine person."

"A mensch."

"That's what I said! Don't you know any Jews? It's a Jewish word."

"I realize that. I just wanted to know what it means to you."

"Same as it means to the Jews!"

"So do you think you'd come back here just to see him?"

"I'd come back here just to pump my gas and see him." She winked. "But you better calm down."

"You'll probably be in my movie."

"OK, honey," the woman said, smiling. She left the station with a great, possibly illegal, gusto, flooring it until she was clean out of sight.

———

THUNDER ROCKED THE world. The rain fell hard and fast. The sky was broken open by great shards of light. Evvie rushed into the store and up to the counter.

"I'm sorry. No more movie," Ranjeev told her. His eyes were sorry, but their expression was fixed. She stood there, stunned. "Why?" she said, but he had turned his back to her to work on straightening the cartons of cigarettes under the clock.

She stood there, waiting, but he didn't turn around. "OK," she said, "good-bye now," but turning away to head out the door felt like falling into a bottomless well.

EVVIE

"HELLO? THIS IS Evvie Muldoone. I met you on a bus a few months back."

"Hello," Rocky sang, emphasis on the *hell*. That gravel voice she'd loved on the bus.

"Yes, this is Evvie Muldoone. I'm calling about your business. The one where you—"

"I got only one business, honey."

"OK."

"If you do it right, you only need one."

Evvie laughed a little. "Well, I've been thinking maybe I'd—"

"Maybe you were sick of all the heartache? Maybe it was time to come to a pro and put an end to this tribulation? Time to start living again and be creative? Get things straight before Christmas rolls around?" A warm lullaby voice, a starry-night voice that could rock you right into another world. She tried bracing herself against it.

"Something like that." She pinched herself. On her lunch break, she had entered an office building, taken an elevator nineteen stories into the sky, and walked down a long, severely empty hall that ended in a glass wall. She stood with her forehead on the glass and watched thick white clouds breaking apart. Why she had chosen this building, this floor, this window to make the call, this day, this hour, she couldn't say.

Rocky sneezed several times. "I suffer fall allergies. Hurricanes stirred things up. Hold on please, miss."

Now he was back. "So, I don't do business over the phone. I can meet you later today, anywhere in the city of Pittsburgh, and we can begin with eyes wide open."

Evvie remembered his eyes. Dark blue. In her mind they were spinning like pinwheels at a fair, and heart racing, she almost hung up.

"I guess it wouldn't hurt to meet for a quick coffee and get some more information."

"Where will you be?"

"I'm working. In a shop downtown. I'm out on the corner now near—"

"Anywhere near the PPG?" Pittsburgh Plate Glass, the building was a magical castle, like a genius child's creation, all black, watery glass bordered in silver, rising high into the sky it reflected. Evvie and Ben used to run through the courtyard fountains in the summer, taking Ben's little cousins sometimes, and for years they'd gone ice-skating there in the winter. Evvie loved to skate but often had ended up falling. Ben had been the leisurely kind of skater who'd put his hands behind his back, a disconcerting and hilarious (if only to Evvie) imitation of a man from another century.

"I'm two blocks from there."

"I can meet you by the fountain in front of the PPG. I find that's a very conducive atmosphere. Very inspiring. Then we go to Bruno's car."

"Bruno's car?"

"That's our mobile office. We have various offices. We work all over the country, miss. In fact, had you called us next week, we'd have been gone. Our goal is we make it easy on the customer, and we have a good time too—we play some nice music, the car smells good, and it's the most privacy you can get in this world. That's important, don't you think? To have a good time in this life? And a little privacy?"

His speech had the slightest twang, like a well-educated cowboy. She was smiling. She liked him more than she should have.

THE PPG WASN'T just one building, but six, sitting upon six city blocks. It was topped off with hundreds of luminous spires. If you stood in front of one of the buildings, it mirrored another, the reflection watery and dreamlike. Bruno and Rocky stood in front of the black mirror glass looking straight ahead, possibly watching a reflected cloud swim its way across another of the buildings. Evvie stopped walking so she could look at them from a distance. She liked that they were looking up, calm enough to be interested in beauty they must have seen hundreds of times before. She saw that Bruno wore a red tie under his coat and stood with his hands in the pockets of his trousers. He could almost pass for a businessman, but something was off. Maybe it was just the shoes—brown-and-white patent-leather saddle shoes, scuffed up. Rocky, however, was dressed in work boots, jeans, a faded brown corduroy coat, pretty much exactly what she liked to see on a man. It was as if he knew that. As if he were trying to speak to her with those clothes. She waved, approaching them, and Rocky nodded his head.

Bruno was taller than Rocky by a few inches, and quite a bit heavier, but even from a distance it was clear that Rocky was the leader. Rocky tapped his foot, looked at his watch, bristled with energy, a disconcertingly bright smile flashing on his face. It wasn't an easy smile but one charged with effort, and maybe a little insanity, or maybe she was just seeing it that way today: a projection. And something about him was so exceedingly charming—it wasn't just that he was handsome—that her knees felt a little weak. She herself was probably smiling an equally disconcerting smile as she moved toward them, the glass building behind her somehow cheering her on. She had loved it through the years, and now it seemed to be returning some of that love. She moved slowly, dreamily, and wasn't sure why; she had always been a fast walker. Was her body trying to hold her back? Or was she somehow extending these moments, making them last, because Bruno and Rocky made such a nice picture? Bruno, at least from this distance, looked not just like Father Joe from childhood, but also a little like her own father. He had an amused expression on his face as he listened to something Rocky was saying.

It was as if she'd already *had* the meeting and now was approaching them to do it all over again. Her whole body relaxed as they all shook hands. At times like this, it was easy to believe in reincarnation, that linear time did not exist at all.

"Yes, it's me again," she told them, sucking in some brisk air. She wore sneakers and her black coat and a blue-and-green scarf around her head that she felt lent her an air of exotic authority. Underneath the coat was a form-fitting rust-colored sweater and her best jeans, chosen very carefully, as if for a date. She had stuffed a credit card into the back pocket of her jeans, along with twenty bucks and a blank check. She had no idea what this would cost her up front—maybe it would be free to simply sit in the car and hear how things worked. She wasn't necessarily going to *hire* them, was she? That would be a *very* impractical joke. But they were certainly interesting people, and why else had their card fallen out of her jacket yesterday into a patch of sunlight on the green-tiled floor in the bathroom? The day's only patch of sunlight? It might as well have whispered, *And now you will pick me up.*

They seemed unusually gentle, but still she was curious to know if they'd reveal themselves as madmen, or legit. *Just ask some questions.* Give them the benefit of the doubt.

"Like that scarf," Rocky told her. His blue eyes actually *twinkled.*

Bruno asked her if she was hungry.

"No, thanks."

The two of them seemed anything but dangerous. In fact they offered the atmosphere a surprisingly powerful current of goodwill.

"She looks different," Bruno said to Rocky, as if she weren't standing right in front of them.

"They all do," Rocky said, then extended his hand. What did that mean?

"As pretty as you are, you look a little malnourished, honey, and that's because food doesn't taste good anymore. Am I right?" Rocky said, and somehow winked without aggression or insinuation. His face was bright and warm in repose. Then he tilted his head to the side, his expression one of sincere concern.

"I also walk a lot."

"So follow us to Bruno's car. We're walking quiet, we're three people having a meeting, we're not drawing attention to ourselves. Three fine individuals," he sang in a high-pitched near whisper.

"That's right." She felt a streak of exquisite happiness shoot through her.

The three of them headed up a narrow sidewalk and around a corner. Bruno's car, parking lights flashing, sat legally parked on the corner, across from an alley where an old man heaved a trash bag into a Dumpster. The car was a green sedan, a Buick Electra from the 1980s, or perhaps even older.

"Nice car, gentlemen. But probably a real gas-guzzler," she said, too loudly.

"Correct. We don't drive it much."

Bruno opened the back door for her and gestured with his arm. "Madame." She stood and looked at Rocky.

"We're just going to sit here, right? And have a meeting? We're not going anywhere?" Evvie looked at Bruno, who smiled at the ground.

"We're just going to sit here," Bruno said, nodding. She saw him look at Rocky, and for a moment was scared.

"Why'd you look at him like that?" she said.

"Because all the ladies ask the same exact question. They all want to make sure they're not going to be *driving* with us. Always the first thing they say. Some of the fellas say it too. But *all* of the ladies."

"Well, you can understand, can't you? I mean, this isn't all that *normal*."

"Of course we understand," said Rocky. "We're not well acquainted at this point. A smart lady such as yourself does her homework. Feels the waters. Take it as slow as you want, sweetheart."

"Thanks." She actually liked him calling her sweetheart. Why did that presumptuous condescension feel good?

"And take my keys," Rocky said, and tossed them over. She caught them. There were at least twenty of them on a Pittsburgh Steelers key chain that was just like Ben's.

"Can't go anywhere without my keys," Rocky said, and winked.

"Thanks." She held them in both hands.

Rocky's head dipped down, and he put one hand up in the air that said, *No need to thank me.*

She slipped into the backseat. Lush olive green fleece had been stapled over the seats, and two pink-velvet pillows sat against either door. The interior had been made fanciful with dangling mobiles, like the space above a baby's crib, and she looked up, dazzled. One of the mobiles was made of tiny plastic records—Evvie leaned forward to read their labels. Old stuff. The Four Tops. Elvis. John Lee Hooker. The Beatles. Lead Belly. Smokey Robinson. These put her somewhat at ease. Especially Smokey Robinson, whose records her neighbor Donnie had played in those years before he'd gone to Vietnam. She'd forgotten all about those songs. And John Lee Hooker, whose "I Cover the Waterfront" she and Ben adored. Another mobile was made of tiny stuffed animals—rabbits, turkeys, bears, and kittens. Still another mobile featured pictures of happy couples—no doubt an advertisement, Evvie thought; they were smiling because it felt so good to be back together.

The two men were in the front seat now, both of them craning their bodies so they could look at her.

"Well?" Rocky said. "Nice office?"

"Very nice. Are those all people you reunited?"

"Most of them. And if you turn all the way around, we got talking people too."

She turned around and saw three framed photos on the back ledge. "Push those buttons on the frames there, and you'll have a little fun. But can we ask you what you want us to call you? You need an alias. We don't want your real name, because then we might slip up and use it during the operation."

"OK," Evvie said, and turned from the smiling photos on the back ledge. "Give me an alias."

Bruno laughed a little.

"How 'bout Starshine?"

Bruno laughed again.

Rocky turned to him. "Do you have something better?"

"No, no, not at all."

"She looks like a Starshine," Rocky said. "Look at those beautiful eyes."

"I like Starshine," Evvie said, and Rocky turned around to give her a nod of approval. Who did he look like? Someone from long ago. Maybe from a dream. Maybe a movie. She couldn't figure it out. It didn't matter.

"She's got little stars right in the middle of her pupils," Rocky said. For a split second she recoiled from his charm and wanted out of the car.

She turned back to the photos. One couple was photographed in bathing suits on the beach. Both were a bit paunchy and pale in sunglasses, with big smiles and drinks held up to the sunshine. They looked unpretentious and sturdy, and she liked them instinctively and felt she'd met people like them before, in Jersey. She wondered if Rocky and Bruno changed these photos according to who the customer was. She pushed the button and the woman said, "Rocky, Bruno, I think of you every day! I wish you as much joy as you brought me!"

"Push it again," Rocky said.

Evvie pushed the button again, and the woman said, "So God bless and keep ya!"

"I appreciate that," Rocky said. "So does Bruno. Are you a believer?"

Evvie thought about this. "I'm not a hard-core atheist."

"That counts," Rocky said, nodding. "That counts."

"Are you a believer?" she asked Rocky.

He reached into his shirt and pulled out a gold cross.

"And you, Bruno?"

"Without my higher power, I wouldn't be here."

Evvie was strangely happy to hear this.

She turned around and pushed another button on the framed picture of a young couple who sat on the steps in front of their nicely painted blue house. Though their heads were inclined toward each other and their hands were entwined, Evvie wasn't all that interested in them. They were too young, too protected by the ignorance of youth, but she pushed the button anyway. No sound came out. "Must be broken," Bruno said. "Those two are from North Carolina."

"OK. Let's get down to business," Rocky said. "What are your questions?"

What were her questions? For a moment her mind was utterly blank. She looked back at the black glass building before which a woman in a red coat paused on the sidewalk. The woman wore white mittens. Evvie looked at her and asked,

"When you kidnap people, you never, ever have a loaded gun. Am I correct?"

"Might as well be a plastic water pistol," Bruno says. "We don't play with fire, Starshine."

"We hate guns," Rocky added. "We hope you're not an NRA supporter ignoring the plight of the ghetto kids?"

"Of course not," Evvie said. "I wish the NRA would go fuck themselves."

Bruno and Rocky laughed at this, turning toward each other with eyes held wide.

"So how did you get into this business?"

"I was waiting for you to ask," Rocky said. "And I understand that you might want nothing to do with this when I tell you the how of it in a nutshell."

"OK."

"Cards on the table. I'm a felon. Served time. Twice." He nodded his head to emphasize the truth of it.

"For?"

"Drugs! You could've guessed that now, couldn't you? You're a smart young woman, I can see you putting two and two together, I can see you looking at my eyes and knowing I'm just the kind of person who would want to go exploring mentally. Just the kind of person who might hear that drugs open a window to reality. Which of course they do. And when you see *reality*, you can hardly bear the colors or the truth. But seeing reality happens to be quite illegal in this land of ours, and a robocop threw me in the brig. Problem is, you get out of the brig, you go for a job, and the man says, *I don't think so. I think you flushed your life down the shitter, son!* Excuse my language."

"And you, Bruno?"

"I was Rocky's cellie."

"We weren't doing anything together."

"We were brothers, talking through the nights."

"That's right."

"And you did drugs, Bruno?"

"I'm afraid I drank. One too many times, in all the wrong places with all the wrong faces."

"Don't withhold," Rocky said, turning to Bruno, his chin lowered down. "Don't withhold a damn thing. We learned you can't do that. Just *tell* it like it is."

"Well, I got in a fight. In a bar. And I was ramified, and broke some glasses, and one man had to get stitches, and next thing I know, I was getting me a steady diet of brake fluid."

"Brake fluid?" Evvie said.

"Brake fluid. Drugs they pump into you when you spend those special months in the brig."

"Brake fluid," Evvie said.

"I never needed any, but they shot me up anyhow," said Rocky. "Like a vaccine just in case. If anything, I needed a good counselor, seein' as I grew up homeless."

"You did?"

"From third grade on, it was mostly an old brown Chevy I called home sweet home," Rocky said. "Parents were addicts. But I educated myself." She saw he was rolling himself a cigarette.

"Rocky's got a high IQ."

Rocky narrowed his eyes on the front windshield. Evvie watched him closely. In profile too he was somehow intensely familiar. His profile was as familiar as the front of his face.

"Well, I do have that, but so do a lot of folks. What you'll really notice most is I'm a creative entrepreneur. As is Bruno. I told Bruno a man can have all the smarts in the world and still be a failure if he doesn't understand people. If he understands people, he can be a creative entrepreneur."

A silence fell. She thought of Rocky the homeless kid. How in third grade, the other kids would've started whispering, *He lives in a car.* She saw his mother dragging him into a public restroom, holding him upside down at the sink to wash his hair, then standing him in the sink to wash his feet.

"In any case, what else do you need to know?"

"Well, a lot," Evvie said.

"Ask away," Bruno said. He had a thick, baby-pink bottom lip that didn't fit the rest of his face.

"How much does something like this cost?" Evvie said.

Rocky laughed. "Something like this? There's nothing like this, miss. There's only this."

"We saw a need, and we filled it. There's no competition. We believe in helping people in creative ways is all."

"And the cost?" Evvie said. She could feel they were stalling. They looked at each other. Were they trying to decide how rich she was? Did everyone get a different price?

"Don't you have a set price?"

"Sure we do."

"Then what is it?"

"Two grand."

"Well, thanks anyway. That's out of my league." Actually, she'd been imagining this was the price. But now it seemed outrageous, as did her presence in the car. To even consider such a thing! She reached for the handle. She would walk through the cold and forget about these two. Forget about the whole thing.

"One grand up front. The other you pay over time. One lady took three years," Rocky said.

"We understand how it goes. We been around the block. I myself had to stand in line for food stamps years ago, and my ex-wife and I, for many a year, had to save up for days just to get a pizza. I was poor. Nurse's aide down at the VA."

"Your ex-wife? Did you ever try to reunite with her?"

"We didn't have the business then. Even if we did, how could it work when I'm one of the workers? And she was much happier with her new fella." Bruno laughed.

Rocky kept nodding his head, as if to hurry Bruno along. He had heard this story too many times. But Bruno still wanted to tell it. The new fella, apparently, had blossomed into a multi-million-dollar casino owner in Atlantic City, see. His ex-wife kept in touch for years just to tell him about all the luxurious vacations they went on, see, but he didn't mind! He was the type who would rather have his peace of mind than be rich. Far as he could tell, rich people were some of the most miserable sonsabitches in the world.

"And you, Rocky, are you married?"

"Very happily."

"For how long?"

Rocky looked in the rearview and held her gaze. His eyes were both dark and bright, with an earnest expression. "Forever. She fell in love with me when I was still locked up in the stony lonesome. Rode on a bus and brought me candy galore and a steady smile." Rocky held up a picture of what looked like an older Hispanic woman in a baseball cap, wire-frame glasses, and silver earrings. Around the woman's neck was a small gold cross. "Read that face. Go ahead."

Evvie shrugged.

"Honest? Pretty as hell turned backward and forward?"

Evvie smiled.

"I sang 'You're the Best Thing That Ever Happened to Me' the third time she visited."

Evvie smiled again.

"Society's fallin' apart, but we don't have to fall with it."

"I guess not."

"You guess not? You *guess* not?" Rocky was smiling at her in the rearview. "Come on, Starshine, you *guess* not? That's not good enough. Is it?"

She returned his smile. "I guess it's not. Apparently."

He laughed. He sighed, and shook his head. "Take her picture, Bruno."

Bruno snapped a quick picture on a tiny digital before she could stop him.

"Why did you do that? I'm not comfort—"

"Don't you know you're beautiful?"

Evvie said thank you.

"Me and Bruno are not part of the Me First crowd," Rocky said, and the non sequitur made her lean back into herself. "We're not down with the greed machine. We're trying to make ourselves a living without dying."

"And now we got the al-Qaeda terrorists on top of everything," Bruno said, and Rocky shot him a look of confused contempt and asked what the fuck that had to do with anything.

Bruno started to answer, but Rocky stopped him, hand up in the air. "I know, you're right, everything is everything."

"Yeah," Evvie said. This was a phrase from a line in the devastating Springsteen song "You're Missing."

"We thought 9/11 was it," Rocky said. "Thought that was the beginning to the end of the show."

"The chickens came home to roost," Bruno said. He had taken off his coat and loosened his tie. He was looking at Rocky.

"That's right," Rocky said.

Did they mean what she thought they meant? She decided they did. At the very least, they were far from the sorts of people who would ride around in a truck singing that song about the U.S. of A. putting a boot in your ass.

"What'd you think that day?" Bruno said.

"I didn't really think," Evvie said.

When the planes crashed, she'd been on the bus not far from here, going to a job interview at a radio station where she'd hoped to spin records in the middle of the night to make a little extra cash. She could still remember the people she rode with. A child in a red jacket speaking loudly about a vampire to an enormous woman who kept saying, "Mmmm-hmmm, that's right," as if the child were a preacher and she in the pew. *This vampire he eat babies!*

Mmmm-hmmm. The woman had her eyes closed.

Ben had called her, watching people jump to their deaths. *Get off the bus and wait on the corner of Murray and Fleming-ton. I'm coming to get you.*

She'd wanted everyone to get off the bus with her. Ben had come fast. They'd gone home, watched the television, and huddled together for two whole days.

Ben!

"God help the little guy," Rocky said, facing her. She saw a rich melancholy come into his face; then his eyes widened in resistance. "In a country like this, God help the average working man."

"That's right."

"We took a wrong turn," Bruno said. "Someday the poor man will rise up." He clapped twice. He looked at Rocky while he spoke. It was clear that Rocky had schooled him on such matters. Rocky, had he been given a few breaks in life, could've been some kind of history professor. It wasn't hard to imagine him pacing back and forth in front of a classroom, his hand on his square chin.

NOW, IF SHE was really interested (and there was no pressure, they kept insisting, she could just slip out of the car at any moment, no need to explain or even say good-bye), but if she was interested, then, like they said, they would need a hundred dollars right away, then a thousand up front before the operation (they kept using this word *operation* and she wasn't crazy about that), and the way the operation would work is Starshine would have to visit her husband somewhere, maybe his work, or his apartment, or even just on the street, but the timing was crucial. If she got the timing wrong, and they showed up and found she wasn't there with him, they were sorry to say it, but they would have to keep the money and she'd get no second chances. This unfortunate policy was because of someone they called the dame from Denver. (Evvie laughed at that and said, "The *dame* from *Denver?*" Rocky laughed with her, and winked.)

They'd worked with the dame from Denver for two weeks. They'd show up, and she wouldn't be there; she was a nice gal, a great gal, actually, a beauty-full lady in heels, said Bruno, but she wouldn't be there, or he wouldn't be there, and, well, after that grand waste of precious time, they got tougher with the rules.

"We had to. We're actually softies. Do you know how many people out there like to take advantage of softies?"

So now they couldn't mess around, they were in demand at various places in the country, they depended on people who respected them as professionals and so behaved like professionals themselves.

"Sure. I can see that." Her voice was thin and off-key and her mind was frozen.

It started to rain a little. She turned and looked out the back window and saw the PPG. One summer night, just a few years ago, she and Ben had met a nine-year-old break-dancer, and talked with him for hours. The boy had regaled them with stories about his intergalactic travels. In the middle of his stories he would stop occasionally and salute the sky above the PPG, suddenly in contact with someone on another planet.

"Can I write you a check?" she said, eyes on the building.

"We prefer cash. First we work out the details. We give you a secure plan."

"You have a say in it. We work on it together," Bruno said. "All our customers are creative people. Risk takers. We value their input."

"OK, OK," Rocky said, reeling him in. "Don't pile on the BS."

"I don't have the cash," Evvie said.

"But you can get it?" Rocky said, calmly, hopefully.

"Tomorrow."

"We'll take the check," Rocky said. "Just this once."

Bruno shrugged. "He must like you," Bruno said, looking at Rocky. "Rocky hardly ever takes a check."

"I can judge a person's character," Rocky said. "You ought to know that by now."

Evvie smiled at him. She could see that this was the truth. She could read his eyes as they read hers. She could see him seeing that she wouldn't steal or cheat. She understood that the two of them had an understanding of sorts. These stirring connections were rare in the world. They always took her by surprise and filled her with relief and gratitude.

"So tell me again how it works. I'm not completely sure about this yet," she said.

For one moment, she felt she was looking down from above, a giant who was contemplating taking her small self by the scruff of the neck and tossing her body out of the car and into the nearest river, where she could swim back to the shore of reason, because, she thought, this is insanely unreasonable, and I know it, but then why does it also somehow feel like *exactly where I should be* and what I should be doing, right now, right here, on this rainy afternoon. Ordained.

She took in a slow breath. The silence in the car was deep and filled with their patience. They'd been right—back when she first met them they'd said the whole thing was like going to the theater. *Thee-ate-her.* She was on the verge of having front-row tickets to a show she'd been dying to see forever, and it didn't matter that she was one of the actors. She had nearly always been one of the actors, and simultaneously one of the watchful audience members.

"I need all your contact information on the check," Rocky said. "I mean, if you plan on writing one."

"I do think I will."

"Give Starshine the book to lean on."

Bruno handed back a large, battered book with Bob Dylan on the front of it, and no title. She opened the book and saw it was Dylan's sheet music. The collected works. She opened to "Idiot Wind," and turned the page to "Sad Eyed Lady of the Lowlands." A song she and Ben had memorized.

"You guys musicians?"

"That belongs to my son," Bruno said. "He left it behind last time he visited. You'd think the kid grew up in the 1960s. Listening to all the music we grew up on."

"You grew up in the 1960s?" For reasons she couldn't explain, she had imagined Bruno singing doo-wop on a corner.

"Graduated high school in 1966."

"Speak for yourself," Rocky said.

"I am." Bruno explained that Rocky was younger than he, but didn't tell his age.

"I don't even tell myself. Nobody should. I learned that from the holy Mexicans. The numbers hypnotize you. Far as I'm concerned, I'm all the numbers in the world, or none of them."

Evvie saw the wisdom of this and said so. She wrote the check, signing her name with a flourish that surprised her.

Now they were even nicer. Now she was one of their customers for real. Now they wanted to know her wishes, in detail, and how she might want those wishes carried out. It was time, Rocky said, for some dreams to come true.

BEN

AS IT TURNED out, Ramona had a talent for modern dance. At least this is what Lauren seemed to believe, and Ben tried to believe it too, sitting there on the worn wooden seats of the auditorium one night in early November. Backstage, Ramona was dressed up as Autumn, with real leaves pinned to her black leotard, and she would be dancing with Winter, a friend of hers named Eugene whom they'd never met but heard a lot about; the kid was so precocious he was reading Noam Chomsky. Ben had watched Ramona practicing one evening on the grass out front, in her bare feet, in the cold; he'd stood on the steps and clapped for her, secretly thinking, Anything but dance, kid. Do anything else. She had not inherited a speck of Lauren's grace. She was a flailer, but unlike many people cut from such a cloth, seemed not to know it. Her chin was lifted like the proudest ballerina. He supposed she was young enough to get away with this performance, but he worried for her nonetheless.

"Good evening, parents, and welcome. Tonight, as you know, we've asked all the children to interpret one of the seasons. Rumor has it we'll see ten Summers, nine Springs, five Autumns, three Winters, and a whole chorus of the seasons all mixed together!" said the woman with gold-streaked hair

onstage. Her pep was forced but emerged from a genuine desire to rouse the audience out of what often seemed (Ben had
been to three of these events already) like a collective parental
stupor; everyone hauling themselves around with a combination of goodwill, exhaustion, and barely suppressed dread that
the evening, under these harsh and buzzing lights, would go on
forever.

"We let the children choose their season, and we had them
write their own script and choose their own music. We couldn't
be more proud of them, and we'd like to thank some people who
made this evening possible, starting with you, the parents!"
In her skirt and high heels she conducted their clapping. The
woman was a complicated presence up there on the stage, black
and elegant, beautiful but also tired-looking, and Ben clapped
and watched her with narrowed eyes and imagined she was responsible for too much in life. She was the sturdy one who took
over administrative tasks and then regretted it, but kept doing
them because she felt she was surrounded by flakes and idiots.
(Probably was.) She peered at them over her reading glasses,
a warm, if weary, smile on her face. He had real empathy for
these kinds of people, since he was one of them. At work he'd
become that person, even as he'd tried not to. I'm not the boss,
he chanted, off and on throughout the day. Do I look like the
boss? he'd sing. Yes, a woman had answered, you really do. He
didn't know the answers to half of their questions, but he was
undeniably the guy who knew where things were. The man he
shared an office with didn't, of course. Always the people who
didn't know where things were ended up right smack beside
Ben. Like Evvie, who'd always been looking for something.
"I'm losing my mind!" she'd holler. "I had my keys right there

on the shelf and now—" And until the last year he'd come running to retrieve whatever it was—the keys, a book, some crucial document or letter from a senator, a photograph. Too eager to help, which his therapist had said was a real problem. He'd always thought of it as a good quality, but the therapist helped him understand that he was always and everywhere searching for approval.

"Uh, look, Evvie, it's right there," he'd say. "Two feet in front of your eyes." He sometimes thought she had some sort of brain damage. Her mother had told him a story about Evvie at age three trying to fly down concrete steps while playing Batman, and he sometimes thought something might have happened to her then.

She'd smack herself in the head and thank him too profusely while he'd lap up the praise.

He'd always been a finder. Even as a boy, if anyone in his family lost something, his mother would holler, "Get Ben! Ben will know where it is!"

Ben was so grateful, right now, that he sat beside Lauren, who was even more of a finder than he was. This organized woman (probably the most alert of all the parents in this auditorium, and certainly the most beautiful, even in the oversize fisherman sweater—very unlike her to wear something like that, actually) had not once, in all these months, lost her car keys.

"Our show will begin in just a few minutes. Again, thank you for coming." She exited the stage in her elegant skirt and blouse, and he was sorry to see her go.

A child behind them started to cry, and lots of younger kids were running in the aisles. "Here he comes," Lauren said.

"Watch out for the handshake." Lauren's ex-husband was walking toward them. Lauren rarely mentioned him, but Ben had retained every last thing she'd ever said about him: He was a bit of a dolt. He lost his temper every time he watched a football game. He was techno-geek savvy. He was late with child support in a way that was passive-aggressive. He was into terrible sci-fi and horror movies, and his name was Carter.

Carter had a ponytail? You'd think she would have mentioned that. He had wire-frame glasses and a Hendrix T-shirt and his handshake was so strong it seemed filled with the intention to break a few fingers. You wouldn't expect it from a thin guy with a ponytail. Oh, but he had muscles. He was an obvious pumper of iron.

"Nice to finally meet you," Carter said, his eyes shifting toward the expectantly empty stage, the spotlight shining down on nothing. Ben had a few seconds to study him. He had the extreme good looks of a man who'd be painted in the Renaissance. His eyelashes were disturbingly long. Finally he looked down at Lauren, briefly, and Ben understood there was a story of pain between the two of them that Lauren had never been compelled to allude to, much less tell in full. He was thankful for that peculiar reserve but knew he could easily be seized by a deadly curiosity.

Carter took his seat down in the first row, and sat slumped, his hands crossed at his crotch, his long legs extended so that they almost reached the foot of the stage.

"So that's the ex," Ben said.

Lauren nodded, and squeezed his hand, and wouldn't look him in the eye.

———

WHEN IT WAS finally time for Ramona to be Autumn, half the families had gone home. Ben was surprised to feel annoyed by this abandoning of Ramona. *We sat through your kids, you should sit through ours.*

Ramona, covered with red leaves, crawled across the stage moaning, "Time, time, time!" Ben hadn't expected this at all. He sat up, utterly alert. She crawled into the spotlight, then slowly rose to stand, her sinuous arms reaching out into the air like branches. They moved until they found their perfect shape, and then she stood there, impressively frozen, a bony birch on a windless night. It was easy to imagine snowfall and a cardinal landing in the crook of her elbow.

Winter, an Asian boy in a white suit a few sizes too small for him and a small policeman's hat, ran onto the stage and blew a whistle. Then shouted, "Dance, Autumn, dance! Before I come, and you can dance no more!" So this was Eugene the Chomsky reader. His voice was high and clear, but somehow possessed its own authority. He blew the whistle again. "I saw the best minds of my generation destroyed by madness!" Eugene cried, apropos of nothing. Ben whispered to Lauren, "That's the beat poet Ginsberg," and Lauren said, "Get out," and the boy shouted the line again, then walked around in circles that got progressively quicker and larger while part of an old U2 song began to play. "With or Without You." The boy circled the dancing red tree of Ramona, and Ben looked over at Lauren. "This is *wild*," she whispered, and bit her lower lip. "It *is*," he said, watching Ramona, who was still a flailing dancer but was somehow in the process of transcending herself. Having shed all self-consciousness, she was good, in that strange way that anyone is good, when their intentions have been unified into a single desire. He'd seen it before, in college, when a homely young woman had unexpectedly stood up at a party and sung a song about the dignity of coal miners. Nobody even knew where the woman had come from, nobody had ever known a coal miner, and the woman couldn't sing her way out of a paper bag, but by the end of her song Ben had thought she was the best and most beautiful person in the room.

Ramona somehow danced fighting, with all her heart, the idea of winter and the idea of all the best minds of her generation being destroyed by madness, while Eugene with his long bangs like a black curtain on his forehead kept repeating Ginsberg and U2 kept crooning, *And you give yourself away*, and Ben was right there with Ramona as she leaped into the air and spun across the stage while Winter blew his whistle and said, "Your roots, your roots, you have lost your roots." Ramona stopped in her tracks and tiptoed backward to where she'd started, and tried to attach herself again to that spot where her roots had been torn. The spotlight revealed the surprisingly anguished effort of her face. So, he thought. Ramona was an actor. Ben vowed then that he would find ways to encourage this talent. And find more ways to show this child that he could love her.

AFTER THE SHOW, Ben and Lauren waited in the bright hall for Ramona. Carter was talking to the woman who had introduced the show. He stood with his arms folded over his narrow Jimi Hendrix torso, nodding and smiling. For an instant Ben imagined him as the lover he must have been, leaning down to kiss Lauren, his eyes closing.

Then Ramona jumped into Carter's arms. Her thin legs

were wrapped around his waist and he spun with her once. It was a display. It was his night to have her sleep at his place, and now he put her down, and the two walked hand in hand out the door. Lauren grabbed Ben's hand and dragged him after them.

"Ramona!" she cried, in the November dark. Ramona stopped, her pale face startled.

Lauren led him over to them on the sidewalk where she stood. Carter looked surprised, and he wasn't wearing a coat. It was forty degrees and he was in his T-shirt. His eyebrows were raised high.

"We wanted to tell you the show was great!" Lauren said. She had the white hood of her jacket up now.

Ramona smiled, her eyes flashing up once, then lowering down. "Thanks." Ben could see she felt awkward. All the feeling he'd had for her recoiled, replaced by a dull sympathy that she had to endure any of this.

"You really blew us away," he said. "Really."

She nodded. Carter stood there, waiting for this to be over. Ramona kept smiling and looking down at the sidewalk.

"We love ya, honey," Lauren said, and pulled Ben away. She'd never pulled him anywhere before. He was surprised at the force of this gesture and yanked his arm back away from her. She looked at him, surprised, and said she was sorry.

"No, no, it's OK," he said.

As they walked toward the car, he could feel he was about to see a side of Lauren that he'd often sensed would one day reveal itself. He'd almost been looking forward to it. So the day was here. The night, rather. The black night with its bright moon and the sound of a train in the distance.

"That asshole! I wish he'd fucking move to *Alaska*! He almost did, you know. Five years ago he almost moved to *Alaska*, and I argued he should stay here so he could see Ramona. Now he acts like he's Father of the Year. You'd think he might have steered her over to at least say *hello* to us before absconding with her like that! He's the most passive-aggressive person walking this earth."

Lauren was trembling with anger, and tears filled her eyes. The night itself seemed to be backing away from her.

"She's all I ever wanted, Ben. She's the only real family I have. And he's trying to take her away." They stood next to the car now, under a huge, bare tree.

"I don't think so, Lauren. He's just—he's a bit of a dolt." This was an unreasonable attempt to make her laugh, but it didn't work. He wanted to embrace her, but something held him back. He reached out lamely and put his hand on her shoulder.

"I almost died giving birth to that kid, Ben. She's the only kid I'll ever have. You'd think that would count for something. Now she prefers him since he lets her live on Ramen noodles and Cocoa Puffs and watch R-rated movies and play video games with him until midnight."

"Lauren, come on! That's not true. And you never know, you could have another kid." She'd never mentioned Ramona as the only kid she'd ever have.

"Doubtful. Like I said, I almost died." He attempted to let this news sink in. Was he disappointed? He didn't even know.

Maybe having a kid only led to grief, one way or another, like he'd always thought. Maybe the loss of freedom would be terrible. Having a kid wasn't what it used to be. He would have Ramona, in a way, and that could be enough. He looked up at the moon. They got into the car.

It wasn't that what Lauren had said was so bad. It wasn't that he couldn't understand her high-pitched emotions. What disturbed him was something subtle that he was trying now to figure out.

"What?" she'd said. "What?"

He'd ducked inside of himself like a creature in a cave, and she could feel it.

"Nothing."

She fell silent, moved back; she had her own cave.

What he'd seen was a kind of revelation, he thought, or should have been. Lauren was revealing something deep. But oddly, it hadn't, and didn't, feel intimate. It didn't feel like she was revealing herself at all. All this emotion, trembling rage and sadness, somehow made her seem more distant, when it should have brought her closer, and brought them closer. He was not, by nature, someone who feared the emotions of other people, so that couldn't be it.

They drove in silence.

"So what, you think I'm over-the-top for freaking out?"

"No."

"Then what's the problem?"

"I don't know."

"Oh."

Another silence fell. They were almost at her house.

"When you figure it out, please tell me," she said.

He took a breath. "It's like you were behind thick glass," he tried.

"What?"

"You were so upset, you were shaking and everything, but it was almost like, I don't know, like you were acting."

"Acting? What?"

"I don't know, Lauren."

"Please talk sense!"

"I'm sorry," he said. "I felt you were unreachable."

"Maybe it was *you* who was unreachable."

"Possibly."

He parked the car. For a brief moment he considered telling her he'd see her tomorrow, but that would be cruel. They didn't spend every night together, but certainly when Ramona was gone they did, and besides, he began looking forward to her body under the quilts, the warmth of her mouth, her touch, which could simplify anything, at least for a while. The smell of her, always a balm. She had changed in the past few months; she was no longer a cautious, utilitarian lover. And in the darkness, he felt she was present in ways she would never be in the light. Maybe that was true of everyone, he thought now.

"Sometimes I feel like I'm behind thick glass too," she said. They sat there in the car, staring at the windshield, and he curbed his thought. *That's because you are. We both are.*

"Like I'm a fish in a tank, Ben, and the world is out there, sometimes looking in, sometimes walking by."

"Oh, Lauren, I know what you mean. But—"

"You do?"

"I do. And it's all right."

They were out of the car, past the lavender door of the fence, and stood on the front porch while Lauren unlocked the door.

"I really never wanted you to see that side of me that you saw tonight."

"I'm glad I did," he said, not because it was true, but because he was starting to feel desperate to close the gap between them.

"I had a dream about Evvie last night," she said. She took off her white jacket and hung it on the wall hook. She stayed there, her back to him.

"Was it a nightmare?" He was half joking.

"It was another visit. She came back to the house with *The Magic Mountain* in her hand. Only she was all dressed up like some kind of *harlequin*, and she had really strange eyes." She turned around.

"Oh. Sorry about that. She has no right to invade your dreams. Especially dressed like a harlequin."

"Yeah, well, people don't exactly need passports to visit people's dreams."

"She won't be visiting again like that for a long time. I mean she won't visit your house. In real life. I can't control who shows up as a harlequin in anyone's dream. Obviously. "

Just days ago Evvie had come by Lauren's house to meet her—having called Ben to say she was ready for this, and couldn't they just have a short visit and start to be friends, the three of them? It was too strange otherwise, she said. He'd agreed, foolishly, seduced by the goodwill and forced cheer in her voice. And as he would have predicted, it had been a disaster. She had dressed up the way he hadn't seen her in years—in a short skirt, a red top with frills, and boots he used to tease her about, since they were so sexy. She'd appeared at the door, and he'd wanted to throw a blanket over her head. She looked good, but he couldn't bear to see all that futile effort. Her shoulders tense, her hands cold and wet as she stepped inside and shook first his hand—like a politician—and then Lauren's. Lauren's dog, Chuckie, had snarled at her, and that too was terrible and a first: dogs loved Evvie and she was proud of that.

Evvie had stayed less than five minutes, said something bizarre to Lauren about belly dancing, then burst through the front door and ran like someone being chased.

"Uh, was that a little peculiar?" Lauren had said, in a defensive voice, and then he saw her eyes were wet.

"Lauren, it's OK."

"Not really. The look on her face when she looked at you—"
She'd gone into the other room and cried.

"WHY WOULD SHE have to visit again?"

"I don't know. Ruth, for one. I need to stay in touch with Ruth. I miss Ruth a lot."

Lauren looked at him and sighed impatiently, then walked through the hall, into the kitchen, and out back where she stood on the white stones that would surround her herb garden next year. He followed her out. In one night, they had gone from a measured, loving couple to this drama. He spoke softly so as not to add to it.

"Look, I think I've shown where my allegiance lies. I'm yours. I just thought maybe since I'd lived with Evvie for almost sixteen years—"

"People live together for sixteen years all the time. And then they don't. And they don't talk on the phone, or try to be friends. They walk away from the past because they know it's like something died, Ben, and you can't raise the dead." She spoke looking down at the white stones. She still wore the Irish fisherman's sweater—too big, and the sleeves were too long. Maybe it had belonged to the dolt.

"You're right, Lauren." The sight of her—for whatever reason—had filled him with pity. This beautiful girl—she looked like a *girl* right now—who'd never really known her parents—this person who deserved to be loved without too many complications. He had the urge to give her a warm bath.

"I'm right?" She looked at him, and laughed a little.

"Yes. What's funny?"

"I don't know. I don't feel *right.*"

"Let's go upstairs." He wanted to wash her hair, rinse it with cups of warm water, then fold her into a warm towel. He'd done this with Evvie, a million years ago.

"If you want to be friends with Evvie, you should be friends with Evvie."

"I don't," he said. And right now, he didn't. He went and stood behind her, his body lined against her back.

"Why do you always smell so good?"

"Wasn't Ramona amazing?"

"Yeah."

"I never did anything like that as a kid. Like, on a stage. Did you?"

"Not like that. Not with a little cop shouting Ginsberg and blowing a whistle."

She laughed. They headed into the narrow kitchen. Lauren first, Ben following close behind.

———

HE WOKE IN the middle of the night. It was not a dream that woke him, but a feeling of gratitude, happiness, peace. It was like he was floating inside of something made of a powerful tincture of those qualities. As if he were contained by them, soothed, and yet astonished. It was not hard to stay perfectly still. He breathed.

This kind of wakening had happened to him only once before, years ago, during the summer after he'd graduated from high school, one hot night when his siblings had been away at camp, and his mother in Gettysburg for a weekend. The house had been all his. He'd done very little—read books, had a few friends come over to shoot baskets, called his girlfriend Etty Glazier on the phone. Earlier that summer he had gone with her family to the beach, and they'd seen a lifeguard resuscitate a child who'd almost drowned. The blue boy had finally started coughing, his frantic mother kneeling beside him bursting into tears as he opened his eyes. The almost-drowned boy had somehow imbued the rest of their summer, his blue face a moon above them illuminating all they did. He'd imagined the night he'd awakened that seeing the almost drowned boy had something to do with it.

Certainly he'd long ago given up expecting this overwhelming presence, or whatever it was, would return. And yet, here it was in Lauren's room, surrounding him for no reason. This time the experience was more intense. He lay there, his mouth open as if he could drink whatever it was.

What was this power that had come into the room to hold him in place? And if it really existed as a force, why didn't it come every night? If it did, maybe more people would believe in God; that was the only way Ben could describe the depth of the sensation. He put his hand on Lauren's shoulder, as if he might transmit some of it to her. She stirred a little. Then turned to face him, her eyes opening.

"You're brave," he whispered to her. He didn't know where the words had come from.

"You're brave," she echoed back, her eyes closing.

"Something's different in the room right now," he whispered. "Something big."

"I feel like you're sleeping in my heart," Lauren said.

"Ah," he said. "Is that what it is." His eyes stung with tears. The feeling, the force, whatever it was, was leaving him. Maybe because he didn't feel that he was sleeping in her heart. Maybe because he had never in his life felt like he was sleeping in anyone's heart. But what did that even mean, to sleep in someone's heart? Maybe he was desolate as the heart of the world backed away from him. He took a strand of her hair in his fingers. "Is that what this is," he whispered again.

The room had contracted; it was just the room. He felt a keen sense of loss and terrible longing, just as he had all those years ago. Twenty-seven years ago, he realized.

The old windows framed the reddish moon, the clock on Lauren's rolltop desk was ticking next to a framed black-and-white picture of Lauren and Ramona, when Ramona was a cheeky infant in a hat with a chin strap. The world was so much more mysterious than he usually gave it credit for. And he had this lover. Breath. This life. And with any luck, time enough to deserve it.

EVVIE

DID GOD NOT only exist but also act like a secret magician stirring things up in the invisible core at the heart of the universe? It seemed now to Evvie that this might be true. Not a God that could reliably give anyone the results they wanted when they wanted them. But a God that might point a human being in a certain direction with a long, invisible finger suddenly dusting the back of the neck, or tracing a quick path down the very center of the person's spine.

Or perhaps a God with unlikely minions who pointed people in certain directions.

Either that was true, or Evvie was going a little crazy, since suddenly almost everything seemed like a sign. Her old friend Jimmy Burkel from her dorm at college, who'd been diagnosed with paranoid schizophrenia, had started out this way—seeing everything as signs, and in moments, Evvie had a sickening fear that she was losing her anchor. She started missing Jimmy Burkel, a brilliant, lumbering physics major. The two of them had been insomniacs together, huddled in a cavelike lounge, lovers of caramel corn, backgammon, and the Psychedelic Furs—this before he started seeing signs.

She tried tracking Jimmy down, to no avail, while developing a belatedly keen empathy for him. This led her to consult the Internet about various mental illnesses, and it seemed she had a touch of almost all of them, and for a whole day she walked around knowing she was a queasy, dubious person on a slippery slope until she recalled that this is exactly what had happened when she was a kid and read about physical diseases. This happened to a lot of people. She was not crazy; she was simply, like many, perhaps most people, highly suggestible. And who wouldn't be, she thought, given all the signs she'd been getting.

1. Back in July, just in time, just after Cedric moved out to live in a house of Russian professionals in Greenfield, she'd seen Tessie the landlady on the street, who just happened to have a room available right across from the room she and Ben had lived in that first summer. What were the chances?

2. Another sign: She found, after many years of having replaced it, the lost earring she had worn on her wedding day. It was there in a box where she'd looked many times before. Now she had the pair. She wore the earrings now—long, dangling white-and-blue beaded earrings.

3. An old Jew in a black coat and black hat, a man who had to be a hundred years old, on Murray Avenue, in the blue light of a crisp autumn day, had walked up and given her a book by Rabbi Nachman of Breslov. His voice was full of stones and secrets. "Take this. Nachman is the great-grandson of the Baal Shem Tov.

When he was six years old, he danced every night upon his great-grandfather's grave." He spoke from the corner of his mouth, which was hidden by a long white beard. The book felt precious in her hands, as did the sight of the ancient man in black, walking away with his serious limp. She looked down at the book's title: *General Remedy*.

4. The woman who had long had a crush on Cedric had confided in Evvie that last week she'd arranged to be locked in the Giant Eagle freezer with him for a half hour. They'd ended up clinging to each other for warmth, and now, finally, after all these years of flirting and trying to send Cedric messages, Cedric had gotten the point. The two of them had gone for an Italian dinner at the Grand Canal in Sharpsburg, after which Cedric had invited her to play video games with him. Evvie had heard this from Cedric's coworker: "I knew it would happen someday. Cedric just needed a woman to be bold." Evvie, testing the coworker, said, "Well, she did get them locked in a freezer on purpose just so they'd have to embrace," and the oracular Giant Eagle employee, not missing a beat, said, "Sometimes when it's love you have to say to yourself, whatever it takes."

5. Diligence Chung walked into Evvie's room and took a seat in the corner on a straight-backed chair where she smiled demurely at Evvie from under the brim of her purple felt hat, the left half of her lit by the streetlight. As usual, she wore a floor-length skirt and a high-necked white blouse, and a large wooden cross around her neck. Evvie sat down on the edge of the bed, where

Ruth was stretched out, observing this.

"Do you want to sing with me?"

"That's OK. I'll just listen."

"I sing with Holy Spirit."

"Great."

Diligence began, in the highest, reediest, most painfully quavering voice Evvie had ever heard, a glass-shattering voice that was somehow also beautifully possessed of innocence. The improvisational song kept circling back to these words:

> *"Your dreams are God's dreams,*
> *making no sense to this world!*
> *Your dreams are God's dreams,*
> *making no sense to this world!"*

And one of the final, electrifying verses said, *"Woman across the hall with nice dog, never giving up on Love!"*

Evvie lay in the dark in the spare room—she had given almost everything she owned away—Ruth snoring gently beside her. *Hello, God.* She had talked to God as a child, when she was very small with her sister in the twin bed across from her and the radio playing to block out the violence below them, only back then she'd believed God was all-powerful and highly judgmental, a God that could easily send you to hell to burn for eternity if you didn't shape up, say your rosary, bless yourself ten times a day, give your coins to Unicef.

This was a different God, who had a strange sense of humor, whose ways were far more mysterious than she'd suspected, and who felt not judgment, but serious regret and pity for what had happened to creation and its creatures. As if he'd made a few dire, essential, if perhaps inevitable mistakes, and knew that now, but there was *no taking it back*. His pity only increased his love. Or hers. She or he was not in control, obviously, and yet, it occurred to Evvie over the course of the past few weeks that he or she was not quite absent, either. And according to Rabbi Nachman of Breslov's little book, God loved the brokenhearted above all. This God liked you to talk to him or her as if he or she were an old friend who was dying to see you. Out of deep sorrow and pity, sometimes, this God found a way to speak up. But you had to listen as if you were always expecting to hear something. You had to listen as if everything depended on it.

EVVIE HAD GONE back to Lauren's neighborhood, found out Lauren's last name from a leaf-raking neighbor, called her on the phone, pretended to be an old friend of Ben's named Val (Val with a midwestern accent), and suggested they all get together at night sometime soon. And Lauren said, "He works late this week and next except for Thursdays," and Evvie said, "How late?" and Lauren said, "Until at least eight o'clock."

"Shoot," Evvie had said, really emphasizing the accent, both enjoying the deception and feeling sickened by it, unmoored, as if the lie somehow cast her into no-man's-land. But there she stood in no-man's-land, pinching herself hard, breathing in the air, anxious and hopeful as a newly arrived immigrant. "Are you sure about that? I mean, can't he try to get off early?"

"No, he really can't. Same thing happened last month. He has to prepare documents and work on the computer. It's a real drag, but he might get a promotion soon. Maybe the week after next?"

"Maybe. Wow, that sounds lonely for Ben. Do the other employees have to stick around too?"

"Oh, maybe one other guy. But sometimes it's just Ben."

She'd told this to Bruno on the phone, and a few hours later, the two of them called her back, sharing one phone. They'd explained that she would go visit Ben, tell him she missed him, tell him she was concerned he was working too much.

"OK."

"So the two of you are in there, having your small talk. We let this go on for about ten minutes."

"Ten minutes," Bruno said loudly.

"Should I tell her about Darlene and Eddie M?" Rocky said.

"Eddie Murdoch?" Evvie said. She was leaning out the window into the cold night to conduct this conversation, with her heart pounding against the close, black sky. "I knew an Eddie and Darlene," she said. "Eddie Murdoch and Darlene Katz?"

"No, no. Not a local tale. We've been in other states. We wouldn't use the real names if it was local. We're discreet above all things."

"Right."

"So we gave Eddie and Darlene their ten minutes—this was in Darlene's apartment, where Eddie had stopped by presumably just to check on her. Eddie had hired us. And by the time six or seven minutes had passed, we saw we'd become unnecessary."

"Why was that?" Evvie really hoped they weren't going

to tell her one of them had dropped dead. Down in the dark street, a man in a raincoat walked by.

"Because they got indecent for each other. Seven minutes in heaven. Darlene jumping on Eddie, Eddie melting right on into it, and the two of us at the window, feeling bad for watching, but what else could we do? We had to see it through."

Evvie looked straight at the big, bright moon. "Please. Don't tell me you watched Eddie and Darlene have sex, because if you did—"

"No, no, no!" Rocky said. "They disappeared! They pulled each other up the steps, and that was that."

"Did Eddie get his money back?"

"We tried to give half of it back," said Rocky. "But he wouldn't take it. He was too happy."

"He called us his lucky charms," Bruno added.

"Wow."

"So, babe, you get those ten minutes. Because we never know. We'd like things to happen nice and easy for you."

"Right. And if they do, you can keep most or all of the money."

"That's sweet."

TONIGHT EVVIE LAY down with Ruth, but clearly sleep was not coming. She walked up to Forbes, entered Hemingway's bar, drank down a beer, then another, then excused herself and went into the ladies' room, where she applied lipstick and held her own gaze in the mirror, as close to being blank in the mind as she'd ever mustered, despite her love of the song that was playing—"Poor Side of Town" by Johnny Rivers, with its

rhyme of "miss me" and "kiss me." She resisted the memory
this song always gave rise to—it had been playing on the loud-
speaker in 1967 when Donnie the neighbor had handed her
a dollar bill at Immaculate Conception's parish bazaar. *Here,
kid, go get some fries!* This surprising kindness had rendered
her speechless, so she'd waited up for him, kneeling at her
bedroom window that night, thinking she'd casually call out,
"Thanks for the fries, Donnie! They were delicious!" but then
fell asleep on the floor before he'd returned.

Yes, the memory was there, circling her mind like a halo, so
weightless it couldn't penetrate fully tonight. It couldn't send
her backward. She was rooted in the present. These moments
of her life that would never come again. Washing her hands
beside her at the sink in the bar's bathroom was an old and
vivid woman in a violet shawl and thick glasses. Evvie gave all
her attention to her. "It's getting awful cold out there, isn't it?"
Whose voice was coming out of her now? She sounded *just*
like Dorothy in Kansas!

"It is. But I don't mind."

"Me either, I don't mind a bit!" Had she always had this ca-
pacity to sound like Dorothy and just never known it?

The woman laughed, looking at herself, and Evvie joined
in. Evvie was not sure what they were laughing about. All she
knew was that soon she'd have hours and hours, locked in a
room with Ben. The happiness of anticipation was worth the
price of admission. Then later, after it was all over, she'd reveal
her Dorothy voice. *There's no place like home.*

She had one more beer and made small talk at the bar, the
kind that Dorothy might make, with wide eyes. Then a call
came, and she saw it was from them and she rushed outside.

Rocky spoke clearly, with the quickened ease of someone who knew his speech by heart, the tone of voice level and reassuring now, like a pilot on a plane. "We'll be wearing masks tomorrow, of course, and you can have a say about what kind of masks you want us to wear. And even what kind of voices you want us to talk in. Remember, this will be like going to a great show, and you should enjoy it. So. Animal masks? Prince Charming? Politicians? We could be Reagan and Bush."

"Not animals. Otherwise I think I'd rather be surprised."

"Good, good," Rocky said. "I love a woman who likes to be surprised. A woman who respects the show."

Evvie fell silent. She looked at the bright, blue-white moon, smiling.

Is this me? Am I still myself?

BEN

THE LAST TIME Ben had a gun pointed at his head he was seven or eight years old, and it was a toy pistol. A lot of boys played at war, but the next-door neighbor pretended with disturbing passion. "Bang, bang, you're dead! Say Sayonara!" the boy would say, trying to make his voice deeper, louder. In a cold flash Ben sees the neighbor boy's face as it appeared in the window of the boy's mother's car the last time he saw him. It was a lost, bloated face, a face that had soaked up the atmosphere in a family that was infamous for being rowdy and broken. They'd moved suddenly, running from the father, there had been violence in the home that leaked out onto the street the night before. From his bedroom window Ben had seen the mother crouching in a nightgown like an animal, and nobody running to help her, though Ben's mother had shouted to his father, "Do something!" The woman sprang up and ran back into her house, and her husband told everyone to mind their own goddamn business, and everyone did. And now, even though this man in his office tonight has a real gun, a Dracula mask, a deeper voice, and is saying, "Don't say a word" instead of "Say Sayonara," Ben hears the old neighbor boy's words swim up and ring in his head. Part of Ben, nervously laughing, eyes roving the office looking for Evvie, hopes the man with the real gun will suddenly step back, rip off his mask, and say, "It's a joke, dude, we're checking your reflexes."

But Dracula mask stays utterly still and presses the gun harder against his temple. Hard, cold, insistent. Ben closes his eyes and feels his stomach drop. He thinks of falling to his knees, desire for his own life bursting inside of him like a great fire. Please. No. This can't happen. He hears the man breathing behind his mask. He opens his eyes. The man is wiry, of medium height, wears white, feminine-looking gloves and black clothing. The bottom of the mask has been sliced off, so he can see the man's real mouth and chin. Was it someone he knew? "Dude, who is it?" Ben tries, but feels something in his heart tumble and rise, circle around and do backflips just to reach a single strand of hope that this is someone's sick idea of a practical joke. But it doesn't feel like a joke, and where is Evvie? "Please," he manages, but the man drills the gun harder into his head and tells him to shut up once and for all and keep his eyes shut. The night's turn of events has the feel of something utterly random. They—he and Evvie—are someone's playthings now, and knowing this, he feels his spine turn to water, and his throat closes up. *God help us God please help us God help us.* He hears another man saying to Evvie, "You'll keep nice and quiet if you like life." Someone bored, crazy, and cruel is going to have some fun with them, then hack them into pieces and throw them in a Dumpster somewhere out of town. Such things happen somewhere in this world on a daily basis. Again he thinks of hitting his knees, pleading for mercy, but somewhere he's read that revealing weakness in these situations lowers your chance for survival. Weakness was something people like this could not stand for. It would all be over unless he could find some strength.

"Open your eyes."

Trembling, he looks across the room to where Evvie stands. She is by the black window in her dark coat, her head pressed on the glass. "Evvie?"

She turns around, stricken. Her face, always pale, is sickly looking. *Evvie!* It was as if the fact of her had never made it all the way through to the center of his consciousness, until now, in these tunneling moments, when she opens her mouth to speak but no words emerge. The other man, a bit larger and wearing a raincoat and a Wolf mask, stands several feet away from her, but has a gun pointed at her head too. Evvie clenches her eyes shut.

The men had come out of nowhere; he hadn't heard their footsteps, hadn't sensed anyone coming into the office, and is now furious with himself. Why hadn't he locked the fucking door downstairs? Why hadn't he had the modicum of vigilance that might have prevented this nightmare? He'd locked the door most other nights, why not tonight? Evvie had been visiting again—she'd dropped by twice this week, and he'd almost enjoyed her company, now that she was less desperate. She'd told him about a new friend at the animal shelter, how she was thinking of a documentary about crows, how she'd actually been going out at night sometimes, to hear music, and some funny stories about Tessie, the landlady he hadn't thought about in years. Tonight she'd shown him photographs of her extended family, but that now seemed to belong to another

day, another year, even. One of the photographs was very old—
Evvie at two, anxious and alien, sitting alone on a patch of
grass. The back of the photo read *Fourth of July! Evvie!* As he
looked at her now, he saw that strange child in her face, and for
an instant he somehow seemed to blame her for the gun at his
temple. Somehow she looked like the kind of person this would
happen to. He'd known that, always. Or so it seemed in these
few moments.

"And none of us says another word," Dracula says.
"That's something we all have to understand. We ain't
nothin' but four church mice walkin' down the steps and out
to the car to take a ride with Jesus. Nobody's wayward. The
correct car is a white caddy with the back door open. Now,
put these masks on. Whoever sees us needs to think we're
four people going to a little costume party. If someone asks
to join us, you say you wish everyone could come dance, but
it's invite only. You say you're feeling lucky and can't wait to
get where you're goin'."

Dracula hands Ben a cheap plastic mask from a child's
SpongeBob Halloween costume. He swallows down a streak
of hysteria that threatens to become laughter and tears. "I can
get you a *lot* of money," he tries, but Dracula shakes his head
and moves the gun so that it rests on the side of his throat. He
gives Evvie an even cheaper-looking mask, some kind of brown
squirrel or chipmunk.

They walk out of the office, two by two, Evvie and the Wolf
up front, with his hand on the crook of her arm, as if using her
for balance. They leave the lights blazing, and walk down the
stairs, then single file out the glass door at the bottom of the

steps. In the dark street the air smells like someone nearby is having a real wood fire. Ben takes a deep breath, and then another. Across the street a young woman in very high heels walks quickly, talking on her cell phone. Other than this, the street is empty for two blocks. In the distance Ben can see an old white-haired man standing alone on the corner near the Dairy Queen. The man is walking slowly toward them, like someone in a dream.

"Get in," says the Wolf, smiling, and Evvie slips into the car.

"Get in," says Dracula, in the deepest voice on earth, and Ben obeys, but not before taking another gulp of the air, then looking up at the sky, and all around at the street, as if some last-minute miracle might reveal itself. He wants his life! It takes everything he has not to cry out in terror.

In the three seconds that he sits there alone with Evvie, while the kidnappers are opening the front doors, he says, "We'll get out of this. Don't worry." But his quavering voice says otherwise and he wishes he'd stayed quiet. She, Evvie, has gone still and silent as stone. He's never seen her that way. He is worried she is in a state of such shock that it's physically dangerous. People can die of shock.

They drive a few blocks down the street and he says, "I think she's sick. I think she needs to go to the hospital. She's not very—"

The Wolf turns around with the gun. "You speak when you're spoken to, boy. And both of you fools can take the masks off and breathe easy. Right now."

Ben and Evvie take their masks off and look at each other.

"Can you tell me why us?" Ben says, still looking at Evvie.

"Why you're doing this? Is it just for kicks? If I knew I maybe could—I have a lot of cash. We can go to the ATM machine."

The car screeches to the side of the road. Dracula puts the car in park so he can turn around with his gun too. "Who's in charge?" he says. "Who's the master of the operation here? Is it you?"

"No."

"Shake your head no, you don't need to say it!"

Ben sits there, blinking. The man's voice is raspy; it's unclear if he's old or young.

"I said shake your goddamn head no," Dracula says, softly, in yet another voice.

Ben shakes his head no.

"Now, let's all go on, all of us quiet. Beautiful. Pretend you're in church. A little church of mice on wheels, checkin' in with the risen one."

"We'll tell you everything you need to know, once we get there," says the Wolf. "If you follow directions, you'll be fine." This was punctuated with the Wolf's high-pitched giggle. Then he turns around to stare at them for a moment. "You people can swim?" Ben looks at Evvie and sees she has her eyes clenched shut. "Yes, we swim." He instinctively reaches for Evvie's hand, and squeezes it tightly. In this moment, he can't imagine ever letting go.

THEY DRIVE FOR well over an hour, and in the back they look out of their respective windows, holding hands, and breathing. The Wolf and Dracula aren't saying a word, except every so often when one of them says to the crazy radio talk show host,

"Fuck *you*." Ben had considered jumping from the car, even though they're speeding down the road at seventy or eighty miles an hour, but how could he jump and leave Evvie alone with these two, even if he could survive such a thing?

They change the radio station to some kind of polka music.

"You said you bought chips," Dracula says to the Wolf. "These aren't chips, these are Doritos."

"I'm sorry—I thought Doritos were a kind of chip."

"No, buddy. No." Dracula eats the disappointing Doritos anyway. "Doritos are not a kind of chip. Doritos are Doritos."

Their lackadaisical way of speaking to each other is terrifying. They must go on these sprees whenever they get a little bored. Ben is afraid to speak up, afraid to jump out, and afraid that if he does nothing, his heart will explode or just give way. He tries to listen to Evvie's heavy breathing. Focus the mind, he tells himself, and then you won't do anything stupid. Just focus your fucking mind.

With his finger he writes on Evvie's palm the letter *U*, and then the letters *OK*. She doesn't respond.

AFTER A WHILE, he can see the rising moon, bluish, enormous, and perched above a line of black trees that rim the field of rolling hills to the right. His window view. He can't get enough of it. Evvie's view is similar, only the line of trees is a bit closer to that side of the road, like a black wall. He sees a solitary house, small and white on the hill with a single lit window. Do the people inside know how lucky they are to be there? Lifting their forks? Evvie's hand is cold and damp. He has an urge to put his ear against her chest to hear her heart beat. He knows it's pounding, racing like his, but probably faster and louder.

"Let's go to Warehouse X," Dracula says. "That has music."

"It's still filthy, last time I checked," said the Wolf.

"No, no. I got Wilma."

"That's not so good! Wilma's too old for that!"

"I paid her well," said Dracula. "And I ain't about to put on an apron myself. Though I did help her out." He says this in a high-pitched, mocking voice.

The Wolf laughed and said he'd have liked to have seen that.

"First they swim, then Warehouse X."

"First they swim," the Wolf agrees.

"Give me one of those cheese sticks, and offer some to our guests."

The Wolf laughs, and briefly glances back at them. "Cheese stick?" he says.

Ben shakes his head no. Evvie doesn't move. Ben wishes they'd said they didn't know how to swim.

"I think Warehouse Y is better," the Wolf says after a silence. "I can get the music from X and move it in easy."

Ben likes hearing this. Maybe these were just perverts who captured people for some kind of sadomasochist disco parties. Nothing involving death. It was unbelievable what people got off on these days.

They're the only car on the road for a long while. Finally one of them changes the polka station back to the talk show. The host is speaking of Osama bin Laden.

"Jasmine thinks he's good-looking. She has his picture up on the wall. Says he has eyes like Jesus."

"Osama bin Laden," Dracula says, and glances toward the backseat for a moment. "Osama bin Laden can't help it. He's a pawn. He didn't want to be himself, but that's what happened. We're all pawns! We have to do what we have to do and it's a crying shame."

The Wolf laughs. Then, as if to punctuate the statement, rolls down the window and fires a shot into the sky.

Evvie squeezes Ben's hand so hard it hurts, and he hears her gasp.

The Wolf rolls his window back up and says to Dracula, "Remember that woman who walked all those dogs at the Point in Pittsburgh? What'd she say when she fired at the sky that one night?"

"I'm shootin' God," Dracula says. "You know that's what she said."

"I'm shootin' God," says the Wolf.

"She was nice," says Dracula.

"I'm shootin' God," says the Wolf. "That wasn't right. I mean, shoot the stars, shoot the moon. But shootin' *God*?" He's whining.

The Wolf turns around for a second and looks at them, then turns back to the front.

"You can't judge a lady like that," says Dracula. "She'd been through hell. And God can take it! God can take anything, and make it *nothin'*. This anyone with a nickel's worth of gray matter will come to know. God can take it!"

THEY PULL THE car off the road, onto a bridge, down another pitch-black road. They stop before a chipped white bench that sits before a river.

"We're not swimmers, ourselves," Dracula says. "You two go on and swim back and forth now. Fitness is important."

They could swim to freedom! Once on the other bank, they could run for their lives. They would risk being shot at, but it was the best chance they had.

"We'll be in a canoe. Just in case. Don't make us use the paddle. Just swim as fast as you can, side by side, over to the other bank of the river. When you get to the other bank, stand there, count to fifty, touch your toes, then dive back in."

The canoe is leaning against a tree, just yards from the white bench. It's small, but big enough to hold the two men. And now they're all out in the cold.

The river is wider than it looks. They swim naked and the water is freezing cold, as Ben knew it would be, but he hadn't counted on it being a great release, a deep, exhilarating entrance into another state of consciousness, where the breath of night that enters him creates a room in his mind, and then expands to become a wide expanse of country under stars, all of it inside of him, shimmering. The stars in his mind burn brighter and bolder, his whole mind filled with the fire of stars, his tears entering the river, Evvie's body right there, slick as a seal, as she gasps, *Ben, are you making it?*, and he says yeah and wants to tell her of this world in his mind, where silence is music and deepening and he can think, think of what to do next, but then a shot is fired and everything collapses into darkness.

They hadn't hit Evvie, or him, or even the water surrounding them. *They're shootin' God*, he thinks. The canoe slides over beside them; he could reach out and touch it. "Go on and swim to the bank. And do what we said. And do it without complaints," says the Wolf.

Under the moon, they stand freezing on the riverbank and count to fifty. The men in the canoe are a few yards away, with guns pointed. *"Dance!"* one of them says. *"This is the senior prom and they're playin' your song! 'You Belong to Me'!"*

The other man—the Wolf, it sounds like—howls with laughter.

A naked, trembling Evvie is in his arms, and they're dancing, and she starts to cry.

"No. You can't do this," he tells her, furious. "Stop your sobbing or we'll fucking die."

"I–I–"

"Stop!"

She gulps down air. She stiffens. They dance like robots until they're told they can stop and swim back to the other side.

THE DEEP PLEASURE of returning to their clothes, to the embracing warmth of the dark car, to the motion of the road, to the trembling of his own body, is enough to make him weep, silently, and for the first time he thinks of Lauren, and Ramona, and wonders if they'll all ever sit at the table again together. But he can't remember their faces. Where their faces might be is a dull sound, a small orange light flashing like a siren. He grabs Evvie's hand and squeezes. She pulls herself together. She's stopped crying and is now sitting beside him with her eyes closed and her teeth chattering and her face lifted up to the ceiling of the car, as if she's praying.

The car pulls up to an ATM machine on the edge of some small town where houses dot the hillside. "Now we get out and you two empty your accounts."

"Gladly," Ben says.

The night is silent except for small-town oblivion roiling in the hills like dark laughter. The guns pointed while first he, then Evvie, empty their accounts to a grand total of $780.

"I have some in the savings account that I'll get you as soon as the bank opens. I have over ten thousand dollars, and it all belongs to you. I want you to have it. And I won't say a word about any of this. And then I can ask a lot of other people for money. I know some really rich people."

Dracula and the Wolf do a little dance to these words, then throw their heads back and laugh. Were they celebrating how rich they'd be or simply mocking him?

"Maybe we'll be back in the morning. If you're well-behaved children we might even take you out for ice cream," says the raspy Dracula voice. "Give me my headache pills," he orders the Wolf, and swallows them down without water, whatever they are.

THE CAR PULLS down a dirt road that cuts through some kind of dead harvest. Maybe it's wheat. It lies down in the moonlight, half frozen, like long bones. It occurs to Ben that this might be the last landscape of his life. He withdraws his affection from what he sees now. He looks at it and tries to see it as ordinary.

But nothing is ordinary. Not the moon, black sky, trees, road, hand he's holding—he's grabbed Evvie's again—and breath he takes. Not any breath. All of it extraordinary, now and forever shall be. He will never be bored again. He will go home and start all over. He will love his life, every spoon and doorway every face every window every breath, as never before.

LAUREN. HE LETS his thoughts be subsumed by the name, lets the name repeat itself in his mind, Lauren, Lauren, Lauren, but still cannot clearly remember her face. He sees a pair of sandals she'd worn when it was warm. Red sandals that left stripes on her feet. She'd painted her toenails red to match. It had taken her hours to do so, she was so meticulous.

He focuses on those small feet, then lets his eyes, like two desperate hands, travel up her body, but finds Evvie's body, and Evvie's face, the face he knows best, shining in his mind the way it used to, when he was away without her, missing her with every cell in his body. His jaw is trembling and he can't make it stop.

The car slows down to twenty miles an hour or less. On the dead ground Ben sees abandoned tires and a cracked full-length mirror that holds the black sky, and farther back, on a knoll, what appears to be a pair of shoes. You usually only see one shoe, but Ben sees a pair, he's sure of it, and they're so unlikely—white patent-leather men's loafers, such as an old man in Florida might wear—that he feels chills shoot through his body. They had murdered the old man because they felt like it, because they could, because they were bored, maybe just to see him die, like in the Johnny Cash song. As he catches sight of two warehouses—large sheds, really—waiting for them in the middle of this godforsaken field, his eyes fill with tears. The sheds look alive, hungry even, like they've been patiently waiting here for a long, long time. They seem to be proud of themselves, proud of taking part in the historical reality of evil, and Ben understands that, up until now, evil had been such an abstraction to him that he'd sometimes argued that it didn't exist; it wasn't a *force*—it was just people gone wrong. Looking at the sheds, he understands such a position can be held only by those who've never confronted it.

"Warehouse X needs a paint job," sings the Wolf. The car bounces over rough terrain, then slows down to a stop.

He holds back tears of pity that he and Evvie have together come to this, tears that he might never get to say good-bye to Lauren, that she would think he'd disappeared on her. He sees her making calls in her kitchen, her profile now coming into view. Lauren. She would try to contact his parents, and they'd know nothing. She would try, then, to contact Evvie, and she'd be missing too, and Lauren would assume they'd run off together. It would make sense to her—another abandonment. He couldn't bear that thought.

"Do we get to make any calls before—" He stops himself.

"Before?" says the Wolf.

"Before shut the fuck up?" sings Dracula.

APPARENTLY THEY SETTLED on WAREHOUSE WHY. Those words are spray-painted on the door, which is heavy and metal and padlocked. The headlights shine upon it now. Chipped green paint makes a circle on the door, decorated with painted red dots, someone's idea of a wreath. *Very clever*, Ben wants to say. Fucking clever maniacs! The edge of his fear is barely controlled rage, so much so that he gets close to making a dive for one of them. He's a killer too right now, he just doesn't have the gun. His eyes slide over to check on Evvie, but she seems to have evacuated her body. Her face is white marble. Her eyes are at half mast. His heart cries out her name, and then, strangely, both of their names together reverberate inside of him, *Ben and Evvie. Ben and Evvie.*

The men both get out of the car and Dracula opens Evvie's door. "Both of you exit out this way."

With guns they point them toward the door. The Wolf opens the padlock and steps inside. "It's nice enough," he says.

"Where's the music?" says Dracula.

"I can go get the boom box myself," the Wolf offers.

"Is that what you call a good idea? Are you stupid enough to forget the operation policy of sticking together?"

Dracula says they *all* have to stick together, and they march single file into Warehouse X. The dank air smells heavily of some kind of wretched chemical. They stand with Dracula in the doorway, the two of them side by side, in front of him, while the Wolf disappears into the pitch-black, whistling. Ben wants to ask what the smell is but controls himself. As long as they don't have to breathe it for long, he doesn't need to know.

The Wolf emerges from the black with a boom box. Again Ben feels hope sear through his body. A simple smile explodes on his face. He has the urge to thank the Wolf man profusely. He wants to break down weeping and explain how much they both love music and how he would do anything in the world to go on living in this world, where it was possible to hear music, that they were both good people who would be *glad* to be of service of any kind and find as much money as they needed, as long as they would eventually be released to life.

"Please," he finally says, childlike. "Please don't kill us." And then, a lie that comes out of nowhere. "My wife is three months pregnant. Don't kill the baby." For a moment this seems true. "It's our first child. Please don't kill us."

EVVIE

SHE'D BEEN TRYING to pray, bargaining with God, God full of spikes, God with his dark laughter, God who had made her this freak, this loose-cannon desperate wretch of a person who had thought a little kidnapping might be good. God the Divine Madman who had given her too long a leash.

And who was she? Had that person she'd become always been there, waiting to take over? Or had some spirit entered her, something she couldn't have controlled? Was a body just a receptacle for various selves who would never stop coming, never leave her alone? No wonder she saw her desperate prayers like shreds of wet paper hanging from a skeleton's bones, and God with his dark laughter, God with his arrows aimed at the head, *oh but God*, oh but if you let Ben *live*, I will die a million times over, reincarnate me as a tortured animal, I will come back willingly to live in hell if you just let Ben live and let them do, let them do whatever they want with me.

She is almost happy when they tape her mouth shut and tie her arms behind her back. Several times she'd been on the verge of grabbing Rocky, of pleading with him, Rocky who'd seemed so—what had he seemed like then? A million years ago when they'd first sat in the car that day across from PPG and she'd been someone else. He'd seemed humane, in his crazy way, humane with imagination and something *warm* coming from him and she had liked his eyes! Windows to the soul! They'd been spinning in her mind like pinwheels at a fair she'd gone to when she was small. He'd made her weak in the knees that day downtown—the way he looked at her. She'd never understood that expression, "weak in the knees," until then. Had she been falling in love with him? She'd dressed up for him that day. Had she been drugged? Under a spell? He'd lulled her, because she'd wanted lulling. And thank you, God, for how he is taping my mouth shut so tightly and thank you, Mr. Rocky. Mr. Dracula. She looks up at the mask. She had never loved Dracula. But she reconsiders. Now she thinks she will love Dracula and live with him here forever until she starves, if he just lets Ben go.

SHE SITS CROSS-LEGGED beside Ben in the dark. Her arms ache, wrenched back behind her. They've taped and tied Ben too. Terror is giving rise, in strange, watery moments, to a great fatigue that is almost a death wish, then suddenly blasted away by a longing so great she thinks it will break her into pieces.

THE WOLF TURNS up the boom box. The Bee Gees? *The Bee Gees?* If she hadn't been taped she'd say it out loud. She would scream it. Next he'd flick a switch and the lights would come on.

But it stays pitch-dark. Much darker than the night. And the darkness is supremely alive, vibrating, as if a murder of crows is circling in the air before their eyes, flapping their wings.

"We're going to have some fun now." Dracula's cool hand reaches for the back of her neck. She whimpers.

"I'm not sure what game to play," says Dracula, in the whining voice of a spoiled child. It's true that he is quite the actor.

"We could play American Idol Meets Survivor. Or we could play Tell Me a Story, Asshole. Or we could get started with something much more fun."

"Any ideas?" he calls over to the Wolf. "Any preferences?"

The Wolf just howls into the dark.

"Who wants to sing a song? A song so good, so pitch-perfect true, it *could* cause a man like me to throw their gun out the window. A song to change the world is what I'm searching for. A song that could make me break down and cry!"

Ben makes a noise behind his taped mouth. Then another, louder noise.

"Are you sitting there telling me you don't have stage fright?" Dracula asks. "Wolfman Jack, this man wants to sing us a saving song of succulence. Turn off the Bee Gee brothers."

Dracula comes over and bends down between Evvie and Ben. He has a hand on each of them, and presses down. Rips the tape off Ben's mouth. "You're a brave man. You must know, my friend, that if you get the song wrong, it's all over. Those are the rules that inspire greatness. Get it right the first time. *Perfect pitch.* And choose the song carefully. You have one minute. Imagine that. And if you fail, imagine that I'm a man who can send your wife special delivery into the arms of her maker. You're in the hands of a special delivery man." He stands up straight and fires a shot at the ceiling.

"Singer, rise!"

Ben stands up.

"What will you sing?"

"Any requests?" Ben manages. This strikes Dracula's funny bone for a moment. He bends in half. Then shoots back up. "Something great. Something you can sing as if your life and hers depend upon it."

Evvie thinks she can feel a silent wind encircle them. What song? What song could he possibly sing?

He begins. His voice is hoarse: "What's Goin' On," a choice that somehow seems inevitable.

He makes it to the word "Brother," and then Dracula begs him to stop. "Please, don't do that!"

Ben stops.

"If Marvin Gaye weren't dead, he'd kill himself. Don't you know another song?"

"I know a lot."

"I bet you know a lot. I bet you even know an old-fashioned song from time gone by."

"I do."

"And you better sing it now," Dracula says.

Ben begins without hesitation.

> *"The water is wide and I can't cross over*
> *And neither have I wings to fly*
> *Give me a boat that can carry two"*

Evvie had taught him this one. Her grandmother had sung it to her in earliest childhood.

> *"And the boat can row my love and I*
> *Love is gentle, love is kind"*

"Not hitting the mark, my friend. Not hitting it."

Ben sang louder.

> *"The sweetest flower when first it blooms*
> *But love grows old and waxes cold"*

"Enough of that!"

Silence.

Dracula doesn't deliver Evvie into the arms of her maker; he's not keeping his word.

"Maybe I'd rather hear you tell a story," Dracula says. "A story about your wife! This woman with stars in her eyes! Maybe one where Starshine was a kid. And she fucked up royally! Something amusing! We heard a story last month about a kid who fucked up royally. And it was a good story, with a monster in it. Tell us a story along those lines. So once upon a time, your wife here was an innocent child."

He'd said *chi-old*.

"And this chi-old did such and such stupid shit, or maybe ran into the arms of the wrong person. A chi-old meets a monster and—"

Ben stands there.

"Begin. We're just getting to know you here is all. Save yourself, partner."

After a long silence, Ben begins. "She rode this red bike," he says.

"Who?" Dracula says.

"Evvie. My wife. When she was a kid."

He is not a natural storyteller. You had to fish things out of him; otherwise he'd turn a story into haiku. How was he going to pull this off? Evvie already knows what story he's trying to tell. Her heart slams up against her chest. It was his favorite story, one she'd told him when they were first together, in a bar near his mother's llama farm. She'd told him the story and he'd listened, then said, *OK, marry me.*

"She thought if she rode the bike fast enough she'd start flying, like Pegasus. The bike was her horse. She would ride the bike five blocks to visit a goat. A city goat who looked neglected. She took the goat presents. Then an old man came and yelled at her to get off the property, so she got back on the red bike and rode home. The bike had a name but I forget it right now. It'll come to me."

Ben's voice was steady and utterly clear.

"An old man with a shotgun?"

Ben pauses. "Sure."

"Go on."

"Some kids need to visit goats," Ben says, an odd scolding tone having seeped into his voice.

"I beggeth your pardon?" says Dracula.

"This is how God must have felt when creating the world," says Ben, his voice strangely calm. "You say words in this pitch-black darkness and it's like everything comes to life. Like the goat and Evvie on her bike are right here in front of my eyes."

"Do you want to die, or tell us an amusing story without a goat in it?"

Ben's voice is getting stronger. "The goat is dead. She loved riding on roads where the trees lined up and seemed to be cheering her on. She felt that trees were cheering her on. I think she still feels that. And maybe they are. Maybe the whole world is cheering us on."

"This better get better fast and speak the fuck up," Dracula says, but his voice is softer now, more like Rocky's voice in the car.

"She went on a vacation to this island of ponies with her family when she was eleven, and they'd allowed her to take her bike. Blackie was the bike's name, even though it was a red bike. In her mind, it was a black horse and she found black streamers for the handlebars and that was his mane in the wind and she rode him all around the town, for the whole week. She took Blackie to see the ocean, the bay, and the old man on the beach who made *The Last Supper* sand sculpture every year. She showed Blackie all the sandy apostles and Jesus. She has pictures I could show you, we could show you, after we give you, after you take us out of here so we can give you more money. So then, at the end of the week, her parents said they couldn't take Blackie back home, since they had a packed car, and besides, the bike was a piece of junk. They suggested they just leave Blackie outside of a grocery store. She tried with all her might to explain that the bike was her horse, her friend, but they didn't understand her tears, except as a sign that she was ridiculous and needed to be sent to her room for the last night of that vacation, since she was too old for such spoiled carrying-on."

He stopped. He took a deep breath. Evvie was amazed that he remembered their exact phrase. *Such spoiled carrying-on.*

"So she snuck out after they slept and rode for hours out past the town, and some man in a car hit her when she was crossing the highway. Hit and run. She lay there for an hour before someone came and took her to the hospital. She was in a coma for five days, and then, when she finally sat up, the first thing she said was, 'Where's Blackie?' "

"Yes! And then what?" says Dracula.

"That's it."

"No, that *isn't* it."

Ben waits.

"I said that isn't it. Has to be more."

"Well, I—"

"What other story can you tell? About her? Your wife? Because that one wasn't good enough. That one just wasn't good enough."

Ben says, "Evvie's third-grade teacher took a poll of her students as to whether or not she should commit suicide."

"What? Is that a joke?"

"No."

Evvie hasn't thought about that in years.

"And what was her name?"

"Her name was Mrs. Finch." Mrs. Finch, who came to school in a long blue gown the day of the poll.

"And why'd she want to off herself?"

"I don't know."

"Nobody ever told you?"

"Nobody ever told me."

"So we'll figure it out. Was it global warming that made her want to kill herself? No, it was not, because we didn't have global fucking anything back then. Was it a monster that made her want to kill herself? Yes, it was, because we did have monsters back then, did we not?"

"Yes," says Ben. "We did."

"And what did the students say?"

"They said no."

A silence fell.

"And that's all you got? A goddamn bike and a suicidal teacher?" Dracula laughs and says, "Inside I'm clapping, I'm giving you a standing ovation," then shakes his head. "Anything else?"

Ben doesn't hesitate. "She sang in an old-age home when she was twelve at Christmastime."

That wasn't true—Ben had done that—had he confused their memories?

"Uh, uh, uh! Stop there. Stop right there. Sit down, Christmastime! Sit the fuck down. You can't steal a show to save your life, can you?"

Ben stood there.

"Can you?"

"Guess not."

"Some people understand thee-ate-her, some do not. At least you could have told us a story with a message. Like the humans go to another planet to escape all their fucking garbage and wars, and then they screw up the new planet even worse than this one, and then they blow up every planet in sight. Hear that? Now I'm giving myself a standing ovation on the inside. Sit down. It's not looking good. God bless you."

Ben sits back down.

Evvie is up on her feet and running. It's so dark she isn't sure where she's running. She'd lost a feel for where the door might be. Dracula chases her; he's telling her this was a very bad idea. But she's fast. She runs forward, then in a circle, then forward again. And she stops running and crouches down on the floor and curls into a ball. He runs past her. But then he's back. He's circling her. He's laughing. He says it's a pleasure to be in the vicinity. He says he admires her guts. Next thing she knows his hand is on her neck. *"You're the one for me,"* he says. *"Maybe that's what you're trying to say."*

Evvie throws herself around as if having a seizure. She makes a horrible noise, and every part of her body is moving hysterically, violently, and now Rocky Dracula retrieves his hand from her neck, and stands over her saying, what the fuck, what the fuck is this, and she is hoping she could be the human sacrifice of the day and then Ben could be free to find the door, could somehow escape the Wolf and his gun, the Wolf who they hadn't heard from in a while and who Evvie thought might even be sleeping. She feels Dracula's foot on her back, the hard shoe pressing down, and it almost feels good. "Stop it," he orders.

And he doesn't shoot her. Just stays bent down looking at the freak show that keeps getting worse and freakier before his eyes. She pours every last desire into the seizure, rolling her eyes and managing to make a low, groaning noise that Dracula does not care for at all, and he says so.

It's too late when they finally hear the door slam. When Evvie looks over, she hallucinates his silhouette against the night sky there for one shocking second. She knows he is outside. Her tears fall hot and fast. Her seizure is over. She keeps making sounds. Rocky stands straight up. He fires toward the door, as if Ben might reappear.

"This wasn't supposed to happen, Starshine. What the fuck were you *thinking*?"

He unties her. He untapes her. He screams at the Wolf.

"He flew by me like lightning," the Wolf whines.

Rocky says he'd trusted her to understand the operation. He'd *trusted* her. He takes off his mask. Now he can't promise anything, he says.

Evvie sits there in the dark, unable to speak.

BEN

BEN HAD TRIED to wave down cars, and trucks, and nobody had stopped. It was dark, it was the middle of the night, and they could see he was out there without a car, and that meant trouble. He'd run for what felt like hours down a long, narrow secondary highway. He was in and out of breath, weeping, at one point screaming Evvie's name out loud over and over again as he walked, then growing deeply quiet, conserving whatever energy was left to him. After that long silence, he began to run against the image of her dead.

FINALLY SOMETHING LIKE a neighborhood began to appear. When he approached a brick house on the end of a cul-de-sac, sensor lights came on, and by the time he got to the front porch and touched the door handle, a robotic manly voice came blaring out from the intercom. *YOU HAVE VIOLATED A PRO-TECTED PROPERTY. LEAVE IMMEDIATELY. THE POLICE HAVE BEEN CALLED. YOU HAVE VIOLATED A PROTECTED PROPERTY.* It kept on repeating itself as he moved to the next house.

Nobody answered in this house, or the next—even as he kicked the white aluminum door with all his might. He'd dreamed a version of this as a child—needing help, going from house to house, someone chasing him, nobody there to let him in. At the fourth house, he slammed down the brass knocker twenty times and pressed down hard on the doorbell so that it rang continuously and shouted, *"Someone has to help!"* until finally a voice on the intercom to the left of the mailbox said, "Who's down there?"

"I need your help! Please! My phone died!"

"What seems to be the issue?"

Ben was aware that someone was hanging out of the second-story window, looking down at him.

Ben looked up. "I need your help. Your phone. Some people— My wife is in serious danger."

The woman ducked back inside, and seconds later, she opened the door with a gun in her hand, her body shapely in her nightgown. When she saw his face, and how Ben put his hands in the air, she lowered the gun. "Really, I promise I only want to use a phone. Nothing else."

Behind her an older man appeared, rubbing his forehead, and asked her to put the gun back in the closet. Then said to Ben, "She's been through some things."

The woman said, "Damn *right* I've been *through* some things." But she put the gun down on the table and turned on a lamp while telling Ben to come in. In the light he saw her hard, drawn-on eyebrows. A woman who pilfered some happiness in a tanning salon, a woman who was now married to this older guy who must have rescued her from some circle of hell. The man, bald and sleepy faced in an undershirt and boxer shorts, handed Ben a cell phone, saying, "Sit down. We'll get you some water. You look like you're going to keel over."

His wife had taken some steps back, and stood with arms crossed, looking at her husband with something like contempt.

Ben dialed 911 and asked for cops to come to where he was now so he could take them to the warehouse, so they could rescue Evvie—

"Where are you?" said the cop.

"Where am I?" he asked the woman, who still stood in the center of the room.

She hesitated. "You're a long way from anything out here."

"What road? Exact address?"

"You're at 120 Ethan Allen Court in Meadow Wood Acres."

HE SAT ON the flowered couch, the draperies behind him holding back the last bruise of night, the woman in the kitchen, watching television, and the man somewhere else. They had given him buttered toast and water. They'd sat with him awhile, and he'd told them what he could—the story spilling out of him too quickly, so that his listeners held their eyes wide open, blinking, saying nothing, but looking at one another, then back to him, then back to one another. "Jesus," the man finally said. Then they gave him privacy, maybe because he seemed a little crazy, his legs moving frantically like windshield wipers on high speed, and he sat there, biting his nails and thinking how he would thank them one day properly, how he and Evvie would drive out here together with some kind of surprise for them, maybe some money and flowers. If Evvie survived, he told himself (and he couldn't imagine a more urgent prayer), then they would circle back to one another without a doubt and live their lives transformed.

———

HE'D *ALREADY* CIRCLED back. It had happened without his consent. Screaming her name to the sky had taken his heart and shoved it up against hers, and now there was only the one heart, the impossible beating heart of this one life, and here on the flowered couch, imagining her back in the warehouse, he wondered who he'd been that he'd ever managed to leave her. And wondered too if this was punishment—this whole night— for daring to abandon this person who was, he saw now, his life. She'd seen the worst of him, and those days returned: the year he'd spent almost six months in deep depression—Evvie washing his feet with a hot washcloth and rubbing oil into the soles, Evvie getting him to eat, one spoonful at a time, and playing deejay until finally, one night, he'd been able to hear music again—she'd played a beautiful grim song, "See How We Are," by X, it was playing in his mind as if she'd walked into this room and placed the headphones on his ears, not a happy song, but it had somehow worked to heal him. . . . And then those days after she'd lost the baby—he'd never called it *the baby* until now—those days after she'd lost the baby he'd given her baths, shampoos, and she'd returned the favor, they were like each other's children, wrapped in big towels, their bedroom in the old apartment filled with fresh, cold air because Evvie liked to swing the windows wide open no matter the season, and she'd wanted to name the baby, and he'd said no, don't do that, and if you do, don't tell me, and she'd put her hand through his hair, soothing him, and saying nothing at all. She'd swallowed the name down, he imagined. He wanted to know what it was. As if it mattered.

Everything mattered. If they could lie in bed and hear "See How We Are" again, two people alive and alone together in their bed with a song, it was all he'd ever ask of life, and even the tedium, even the loneliness, even the despair would be recognized as the gifts they finally were.

In those first years when he'd lie awake at night with her, something old in him, something older than time and unreasonably, unspeakably hurt, some inexplicable isolation he'd never been free of, had been nearly soothed away by her as by nobody else. He'd allowed himself to fall into her strange, slow fairy tales, where the two of them were magnificently lost in the woods but finally taken care of by kindly giants and fairies with learning disabilities and hilarious cooks who spoke in riddles, everything in those fairy tales described meticulously, so that all these years later, though now he trembled and held his stomach tightly and felt cold all over, all these years later he could see the red and white shoelaces of the one giant's peach-colored shoes. And how he and Evvie, lost children who had stumbled into a new mountainous world, slept in a cradle in a tree-room, the window a space between the thick, green branches that hung down to make walls, and through that green window, snow falling on the peaks across from them, and it fell like music, Evvie said, little notes of endless music, can you hear it, and he could hear it, and then she said a fairy was peeking at them from behind a leaf, and he could see it.

AND SHE'D BEEN there the day he'd been told by an old professor that his piano playing was technically fine but *lacked some essential, ineffable quality*, and he'd resisted Evvie's tirade against the professor—*Fuck that fucker, Ben!*—until she'd done a wickedly accurate impression of the man and he'd ended up laughing then and now right here on this couch as he closed his eyes and there she was on Blackie the horse coming to get him, the long plastic mane flowing in the wind, he would like to ride with her on a horse of his own, but he has to go throw up now.

"Can I use your bathroom?" he called out. Too loudly. The man appeared in the doorway, ushered him toward a small bathroom, and before he could even think to turn on the light, he vomited into the white bowl. Then again. Flushed the toilet and then washed his mouth out. Stood up, found the light, and looked at himself for a long moment in the mirror. *Who are you? Really. Who are you?*

TWO COP CARS showed up, four cops, an ambulance, and two paramedics, a fire engine with three or four firefighters.

Ben rode in one of the cars, leading the convoy, sirens blaring.

One of the cops said barely two words and drank a can of Red Bull, drumming his knees and bouncing his head. He looked out the window. The driving cop talked football like they were on their way to a game.

Before they'd left, Ben had blurted the whole story out in the driveway of the people's house. The cop shook his head and whistled after the story was over, then said, "We'll get 'em," but then looked over at his partner with an odd smile, and for a moment Ben wondered if they thought he was making the whole thing up. Another nutcase. The people in the house had stood there at the doorway, watching this, and then, when the car pulled away, the woman had burst through the door and waved good-bye. Ben thought he would never forget that.

He directed the cops to the best of his ability, but his directions were undergirded by a sense of panic that really he had no idea where the warehouses were, that he may have turned left to get into the neighborhood and not right, but there was nothing to do but trust that eventually he would spot the road that led to Evvie. It was close to dawn, and the black night air gave rise to the bruise of morning, and Ben counted deer, six of them, a whole family, in the triangular field to the left. Their silence, their mysterious movements in the predawn cold: something to report to Evvie. And then it came to him that he would also need to tell Lauren—not about the deer, but about all of this, of course, and how strangely it was unfolding inside of him, and he saw himself across from her at one of her beautifully prepared tables. He reached his hand to touch her face, and remembered he loved her, remembered that nothing is simple, that he had things to sort out, that sorrow was coming. And yet Lauren, and Lauren's table, and Ramona, and their square house with the garden out back, all seemed small, almost miniature, almost devoid of meaning when held next to the idea that Evvie, *Evvie*, could be dead.

EVVIE

SHE WENT WITH Ben to his apartment, finally, at dusk. They sat together in the shelter of their shock, in the darkness, holding hands, talking, and at one point, Ben resting with his head against her chest after he'd told her he would never underestimate what factory farmed animals had to go through again; being in that dark warehouse, utterly powerless, sensing they were going to be killed, was a terror he'd felt viscerally, like any animal would.

She stroked his head and listened to him breathe.

"Yeah," she said.

"It might take a long time to recover."

"Yeah."

AFTER SOME TIME passed, he said he was going to Lauren's. He'd already called her on the phone but didn't say much; he needed to see her. "I need to sort this out. Will you be OK here?" His eyes held their confusion and love in equal measure. "Maybe we should call someone to come be with you? Cedric or someone? I really don't want to leave you without—"

"No, I'm fine. Please. Stay as long as you want. I'll rest."

He'd already wept in her arms and told her he was sorry

and that they'd be together again. They'd find a way. They'd
already found it! He'd already explained how their whole life
had been returned to him. She'd not been able to say much at
all. He kissed her good-bye at the door, on the mouth, and she
felt this kiss try to turn into a promise of future kisses, but she
couldn't taste it. A new barrier, heavy as iron, was erecting itself in her heart. As soon as he left, she got online and wrote to
Celia.

I DECIDED NOT TO DO IT. IT'S TOO CRAZY. AND WHO KNOWS
WHO THESE KIDNAPPERS ARE IN REAL LIFE. THEY COULD BE
INSANE. THEY SAY NO GUNS, BUT WHY SHOULD I BELIEVE
THAT? THE ONE GUY HAS BLUE EYES THAT SPIN. THEY MAY
NEVER STOP SPINNING. I'M NOT ABOUT TO FALL FOR HIS
CHARM! EASILY COULD BE SOME PSYCHO SOCIOPATH. THE
WORLD BREEDS SOCIOPATHS.

IF BEN WANTS TO COME BACK SOMEDAY, FINE. BUT I'M NOT
GETTING INVOLVED IN ANYTHING CRAZY. I JUST WANT HIM TO
BE HAPPY. I REALLY JUST WANT HIM TO HAVE A LONG, HAPPY
LIFE. AND THAT'S IT.

She sat and stared at the screen, then added,

OTHERWISE, NOT A LOT GOING ON HERE. I MIGHT ORDER
SOME PIZZA. AND I'M THINKING ABOUT A NEW CAREER—
MAYBE SOMETHING IN THE HEALTH CARE INDUSTRY, SINCE
SUPPOSEDLY THERE WILL BE TONS OF JOBS.

Again she sat back and looked at these words. She had never
seriously considered health care until the words came out of

her fingers, onto the keys, then onto the screen. But now she thought, that's exactly what I'll do.

She signed off with, YOU MIGHT SAY WHY HEALTH CARE, BUT IT JUST DAWNED ON ME, CELIA, THAT WHAT I REALLY WANT TO DO IS QUIETLY HELP PEOPLE IN CONCRETE WAYS.

THE SOUND OF the warehouse door, when it finally had opened, was still inside her, repeating itself, a reverberating screech shooting upward from her stomach, past her heart, into her head, then into the atmosphere like a comet, and she knew now how sound could leave a scar, because each time it repeated itself inside of her, she felt a little different. Some people heard sound as color, and maybe she was turning into one of those people, since the scar seemed to be red-orange, and getting brighter with each repetition.

She walked a tightrope back and forth in Ben's apartment tonight, Ruth staying close beside her, sweet Ruth, who looked at her with the same old eyes of compassion, but also somehow asking a question of Evvie that Evvie couldn't answer. *What is it, girl? What do you want me to say? I know I don't deserve you, but I will someday. I will.*

THE COPS HAD yelled, "Police!" and shone an enormous, blinding flashlight into the darkness.

The flashlight had wandered all over the warehouse, leaving no corner unchecked, bathing her finally with the cold miracle of light. She'd been huddled in the corner, alone. She'd fallen asleep. She'd not been raped.

Then she'd heard Ben. "Evvie?"

"You can come with me," a cop said to Ben. They approached her, single file.

And then Ben crouched down and held his hands out. She took them and stood on wobbly legs. He took her in his arms.

She couldn't think of that reunion now. She might never be able to tame it into memory, even if she lived to be a hundred.

SHE'D HAD TO go to the police station, and tell the story of the night.

It was not difficult to lie—or to refrain from telling the whole truth—because the self who'd hired the men to show up in masks at Ben's office was dead.

In the room with the tiny window, she knew she was being watched as she told the story verbatim except for those details that would have implicated her, or the person she used to be. She told the story with restrained passion and tears and the bedraggled detective had patted her hand and said he knew it was hard, but she was doing a fine job.

"HI!" SHE FROZE on the tightrope in a patch of evening sunlight, one leg held out to the left, as if to keep herself from falling.

"Hi."

"How was your visit?"

"I don't know. She's freaked out, of course. And I haven't told her what my plans are yet. I did tell her I was with you right now."

"OK?" She hadn't meant it to be a question. Her heart slammed in her chest as she bent down to embrace Ruth. She lined her head next to Ruth's head. Diligence Chung had taken care of Ruth while they'd been kidnapped. The dog smelled like the young woman's soap, or perfume, or holiness.

"I want to be careful. I'm sure if I go slow—"

"The thing is, is, I'm on a tightrope. Ben."

Evvie was walking again, arms outstretched like wings. "Mr. Ben, my old friend. I'm on a very thin tightrope."

"Come here, you're shaking. You can't stay on a tightrope when you're shaking like that. You're just in shock."

"Because everything inside me is broken and it's absolutely my fault." She kept walking the rope. Ruth, beside her, gazed up anxiously. "You have no idea."

He walked over and stood behind her. "You don't need to have survivor's guilt. We survived. It's the best thing we—"

"I didn't survive."

"Sure did. You're right here, Ev. Come on."

He put his hands on her shoulders, and she stopped walking. "You survived and you're the reason I survived," he said. "I still can't believe it."

"I can't either." She looked at the floor.

"Take a deep breath, Ev."

But her breathing was shallow, more like a dog's panting.

"Is it going to snow?" she said, but it came out shrill. She knew she couldn't do what she most wanted to do, which was turn her face into his chest and sob until she felt a kind of vanishing. Tears so plentiful and fierce they would be in lieu of confession. What good would confession do anyway? She could tell a priest and spare Ben the pain of knowing. She'd caused enough pain for one lifetime. It was time to start to live their lives again, and be happy.

They stood there for a while, his hands massaging her shoulders. Tears, way back in her head, were trying to travel forward but came up against a dam.

"I heard we're getting a storm," Ben said. His voice sounded like the old Ben. He had been returned to his old self, the one that wasn't trying to run from her.

"Kick me out," she said.

"Evvie, what are you talking about?"

"I want to sleep on the streets. I want to be out there alone. I always have."

He placed his hands on her upper arms and pressed hard. "You're in deep shock."

"No, that's wearing off." Her voice was low and steady. "Unfortunately."

"Well, I'm in deep shock. And I'd like to stay here for a while."

"You should. You should stay here as long as you like. But you should kick me out because I don't deserve to be in your presence."

"Is this what they did to you? Made you more of a masochist than you ever were before? Is this what you're going to let those motherfuckers do? You don't think that—"

"I met them on a bus. Way back in early spring. You hadn't been gone long. They showed me this pamphlet."

"Met who? Evvie, go lie down. You're delusional. I'm tired. We need—"

"This pamphlet about how to get your lover to come back, really."

She spoke in a stage whisper, but the words scalded her mouth and lips as they entered the air. It was like she'd jumped off a bridge and the fall was taking a long, long time. Ben took her by the hand and led her into the bedroom. "You don't need to make up a story. We're both in a crazy state right now. All we need is a good sleep," he said, and sat her on the edge of the bed, and knelt down to take her shoes off, one at a time. He set them by the door. Then was back to take off her socks. "Just get under the covers and go to sleep. I'll be in soon." He put his hand on her forehead, then through her hair. Then turned her onto her stomach and rubbed her back. "I hate that you had to go through that. All those hours not knowing whether you would live or die."

Evvie again felt the presence of tears, far back in her head. She held her eyes wide open in the dark room. He felt her pulse. He rubbed her back, but she couldn't feel anything.

"You should go spend the night with Lauren."

"That wouldn't be right."

"You could figure stuff out. You don't know how things will—"

"I have to find the words to apologize to her. That will take a while. I have to wait and figure it out. I don't have any—"

"I wish you'd go. You can't just—"

"Shhh. Evvie, your voice is really strange. Just try to take some deep breaths. I'm really worried about you."

HE STOOD UP after a while, and left the room, leaving the door partway open, so that Evvie could lie there taking in the hallway, the light, and occasionally glimpse Ben, who kept coming to the door to check on her, wringing his hands, as if she were his own fevered child.

BEN AND EVVIE

LATER BEN LAY down in the dark to join Evvie for a long sleep. Evvie was on her back, eyes closed, breathing shallowly, and when he said, "Ev?" a smile came to her lips. "You OK?" he said, and she didn't say anything. When Lauren called his cell phone, before he even got his hello out, she said, "Who's Val?"

"Who's Val?" he said. "I told you last week. I don't know a Val."

"You have to remember. Your old friend Val. She has a thick midwestern accent?"

"I never knew a Val."

"Think. You had to. She called you. I have a feeling—"

"I'm thinking. Hold on."

He covered the phone and said to Evvie, "Did we know a Val?"

Evvie didn't respond.

"Why are you so determined to know?" he said to Lauren, sitting up.

"She was going to come visit you. She wanted to know your work schedule. She wanted to know exactly when you'd be at your office."

"Val. Val."

"Val," Lauren said. "That's all she said. And she said it in this really, really strong midwestern accent. Like that woman in the movie *Fargo*."

"Val," he said, and got out of bed, and something inside of him began to stomp out a rising knowledge that for some reason Evvie had called Lauren and said she was Val. Evvie who'd always loved lapsing into that Fargo accent.

"Look, I'll think about it and call you when I remember."

HE PUT THE cell phone down and sat on the edge of the bed in the darkness.

"So why'd you say you were Val?" he said. He didn't want this conversation. It was bad timing. They needed to recover before anything like this. But Lauren's voice had been penetrating. The voice of a detective.

He spoke more clearly. "Why'd you say you were *Val*?"

"Because I needed to do my homework."

"What's that mean?"

"I needed to find out when you would be in the office. When you would be working."

"Because?"

Evvie was out of bed now, pulling on her jeans.

"What are you doing?"

"I'm getting ready," she said.

"Evvie?"

"I had to find out when you'd be in the office because I'd hired those guys, those kidnappers. I thought they were safe. They swore they'd never use guns. They said it was like some kind of performance theater. They were just a couple of guys who couldn't get jobs because they'd been to prison and nobody would hire ex-cons. So I thought I could give them some business and just see what happened because they seemed really safe and honest and just interested in *thee-ate-her* and stuff."

"You're dead serious, aren't you? You thought you'd *give the ex-cons some business.*"

"I'm dead serious, Ben." Evvie stood over in the corner. She had her arms crossed. "I just need to find my coat and then I'll exit."

"You'll exit?" He turned and punched the wall. "You're not going anywhere!"

He walked over to her and stood a few feet away from her. He took one step forward. He thought he would shake her. He thought he would slap her. He thought he would knock her head against a wall. But he didn't want to touch her.

"What the fuck are you saying, Evvie?"

She didn't say a word.

"You're serious, you're telling me the serious goddamn truth, and I can't believe it! I know it's true but I can't *believe* it! I can't believe *anyone* would be so fucking stupid."

"I can't either, Ben. I can't believe it, either!"

"Why, Evvie?"

"Why is a great question, Ben. I can't answer it. I—"

HE WALKED OUT into the living room. He sat on the end of the couch, his head down in his hands, and began counting. If he sat there and counted and counted, maybe this all would be revealed as a dream, maybe the numbers would line up like ladder rungs and he could follow them out of this apartment, climb out of this conversation, and into another world of peace and quiet sanity. This could not really be happening. This was an Evvie nightmare. He'd had them before. He'd once had a dream where Evvie was crawling down a highway on hands and knees, traffic driving around her and people shouting out the window, and she'd just kept on crawling. This was like that nightmare, only worse, and so much longer. But it was quite possible that soon there would be an awakening, soon he would be in his bed sitting up and saying to himself, *That was the strangest dream of my life*. Only it wasn't.

It wasn't a dream, that was just a foolish hope and the hope was leaving him and Evvie was actually saying, as she slipped into her coat, *"I'm sorry and I'll be sorry forever and I'll find a way to make it up to you and I don't blame you if you want to kill me but I'm already dead and on my way so see ya."*

"Where do you think you're going?"

"Back home. To my room? Tessie's?"

"Is that right? That's what you think?"

"That's where I live."

"No, you live in a nightmare of your own making, Evvie."

"You could say that."

"You don't understand, do you? You don't understand—"

"Obviously a person who is capable of hiring madmen to kidnap her husband understands very little. So—"

"I mean you don't understand that you can't just go home. You just can't stroll out of here and go home, Evvie!"

"You want me to stay?"

"I have to call the cops!"

"No, you don't! I'll go to jail, Ben! I can't go to jail!"

"Why can't you? You're a criminal!"

"Stop it!"

"Stop it?"

"I just went crazy, Ben! I told you, they lied to me! They said they would never use a gun, they said it was like theater, and I never would have hired them otherwise! They were totally convincing! Nice guys! No words could explain how convincing they were!"

"The whole idea of it is criminal, Evvie. Can't you see that? I don't even know who you are anymore. That you would think, 'I'll just pay these strangers to fucking kidnap my husband and me.' It's not about how convincing anyone was! And how much did you pay them anyway? No, don't tell me. Don't tell me! You can tell everything to the cops. Because I don't want to know a goddamn thing."

"You can't call the cops, Ben. I'll do anything. Please."

"If I don't call, then I'm a criminal too! Did you stop to think of that?"

"You can put me away."

"Put you away."

"Take me to Western Psych. I'll commit myself or you can commit me. All we have to do is say I'm a danger to myself or others. Which I obviously am. I'll stay locked in there for months, Ben. Whatever you want. I'll take medication, I'll get therapy, I'll never even come near you again."

"Just shut up."

Ben paced in the same space where Evvie had been walking earlier. For a long time, he moved in silence. Evvie leaned back against the wall by the door, and waited.

HE'D TAKEN SOME time, but then they were in the car, headed to the hospital. Ruth sitting up straight in the backseat. "Do you mind if I get a few things first? From Tessie's?" With nothing left to lose, she could ask this. She could ask anything. She could be the person with a million requests, the most annoying of all people. It didn't matter.

He nodded. He pulled in front of Tessie's house and said he'd wait for her. "Don't take more than a minute."

And when she got out of the car and walked up the path, he rolled the window down and called, "And don't even think about trying to escape!"

She stopped on the path and looked back at him. She hadn't considered such a thing. But now she did. What if she just walked into Tessie's house, climbed down the back fire escape, and started to run through the crowded backyards, hiding behind this trash can and that tree, under those steps, up on that porch. . . . What if she left as a fugitive for a whole different place where she could reinvent herself as someone strong and capable and solitary? This all flashed through her like a sneeze.

She turned and headed toward the house. Tessie came to the door of her apartment, stuck her face out halfway, and asked Evvie where she'd been.

"Oh, out and about."

"Waltzing around like Pittsburgh's queen of Sheba?"

"Not exactly."

"You look like a ghost."

"Caught a chill." Evvie headed up the steps.

Did they let dogs go to psychiatric hospitals if the patients were especially attached to them? Could she fake blindness and Ruth could be a Seeing Eye dog? After all, she was metaphorically as blind as a person could be. Her heart began to race. It beat so hard she was afraid it would burst out of her chest. She walked into her empty room and lay down on the bed, wondering if she was really having a heart attack. You could definitely have a heart attack at forty-two.

Ben would not believe her. But she couldn't move. She could not move off the bed or her heart would crash through the wall of her chest and land on the floor. Ben was probably out there thinking she was up to something. Thinking she was escaping. He would be furious. He would be thinking how he'd sic the cops and some hound dogs on her trail. But here she was, pinned to the bed, fighting to breathe.

SHE HEARD HIS footsteps coming up the steps. "Evvie?" and for that split second, because his voice was so familiar, because his footsteps had a sound as intimate as breath, it seemed that none of this year had ever happened, and he was returning from his long day to be with her. After this second was gone, there was only her heart, and her terror, and him at the door starting to say something, then falling silent when he saw her face. She saw her face in his, just as if his were made of mirror, and clenched her eyes shut against the image. "Ben, my heart. It's beating so fast."

He didn't say anything. He stood there, taking his breaths, his eyes downcast, his mouth pulled in tightly.

"I might be having a heart attack."

Still he didn't say a word.

"Evvie. I'm not coming to your rescue. It's not all right. Nothing will ever be all right again."

"Ben?"

"Can you just gather what you need so we can go?"

"Soon. Just let me—"

"I don't like prolonging agony."

Behind him, Diligence Chung appeared in her purple hat.

"Is she sick?" Diligence said, her face impassive and her voice high and gentle.

"Yes," Ben said.

"I can sing," Diligence said. "It maybe help her." Diligence stood there and sang in her long skirt and her hat. Her pale, serious face filled Evvie with longing. Next life, I will be like Diligence.

> *"Woman across the hall with nice dog*
> *Never ever giving up on Love!*
> *For God is with woman and dog*
> *Who never giving up on love!"*

"Thank you, Diligence."

Diligence scurried back down the hall.

The song had allowed Evvie to rise from her bed and stand up straight. Her heart was still threatening to explode, but she was capable of putting a hairbrush, some clothes, some lipstick, and a few books into a white plastic bag, and then, into an old brown suitcase, she packed up everything else.

EVVIE

ON A JULY evening, the day before Evvie's forty-seventh birthday, she stood under a red flowered umbrella in a playground. The rain poured down soft and steady and the children loved it, running and crying out to one another below the hot and hovering night sky. A nearly full moon was low and orange and surrounded by shreds of high purple clouds sailing off to the north in a high wind. Evvie watched the kids, and also the cars streaking by on the highway across from the playground. Tomorrow, for her birthday, she was headed to the ocean.

The playground itself was sprawling and featured a sliding-board dinosaur, several swing sets, climbing walls, cubbyholes, and a ground covered with green foam so that children could fall without getting hurt. She knew a few of the parents who were here tonight, talking under the green pavilion, but preferred the drumming of rain on the sturdy flowered umbrella. Her nephew Hugo, Cedric's son, was waving to her over on top of a jungle gym. She waved back, nodding and smiling her encouragement. And then someone else was waving.

SHE HADN'T EVEN talked to him in more than four years. But he was walking toward her, and following close behind, a small child, galloping, curly-headed, barefoot. Maybe two years old. A girl?

"Hi, Ben!" The words came up from her depths. And then her heart began a loud, steady drumming, the sort of drumming that sounds out at the beginning of a parade. She might have started marching in place, were she not frozen.

"Hey!" He stood there, a yard away, apparently stunned. The child hid behind his leg.

THE LAST TIME she'd seen his face was four years ago when he'd shown up in the hospital one night for the visiting hour, just five days after she'd signed herself in. He'd brought her some dark chocolate and a loaf of French bread. They'd sat together— she on the side of the bed in a pale blue hospital gown and gray socks, he in his jeans and dark green sweater and wristwatch, seated on a straight chair far across the room, his arms folded tightly. The window by the bed framed the black night. The room sucked up all the words they tried to say to each other.

He'd leaned forward, elbows on knees, then pinched the bridge of his nose.

Then somehow, they'd started to laugh. Neither had said anything funny. Maybe they'd just looked at each other for a moment too long, and a sense of absurdity had overtaken them. But they'd laughed until their sides ached, both of them bending in half, laughed until Evvie had ended up sobbing. He'd stood up, walked over to the bed, held her hand, sat down next to her, waited for her to calm down, then rose and said he had to go, that he hoped she'd get out soon but not too soon, that he hoped she'd never do anything that crazy again, and please, please don't call him for a long, long time.

Of course she'd honored his request not to call. Would have honored it without his asking. And that same year, when she saw his back while waiting in line at Panera Bread, she rushed outside and started walking in the pouring rain across the busy parking lot over to Barnes & Noble.

Once, in the grocery store she dove into a frozen foods freezer while he wheeled his cart past, humming with an iPod on his head and a long list in his hand.

Another time she saw him and Lauren (in silver clogs) walking hand in hand down in the Strip District one sunny Saturday. They were headed toward her on the sidewalk, and she'd ducked into Pennsylvania Macaroni Company, where she'd taken an hour or so to buy some cheese and olives until the coast was clear.

Standing in the cold at a stoplight on Penn Avenue, she once saw him waiting in his car for the light to change. She almost cried out "Ben!" but instead bent down to tie her shoe for a long minute before he pulled away.

She was the antistalker, guarding the great distance between herself and the one she loved, keeping him safe from anything she might do or say, ever again.

And she had Ruth, sole custody. As it turned out, Lauren's dog was jealous of other animals. Once, early on, Ben had sent Ruth a box of bones in the mail, care of Evvie's mother.

"wow, so how have you been?"

"Good. This is Molly. Molly, this is Evvie."

The child clung to his leg, but peeked up at Evvie, the eyes great dark pools reflecting the evening.

"Hi, Molly. Nice to meet you."

"What are you doing here?" Ben looked around anxiously, as if hoping she was there with a child and not some crazy lone person haunting the place. Evvie wanted to explain to him all the ways she'd changed. All she'd seen and done. How she was nobody to fear, ever again. She was hardly the same person anymore, but how to convey that when his presence rendered her nearly speechless? "I'm here with Cedric's son. Hugo. He's over there with that blond kid." She pointed. *I'm no longer who I was. I'm better. I'm sorry I couldn't have been better with you.* She felt like the Tin Man, moving her arm. The few words she managed to say felt heavy; she had to push them into the summer evening, which felt suddenly, impossibly, thick.

"I saw you one day with the guy—I think he's the guy who worked at the convenience—"

"Yeah. Ranjeev. He doesn't work there anymore."

"Your significant other?"

"In a way. We take long walks together."

"Long walks."

"Yeah. He had to quit that job before I could finish that movie I tried to make. I'm working on something else."

The small girl kept gazing up at Evvie. Evvie smiled down at her for a moment, waving.

"So what's your new—"

"My friend Gigi is manager of this cable station and hired me to do a film on a hospice."

"Wow. Great."

She wanted to tell him that Celia wanted her to travel to Poland with her next summer, that she'd long been saving up for it, that she'd helped organize an animal rights convention in Cleveland, that one day she'd maybe go to India with Ranjeev.

Wanted to tell him about Ranjeev's cousin, a woman who built her own bicycles and was teaching Evvie how to do so, that she missed his mother, and that it hurt that he didn't know any of this, seemed utterly wrong that he didn't know anything about her life now.

"And how 'bout you?"

The child was in his arms. She was so beautiful and substantial, Evvie couldn't stop staring. She was the sort of child who stared back with calm interest, holding your gaze, stilling the world.

"Same company. Got promoted. It's OK, but I'm looking for something else. I'm doing some metal sculpture like I did in college. Sound sculpture. I wish—" He stopped himself.

She smiled at the little girl, and after a hesitation, the little girl smiled back. A little pirate smile. Evvie melted a little. "Wow, I'd love to see it. Maybe we could have coffee sometime and then go visit one of your sound sculptures."

Ben didn't say anything.

"Or maybe not. Sorry. I—"

"Would be tough to explain that to Lauren, considering."

"Yeah. Considering."

"But it's not like you're not—"

"What?"

Ben lifted the child up high on his shoulders, her small hands clutching on to his hair. Behind her was the moon. Ben looked at Evvie. His face filled with a collision of feeling.

"Not like I'm not what?" she said, wincing up at the little girl now.

Evvie swallowed. Ben looked off to the side, then back at Evvie.

"So I better go," he said, tugging on the small feet of the girl. "Say good-bye to Evvie, Molly. And wish her happy birthday. Her birthday's tomorrow."

"Bye-bye. Happy Birthday!"

Evvie tried to say good-bye, but could only wave.

HUGO WAS OVER by the swings, waiting for one to be empty. He was five, a durable little dark-eyed kid with a round face, curly gold hair like Cedric's, baggy green shorts, and sneakers with flashing lights. He watched Evvie walk up to him with his steady, curious gaze that often seemed to belong to someone older. "What's wrong?" he said, when she got closer, and she smiled down at him and said that nothing was wrong. He took her hand. His hand was sweaty and warm and always a surprise, the way it held to hers, the way it trusted. She was his favorite, the aunt who was paid to walk twenty-eight dogs a week and sometimes invited him to come along. He had memorized all the dogs' names and would be more than happy to chant them upon request.

Soon, there was one swing open. The rain had become mist. Hugo ran toward the swing, sat down, grabbed hold of the chains, and told Evvie, "Push me!" She walked over behind him, and started off with a steady push. "Higher!" She pushed him higher and higher until the chains twisted and buckled and he screamed with joy, his legs kicking the air. After a while he was singing a song about a red bird, something he'd known forever.

TOMORROW SHE WOULD drive to the beach with Ranjeev, who liked most of all to take long walks, rain or shine.

Ranjeev liked silence.

You could learn from silence if you stayed quiet. It had so many qualities. One day it was the silence you might hear after an earthquake, while other days it surrounded you, curative and lit with blinding sun, like a warm blanket draped over you on a winter morning in your bed. Still other days, in the middle of silence, a distant siren sounded, as if someone light-years away was coming to retrieve the injured world, Ranjeev said. Do you hear it?

You had to learn to listen, and how to take it in—the silence, the siren. You had to breathe.

Silence could hold everything about you, no matter how strange, how wrong, how broken, and it wouldn't let you go.

If you listened to it long enough, day after day, year after year, the voices in your mind getting smaller and quieter, you might find moments where silence turns into God, Ranjeev had explained.

THE SWING BESIDE Hugo emptied, and she walked over and took it. And she was here and nowhere else. Here in this playground on the swing beside Hugo, who was belting out a song, here in the darkness beneath an orange moon that was wet as fruit. What she carried, this love that wouldn't, couldn't die— sometimes it was pain that flashed in her heart like a diamond. She clung to the chains of the swing and started rising up into the sky.

"Sing!" said Hugo.

ACKNOWLEDGMENTS

Thank you:

Nicole Aragi, best imaginable agent, for your patience, encouragement, and brilliant editing.

To the folks at HarperCollins, especially Gail Winston, for your excellent sensibility as editor, and your contagious enthusiasm. Maya Ziv, for your grace and generosity as you worked on so many details. And Shelly Perron, phenomenal copy editor.

Thanks to those writers who helped me as I worked: Don Challenger, whose own writing and great humor inspired me to begin; Jane Bernstein, for ongoing support and perceptive comments on the first draft; Lawrence Wray, for reading the first draft and steering me past my blind spots, and for buying an Evvie coat; and Charlotte Daniels, for reading early on, in the middle, and then again at the end, and for giving me the gift of a week in her perfect cabin where I finished the manuscript.

Thanks also to Patrick and Patricia Tierney, who listened to the first pages of this aloud and told me to keep going, and to Cynthia Taibbi, who read the finished manuscript.

Thanks to my family and all my friends, far and near, for your invaluable support and presence in my life.

And to those who lived with me as I wrote: Patrick, for sustaining love, faith, and friendship; and Rosey and Anna, for outlandish comedy and kindness.

Finally, a heartfelt thank-you to Drue Heinz, whose generosity and support of fiction made possible the career of so many writers, including mine.

ABOUT THE AUTHOR

Jane McCafferty is author of the novel *One Heart* and two collections of stories, *Thank You for the Music* and *Director of the World and Other Stories*, which won the Drue Heinz Literature Prize and was published by University of Pittsburgh Press. She is the recipient of an NEA award, the Great Lakes New Writers Award, and two Pushcart Prizes. She lives in Pittsburgh, where she teaches at Carnegie Mellon University.